# Temptation Island

Also by Lorie O'Clare

PLEASURE ISLAND

SEDUCTION ISLAND

UNDER THE COVERS
(with Crystal Jordan and P.J. Mellor)

FEEL THE HEAT
(with P.J. Mellor and Lydia Parks)

Published by Kensington Publishing Corp.

# Temptation Island

## Lorie O'Clare

APHRODISIA

KENSINGTON BOOKS

www.kensingtonbooks.com

APHRODISIA BOOKS are published by

Kensington Publishing Corp.
119 West 40th Street
New York, NY 10018

All Kensington titles, imprints, and distributed lines are available at special quantity discounts for bulk purchases for sales promotion, premiums, fund-raising, and educational, or institutional use.

Special book excerpts or customized printings can also be created to fit specific needs. For details, write or phone the office of the Kensington Special Sales Manager: Kensington Publishing Corp., 119 West 40th Street, New York, NY 10018. Attn. Special Sales Department. Phone: 1-800-221-2647.

Aphrodisia and the A logo Reg. U.S. Pat. & TM Off.

ISBN-13: 978-0-7582-6138-0
ISBN-10: 0-7582-6138-1

First Kensington Trade Paperback Printing: August 2011

10 9 8 7 6 5 4 3 2 1

Printed in the United States of America

# 1

"Jenny Rogers, are you ready for your last chance for happiness?"

Jenny gripped her podium, all too aware of the sensitive microphone so close to her mouth. As Joe Jobana—the middle-aged game show host, who looked a lot better on TV than he did in real life—asked the well-known question, the studio audience chanted along with him.

"*Are you ready for your last chance for happiness?*"

Her heart thumped so loud she was sure the mic would pick it up. "I'm ready, Joe," she managed, remembering to smile when the gaunt man standing next to the two cameramen ran his fingers along the side his face, gesturing for her to look happy and excited.

"I bet Jenny is always ready," Joe Jobana said, grinning and giving a knowing look to the studio audience. "Are you always ready, Jenny?"

The paperwork she and her nana had to sign when they bought their tickets for the show had stressed repeatedly that she always agree with Joe Jobana's jokes and one-liners if she was chosen as a contestant. At the time, she couldn't figure out why they'd tell her that over and over again. Now it made sense. His jokes were funnier when he was making fun of other contestants and not her.

Jenny was here for her grandmother. Ever since Papa had died a few years ago, Jenny spent as much time with Nana as possible. Nana's favorite show was *Last Chance for Happiness,* the popular game show, and it was all she wanted to talk about. Nana adored Joe Jobana. During weeks when Jenny ended up working overtime at Bernie's—the grocery store where she'd worked since high school, and located five blocks from her apartment—Nana recorded *Last Chance for Happiness* so Jenny wouldn't miss any of the episodes. Jenny and Nana would shout out the answers and make fun of contestants when they got the answer wrong.

It was far from the highlight of Jenny's life, but it sure made Nana happy. When she knew Jenny was coming over to watch the show, she'd cook dinner, bake cookies, make a day out of preparing for their time sitting together and watching TV. Jenny knew it was the only time anymore that Nana, who used to live in the kitchen, did any cooking.

Nana pointed out continually how Jenny could walk away with the grand prize. She seldom missed an answer. Nana got all of the answers right, too. If Jenny pointed that out, Nana simply waved her off, grumbling something about her missing more than Jenny did. Jenny knew it wasn't true. The Rogers might not go down in history for much else, but they could definitely make their mark as masters of useless trivia.

One glance at Nana, sitting front and center in the studio audience, her hands balled into fists in front of her face as she bounced up and down in her seat, and Jenny smiled.

"I'm always ready, Joe," she said, trying for the same knowing smile he'd given the audience.

Her response worked. The audience roared. Joe Jobana

laughed and said something into his mic as he faced the camera. He sauntered over to his podium, although in truth he walked stiffly. It was amazing how different he was in real life.

"If you answer correctly, your *last chance for happiness will be* . . ." He stressed the last half of his sentence, and the crowd again chanted.

*"Last chance for happiness!"*

*"Last chance for happiness!"*

The last thing Jenny wanted was to be on *Last Chance for Happiness*. It was bad enough having gone through high school being known as the class nerd. In her yearbook she had been voted most likely to always win at Trivial Pursuit. But when Nana surprised her with tickets to the game show, Jenny couldn't disappoint her. She had suspected foul play when her name was called at the beginning of the show to be a contestant, but Nana swore *Last Chance for Happiness* was on the level. There wasn't any way to fix it. It was just a stroke of luck. Jenny suspected it was karma getting back at her for spending her life with her head in books, but she had kept her thoughts to herself.

Jenny watched Nana, who now stood along with everyone else in the three rows. The studio audience was a lot smaller than she thought it would be. Nana glowed with happiness. It made sweating under the incredibly hot lights while cameramen zoomed around her all worth it.

"An island giveaway!" Joe Jobana yelled.

Jenny jumped. The camera wasn't on her at the moment. There were three men riding the cameras, which rolled across the cement floor on squeaky wheels, while crew members hurried around them making sure all props were in place. The cameramen zoomed in on two sexy ladies who waved their hands around large posters that said ISLAND GIVEAWAY.

"That's right, Joe," the announcer's voice boomed. "To the wonderful island of Hawaii!"

Jenny stared at the cardboard posters, trying to see them as the cameras blocked her view. She'd been told not to stare at the monitors that allowed everyone to see what the viewer at home saw, but there wasn't any other way to tell what they were describing.

"You'll be staying at the exquisite Honolulu Paradise, where everyone's dreams come true. Bask on the beach, enjoy the lifestyle of the rich and famous," the announcer continued. "Because this is your last chance for happiness!"

Once again, the audience chanted along with the announcer. *"Last chance for happiness."* Nana yelled loud enough Jenny heard her over the dull rumble.

"Now, Jenny." Joe Jobana looked at her seriously. "Are you ready for your question?"

She didn't feel like smiling. This was the moment. Her head itched from the heat of the lights glaring above her. The cameras were moving in so close she couldn't see anything else. And the gaunt man who'd been gesturing at her wildly throughout the show was giving one hell of a performance right now as he waved his hands in the air to get her attention.

"I'm ready, Joe," she said, wishing she had water. Her mouth was suddenly too dry.

"I knew you were." Joe laughed. "Here is your question. On August sixteenth, 1977, many believed their last chance for happiness came to an end. Miss Jenny Rogers, for the grand prize Hawaiian vacation, what monumental event occurred on August sixteenth, 1977?"

Jenny shook so hard she almost knocked over the podium. She gripped it, her hands sweaty as she stared at Joe Jobana. That wasn't the question she needed to answer to win a trip to Hawaii. The show was never this easy. She stared at the powder plastered on his face and the way the lights reflected in his thick, shiny black hair. Any second he would add something to the question, something obscure that no one would know.

Looking at the audience, lights suddenly blinded her, preventing her from seeing her grandmother. Jenny didn't need to see her. Nana was laughing. Jumping up and down and laughing.

Who would have expected the day her Nana thought the world had ended would turn out to be Jenny's last chance for happiness? It was too much to believe. She and Nana would be leaving for Hawaii. It was all too good to be true.

"Time's running out, Jenny."

She shot her attention back to Joe Jobana. She hadn't answered the question yet.

"On August . . ." Her voice cracked. Jenny cleared it and the microphone hummed. The gaunt man made a face at her, obviously disapproving of her unladylike grunt. "On August sixteenth, 1977, Elvis Presley died."

Jenny stood just outside the terminal at the Minneapolis-St. Paul Airport. It had taken over an hour to drive there, almost as long to park, and she was starting to understand why everyone told her to arrive three hours before her flight. As disappointed as she was that Nana refused to go with her, she couldn't deny how exciting all of this was.

Nana wasn't about to get on an airplane, especially one that would be flying over the ocean. She didn't like Hawaiian food. There was no way she'd go so far from Papa, who was buried in the cemetery just outside Parkville, Minnesota, where they lived. Jenny wished Nana would explore a bit of the world. She could count on one hand the amount of times her grandmother had left Parkville, one of those times being to attend *Last Chance for Happiness* with Jenny. Nana wouldn't be persuaded, though.

"Well I'm not turning down a free trip," Jenny had decided, gripping the plane tickets in her hand. "Maybe I can sell the second ticket."

"That's a good idea." Nana had sat in her favorite chair,

watching Jenny on *Last Chance for Happiness* for the tenth time since they'd returned home. "You can buy more film and take more pictures. We'll make a photo album of your trip once you're home."

The plane tickets were nontransferable. No one in Parkville would cash the two-hundred-dollar voucher that came with her tickets. She had her confirmation for her hotel room and the shuttle that would take her there. There were meal vouchers and drink vouchers. Maybe it wasn't so bad that she couldn't do anything about the second ticket. It wasn't like there was anyone in Parkville she wanted to take with her other than Nana. Jenny didn't have any other family, her parents having died in a car accident while out of town when Jenny was a baby. With Papa gone, it was her and Nana. She hadn't paid for the ticket, so she wasn't out anything.

Jenny pushed her suitcases forward with her foot as the line moved until it was her turn to show her ID and plane ticket to the attendant.

"Enjoy your flight," the attendant told her, after a team of men in uniform had gone through all of her luggage and determined she wasn't a terrorist.

Jenny struggled to put everything back into her suitcases as the airport employees went on to the next passenger. Once she managed to at least get them closed, with all her contents inside, she grabbed her luggage and entered the secured area where the other passengers sat and waited to board the plane. Jenny found an empty seat that faced large windows. There were so many planes outside.

"Are you going to Hawaii, too?" she asked the woman sitting next to her. She appeared to be about Jenny's age.

"Hmm." The woman leaned over and pulled a laptop out of her luggage and shifted her body so her back was to Jenny.

Fine. Jenny didn't want to talk to the woman, anyway, especially if she was going to be a bitch. Glancing at the crowded area, she wondered how all these people would fit on any of the planes parked outside. Wasn't everyone inside this closed-in area for the same flight?

Several men in suits stopped in front of Jenny. An old lady took the chair across from her and spoke to the men, who apparently were there to assist with luggage and help the elderly woman.

"I'll make sure your seat is ready," one of the men in suits told the old woman. "We'll get you on board so you can get comfortable."

"I'll sit there and wait or sit here and wait. One chair is the same as the other."

Jenny wished Nana were here. Obviously older people flying received better treatment.

"You'll have privacy on board. You can choose which movie you wish to watch and have a drink. It's rather noisy here and so many people mean germs."

"Marc, I don't plan on getting sick again. Quit worrying. It lowers your immunity and you'll get sick."

As if to prove her point, Marc sniffled and turned from the old lady, covering his nose so he wouldn't sneeze. Jenny met the old lady's gaze and grinned.

An hour later, Marc was starting to get on Jenny's nerves. She knew from him pestering the attendants that waiting this long to board the plane wasn't normal. The other man standing by the old woman's side looked equally annoyed. Not to mention those sitting around Jenny were growing antsy and some had started pacing.

Finally, a male attendant announced that the plane was going through some final mechanical inspections, and they hoped to have all passengers boarded within the next half hour.

"This is really unacceptable." The woman next to Jenny swore, speaking louder than was necessary.

"I'd rather have the plane safe than the airline hurry us

aboard and risk our lives," Jenny mumbled as loud as the lady just had. She'd spent hours reading about airplanes and correct airport behavior, of which she was seeing none.

The woman looked down her nose at Jenny. "They're probably just trying to sober up the captain," she sniffed.

"I doubt that," Jenny said, although she prayed that wasn't the case. She'd also read how flights were being delayed for this reason or that. However, Jenny had intentionally avoided all information the Internet had to offer about plane crashes.

"I have meetings scheduled, and the board isn't going to wait," a man sitting on the other side of the bitch next to Jenny complained.

Jenny refused to let grouchy travelers ruin her vacation. She stared across the aisle at the old woman, who appeared to be nodding off. Marc fidgeted on one side of her, and the man on the other side of her stood like a statue.

Another hour passed before the attendant returned to the counter and turned on the microphone. "We'll start boarding now," she announced, and the room went into motion as everyone began gathering luggage and standing. She announced which rows would board first, and half the room almost attacked each other hurrying to the counter.

"You'd think they were worried someone might steal their seat." Jenny laughed at the sight of it all.

"You don't fly much, do you?" the woman next to her snapped.

"I don't need to fly much to know there is an assigned seat on my ticket." Jenny gave the sweetest smile she could when the woman rolled her eyes at her.

"Some of us are on business trips and have deadlines," the woman retorted, sliding her laptop into her suitcase and inching to the edge of her seat.

"If I had the kind of job that sent me to Hawaii, I'd consider it a vacation."

"Which is obviously why you don't have the kind of job that flies you to Hawaii." The woman stood, fighting to gather all of her luggage, then hauled her bags closer to the counter.

"I would hate being in any kind of meeting with that woman," Jenny mumbled.

The old lady wasn't as asleep as she appeared when she looked at Jenny and grinned.

More people hustled toward the counter when the attendant called off the next section of rows. Jenny looked at her ticket for at least the twentieth time when her row was called, then gathered the overnight bag she'd chosen as her carry-on so she wouldn't have to pay extra for having too many suitcases. Her free trip to Hawaii allowed for only one suitcase and one carry-on bag.

A large man pushed his way through the crowd and bumped the bitch who'd been sitting next to Jenny. The bag holding the woman's laptop fell to the ground, and several people walked over it indifferently. Jenny hurried forward. Just because the lady had an attitude didn't make it fair when others started acting like children.

"Here you go," Jenny offered, squatting and blocking anyone else from running over the bag, which had fallen open.

The woman cursed under her breath as she frantically shoved files and shoes back into the case while trying to keep the laptop in place.

"Try placing the shoes like this," Jenny said, grabbing a pair of heels that had toppled loose from the woman's other belongings and showing the lady what she meant. "Toe to heel and heel to toe," she explained.

"It won't matter how they're in there if I miss this meeting." The woman ignored Jenny's suggestion and slammed the case closed.

Jenny stood, deciding some people just couldn't be pleased. That's when she noticed the crowd wasn't moving. For whatever reason, there appeared to be another delay in boarding. The crowd was growing hostile, and complaints were easily overheard as those around her began demanding to get on the plane.

"I guess I would be grouchy, too, if I hadn't won this trip and was going to Hawaii for free."

"How nice for you," the bitch snapped. "I bet if you arrive late, though, your reservations will be canceled." She smiled at Jenny for the first time.

"I won them off *Last Chance for Happiness*. The reservations are for several days." Jenny pulled her itinerary out of her purse and flipped it open, looking at it, although she'd memorized every word since she'd received it.

"And if you're taking the shuttle to your hotel and miss the last shuttle run, you'll be stuck in the airport all night." Again the woman grinned.

"When is the last shuttle?" Jenny didn't see a schedule for the shuttle in her paperwork.

"Let's put it this way. If that plane doesn't get off the ground in the next thirty minutes, you better put that small-town attitude away and learn how to flag down a taxi."

Jenny didn't have the money for a taxi. Until she found somewhere to cash her two-hundred-dollar voucher, which she hoped someplace would once she arrived in Honolulu, she had only ten dollars to her name. And what was it about her that gave away that she came from a small town? Were there no nice people in big cities?

Boarding began again and the attendant took more tickets. People pushed forward, anxious to get on the plane. Jenny didn't do much traveling, and it amazed her that so many people opted for this means of travel. Suddenly, home sounded real good. Her life was in order. She wasn't unhappy. Maybe she didn't have thrills and excitement to look forward to on a regular basis, but that hadn't bothered her too much in the past. If she needed an escape, a good book always took care of it. She didn't need this trip to Hawaii. She hadn't even asked for it.

The old woman still sat in her chair with her two men on either side of her. Jenny let a few people push past her. She had an assigned seat. It wasn't going anywhere, and she didn't need to get wrapped up in the attitude of some travelers.

Someone bumped into her and grunted something as they adjusted their shoulder bag and continued past her. Jenny backed up, taking the nearest seat, and glanced at her itinerary.

"Have you ever been to Hawaii?" The old woman was sitting in the chair with its back to hers.

"No," she said, smiling as she twisted around to make eye contact with the older woman. Jenny didn't realize she'd plopped down so close to her. "I've never flown before either. A bunch of new adventures today." She laughed, but felt the strain in her voice.

The old woman's watery gray eyes were alert, with just the perfect amount of make-up around them, not cakey the way Nana's often was. Her nails were nicely done in a pale pink, and she wore enough jewelry that it probably added a few pounds to her weight. The diamond ring on her wedding finger was enormous. She gave Jenny an appraising look. Jenny got the impression this was a woman accustomed to controlling the world around her without ever raising her voice.

"You're excited." The woman didn't make it a question.

"Honestly, I was starting to wonder if all of this is worth it. I would love to see another part of the world, learn how people are there and how they live. I guess I've already learned how businesspeople act in airports." Jenny gripped her itinerary and glanced at the congestion around the counter and then at the corridor where passengers disappeared to board the large plane she could see outside the windows. "Honestly, it seems there should be an easier way to do this. I guess I'm used to how things are done at home. If there is a crisis, everyone getting upset doesn't help solve it."

The old woman had a husky, deep laugh. "There is a better way to do this," she said, her mouth barely moving when she spoke. "I try to fly commercial occasionally to keep in touch with the world, but it simply reminds me why I own my own plane. Just like you and your town, I can also fade comfortably into my life and forget how the rest of the world behaves. I think it's healthy to take a look around you from time to time. None of us are perfect, my dear."

"Is that why you're traveling? Or do you have family you're going to see?"

"A bit of both. Although I'm not sure if things will work out as I wished." The old lady cast her attention in the direction of the aggravated people huddling around the attendants at the counter.

"I'll call right now to make arrangements for your private jet," Marc said, jumping toward the old woman as if her every need was all he lived for.

The old woman raised a delicate, wrinkled hand, waving it in his direction, but she didn't look at him. Marc grabbed his cell phone, focusing on his shoes as he placed a call.

"I couldn't help overhearing your conversation with the young businesswoman you were sitting by for a short time."

Jenny grinned. "I thought you were sleeping."

"Just resting my eyes." The old woman didn't smile in return. "I get tired easy these days. But how exciting that you won a prize in a game show. You must be very smart, or was it a game of luck?"

Jenny wasn't sure the old woman would appreciate how she was raised on Elvis trivia, as well as other bits and pieces of information that had mattered to Nana. "I don't know how smart I am," she said, lifting a shoulder lazily. "It would be more accurate to say I know a little bit about a lot of things."

"What is trivial to some obviously isn't to others. It got you here."

"At the moment, I'm not sure if that's a good thing or not. But the game show was a learning experience, and it made Nana happy." Jenny shook her head, wondering again what people saw in traveling this way. "You're right. I can't let something like congestion in an airport ruin my vacation. And I know I'll love Hawaii."

"Yes, you will. May I see your itinerary? Possibly I've been to where you're going and can offer suggestions for you."

Jenny handed over the folded papers that she'd clung to since arriving at the airport. Immediately Marc leaped forward, handing the old woman a pair of glasses. The woman accepted them, not once looking away from the papers. Then, placing the glasses on the end of her nose, she read through Jenny's reservations, taking her time and reading every word. She glanced back more than once as she perused the pages.

"Interesting." She folded the papers as Jenny had them and handed them back to her. "Have you watched this game show for very long?"

"Oh, yes. Nana and I watch *Last Chance for Happiness* almost daily and have for longer than you probably care to know."

"There's something wrong with a business when they treat their loyal fans so poorly," the woman said, sounding as if she spoke to herself. Then she raised her watery gray eyes to Jenny. When she offered a small smile, there were creases visible in her pink lipstick. "It sounds as if your nana is a very lucky woman to have such a devoted granddaughter."

"Nana raised me," she said, and refrained from offering her life story. This woman didn't want to hear how her parents had died when she was an infant. "We're all each other has now," she added, not wanting the lady to think Jenny was some over-attentive relative.

"Why isn't she here with you?"

"Nana won't travel. It was enough for her to go see her favorite game show in person."

"Your nana is a wise woman. Sometimes the adventures should be left to the young people."

Jenny nodded, since she wasn't sure what to say and glanced at her itinerary, wondering what the old woman saw that didn't impress her. Jenny had read through the papers so many times she almost knew every word verbatim. She hadn't seen anything wrong.

The attendant began speaking into her microphone again. "May I have your attention, please. The flight is overbooked. If anyone would like to come forward and release their tickets, I can instruct you where to go for compensation. Our pilot sincerely apologizes and wishes to thank all of you for flying with Hawaiian Airlines. If you'd like to relinquish your tickets, we will arrange for you to take another flight. Anyone interested, please come forward to the counter."

An uncomfortable silence followed, and Jenny glanced at the many travelers who were also looking around, watching to see who would come forward and give up their seat.

"Maybe I should give up mine." Jenny fingered her plane tickets. "I don't mind arriving on a different plane."

"You don't want to do that, my dear," the old woman said, patting Jenny's hand. "I think you'll find your tickets are nontransferable and nonrefundable. Not to mention, if you don't arrive by six p.m. tonight, Hawaiian time, you'll lose your hotel reservations."

The old woman's hand was cold and soft. Jenny glanced at the clock on the wall and did the math to calculate the time difference. She already knew how long she'd be in the air. She and

Nana had discussed that when Jenny tried convincing her to go with her. If she wasn't in the air in the next half hour, her hotel reservations wouldn't be any good, at least according to the old woman.

Jenny focused on her itinerary, reading it again until she found the small print the old woman referred to. It did, in fact, say all hotel reservations would be null and void if she didn't check in by six p.m., unless she wished to pay the fees permitted by law to extend the reservation for late arrival. Jenny wondered why the people with the game show, who'd gone over the prize and all of its benefits with her, never mentioned this.

The hands on the wall clock moved forward, and with each minute that passed, Jenny's stomach twisted into a tighter knot. The attendant wasn't allowing anyone else to board. Finally, standing, she worked her way around the crowd of irritated passengers and approached the attendant.

"Excuse me," she began, trying to get the attendant's attention. Finally she stuck her plane tickets in front of the woman's face to get her to look up from her computer. "I need to leave or my hotel reservations in Hawaii won't be any good."

The attendant glanced at Jenny's tickets. "If your cell doesn't have a signal here, you can use that phone to contact the hotel and make arrangements for late arrival," she offered, pointing to a phone at the end of the counter. "The plane probably won't depart for at least another hour."

"Another hour? But . . . ," she began, prepared to present a convincing argument, whatever it took for the woman to change her mind, contact the pilot, and inform him it would definitely be in their best interest to leave right now.

The attendant had already returned her attention to her computer screen, as if Jenny weren't still standing right next to her. What was the point!

The truth had sunk in. Her pleasure vacation wasn't going to happen. There would be no Hawaii. She'd spent the past few weeks preparing. It had been all she'd thought about, or talked about with Nana. "Thank you," she muttered, moving away from the counter.

Jenny returned to her seat, suddenly wondering if she should give up this easily. She'd won the grand prize on the show. That meant something, or she was pretty sure it did. Maybe a few phone calls would fix all of this. After all, during all her reading about flying on an airplane, she had taken time to read about several lawsuits, a few of them involving planes not leaving on time. As far as she'd read, no one had won a case against an airport, but it was making the airlines a bit more determined to keep the general public satisfied.

Not to mention, the game show people wouldn't want an unhappy grand-prize winner on their hands. They had promised her a trip to Hawaii. They had to make sure she got there and had a place to stay. She had noticed, even if she'd missed the part about arriving on time, that the small print went out of its way to protect the game show people. Jenny might be small-time, but she wasn't stupid. She had rights, too.

Her phone did have a signal, and she started with the hotel in Honolulu. After writing down how much it would cost to arrange for late arrival, she hung up and searched for the number for the game show committee. Then, placing that call, she agreed to hold when the secretary told her she would see if someone had time to talk to her.

"This is Morgan with *Last Chance for Happiness.* How may I help you today?" a woman asked cheerfully, speaking very loudly into Jenny's ear.

"Hi, Morgan. I'm Jenny Rogers. I won the grand prize on *Last Chance for Happiness* a few weeks ago. I'm at the airport now, getting ready to leave for my Hawaiian vacation, and there is a problem with the plane. It appears it won't leave in time for me to make my reservation at the hotel in Honolulu."

"*Last Chance for Happiness* is not responsible, or liable, for any businesses connected or associated with any prizes that are offered through the game show."

"I understand that," Jenny said, nodding. "I wondered if you could help me arrange to have different reservation times so that I won't have to pay for late arrival."

"All prizes are final and the disclaimer you signed says you agree not to hold *Last Chance for Happiness* responsible or liable for how any business disburses a prize won on our show."

It sounded as if Morgan were reading from a script. Jenny tried another tactic. "Possibly I could exchange this vacation for another vacation prize the show offers. I don't have the money—"

"All prizes are final," Morgan interrupted. "When you signed your disclaimer, you agreed to receive any prizes from the show without hesitation or malice. You agreed not to hold *Last Chance for Happiness* responsible or in any way to pursue litigation against the show or its employees regarding any prize conflicts. You also agreed not to assume in any way that *Last Chance for Happiness,* or its employees would be responsible for any taxes or additional charges instigated by any business or corporation directly, or indirectly, associated with *Last Chance for Happiness.*"

Jenny got it. "Okay. So you're saying you won't help me if my flight doesn't leave in time and therefore I can't make the reservation deadline."

"*Last Chance for Happiness* is not responsible—"

"I understand," Jenny snapped.

"Wonderful," Morgan said cheerfully and way too loudly in Jenny's ear. "Thanks for enjoying *Last Chance for Happiness,* and make sure not to miss our next show!"

Morgan hit a high note that pierced Jenny's ear. Jenny thanked her, although she wasn't sure what she was thanking her for, and hung up the phone. She didn't need to glance at the clock again to know what to do next. Her choices were limited. Hell, they didn't exist.

Stuffing her phone back in her bag, she took one last wistful look at the large plane outside before standing and starting toward the doorway leading back to the busy hallway. Nana would be shocked to see her, but there wasn't any point in staying at the airport. Regardless of when she boarded that plane now, it wouldn't matter. There was no way she would arrive in Honolulu before six p.m.

"Miss Rogers." Marc, the old woman's assistant, reached her side before she exited the boarding area. "Ms. Winston would like to see you." He took her arm, turning and guiding her back to the old woman. The way he moved indicated he was confident Jenny would be honored to give the old woman an audience. Marc tried taking Jenny's bag from her and at the same time guided her into the chair next to Ms. Winston.

Jenny grasped her carry-on firmly and took the seat, frowning at Marc as he stepped backward.

"Miss Rogers," Ms. Winston began, her back as straight as a yardstick as she sat facing Jenny with her hands clasped in her lap. "I've decided you will fly instead of me on my private plane."

"What?" Jenny gasped.

"This will work out rather well, I think. Fresh eyes can often see what jaded old eyes cannot. Give Marc your bag. Marc and Sean will escort you. Once you're settled in, I will call and make sure everything is okay." She stood, as if that were all that was needed with this discussion.

The silent, tall man took her arm, guiding her toward the exit.

"Wait." Jenny dug her feet into the carpet. "Ma'am, Ms. Winston. This is very kind of you, but I can't ride on your private plane."

"Why not?" Ms. Winston arched her penciled-on eyebrows, sounding sincerely surprised. She didn't look like she'd ever been one of those mean business tycoons no one dared cross, but there was something about her.

Jenny guessed few had ever argued with this woman's decisions once they were made. "Ma'am, I don't know you," she said, trying for polite yet using the same decisive tone the elderly lady used. "You're very kind to offer your seat, and your plane, but I can't pay for the ticket, and I won't accept it for free."

Ms. Winston stood and held out her hand. "I am Samantha Winston, owner and CEO of Winston Enterprises."

Jenny didn't have a clue what Winston Enterprises was. "It's nice to meet you. I'm Jenny Rogers." She felt foolish since the old woman already knew her name. "But you can't just give me your plane ticket, and no offense, but introductions don't mean you know someone."

Samantha Winston raised one perfectly sculpted eyebrow. "I can't?" She laughed, her throaty chuckle almost sounding painful. "You've got scruples. Too many young people want something for nothing. I'm glad to see you understand everything in life is earned."

Jenny nodded and held her bag against her chest. She knew all too well how everything was earned. Ms. Winston had been friendly and helpful, but did that mean Jenny could trust her?

"I will arrange for you to earn your ticket once you arrive on the island." Samantha waved her employees on, who once again tried escorting Jenny away from the old woman.

Jenny held firm and wouldn't budge. "What do you mean by that?"

Was she really considering this?

"I have some sensitive matters I planned on addressing while on the island. I believe someone with fresh, young eyes will offer a perspective I wouldn't be able to see. You will attend these meetings in my place."

Jenny stared at her. Nana couldn't wait to see pictures from Hawaii. She would be disappointed Jenny didn't go, but she would understand. "Ms. Winston, you're very gracious. But I can't accept something like this from you. And if you own the plane, why don't you go with me? If you wish me to earn these tickets, which I'm not saying I will do yet, it would be a lot easier for you to delegate if you're there with me."

Samantha Winston smiled. "I've decided to learn something from your nana and allow the young people to explore and report back to me. I have a feeling I'll enjoy hearing what both of you have to say."

"Both of us?" Jenny frowned, wondering if she'd completely lost her mind for even considering this preposterous invitation.

Samantha waved her blue-veined hand in the air and began wheezing. The men were at her side immediately, both of them looking more worried than concerned, as if they'd seen the old lady have fits like this one too many times. Although she almost collapsed in the larger man's arms, the moment he'd helped her into one of the seats, she glared at him and he backed off silently.

"Your plans were to see a part of the world you've never seen before," Samantha continued, although she spoke so softly now that Jenny was forced to take the seat next to her to hear her. "I think I can help you do that more so than if you'd followed your initial itinerary. I'm an old lady, and despite of how things may appear right now, I'm not ready to leave this earth."

Jenny was inclined to say something, assure her she looked far from her deathbed. Samantha did look frail, though. Her small, thin body was almost dwarfed in the seat she reclined in.

Still, there was an elegance about her. Jenny wouldn't be surprised if this woman fought death down to her last breath.

"As I mentioned, you wouldn't have this trip for free. You would be doing me an immense favor if you went in my place and reported to me a few times a day, telling me your impressions of everything."

"You said something about meetings." Jenny couldn't believe she was considering this. The smart thing to do, the right thing to do, would be to get up right now, thank the old lady for her offer, and return home. "I don't have any experience with business meetings of any kind."

"Perfect." A glow appeared in the old lady's eyes, proof she wasn't on her deathbed yet. "You won't need experience. In fact, it is your fresh outlook on life that makes you the perfect candidate. The meetings I'm talking about are personal. You'll meet with individuals who wish to see me in order to achieve some personal goal. Your meeting them first will help me see if they are sincere." Samantha placed her frail, shriveled hand over Jenny's. It was cool, and her grip was firm when she gave Jenny's hand a gentle squeeze. "It would be an incredible favor to me if you would agree to fly to the island, meet with these people for me, then let me know what you think of them."

Jenny had so many questions she didn't know where to begin. Marc's phone beeped, and he pulled it from his waist and answered it.

"The pilot is ready," he informed Samantha after he ended the call. "A couple attendants are on their way to escort you to your car."

"Very good, Marc." Samantha reached for him, and he practically leaped to her side, offering his hand and helping her to her feet. "Are you sure this is a good idea?" he whispered, but not so quietly Jenny didn't hear. "It would be no effort to reschedule this trip until you're feeling better."

"Nonsense." Samantha slipped her hand out of Marc's, then patted his arm affectionately. This man might be on the old lady's payroll, but there was a small exchange of affection that wasn't missed. "Look at her. Jenny's craving to see the world is fresh. Her opinion isn't jaded by money. She won't judge someone unfairly. That is so important. Not to mention, the people I'm to meet will more likely show their true colors when meeting her instead of me."

Marc lowered his voice, leaning into Samantha when he asked, "Do you think *he* isn't for real?"

"Shush," Samantha snapped, aggravated. "He's for real. His motivation is yet to be determined, though. Jenny will unveil that for me."

"Very wise, ma'am." Marc took Jenny's arm. "If you'll follow me, Miss."

She didn't have much of a choice since he'd just taken her bag that had her purse attached to it. When Marc approached, a male flight attendant, or maybe he was a pilot, opened a door at the other end of the room and nodded to Jenny when she hurried into the hallway after Marc.

"Who is the *he* you two were talking about?" she asked Marc.

"You don't question Ms. Winston. She will explain what she needs you to know when she sees fit. You should be honored she saw the qualities in you to tend to these tasks. Ms. Winston doesn't make bad decisions." Marc didn't turn around but continued at a comfortable pace to the end of the hallway. It opened into the plane. She felt a slight vibration under her feet, and she was surprised at how the plane looked inside.

Marc murmured something to a woman standing in a comfortable living room setting. The woman nodded and smiled at Jenny.

"Please, Miss Rogers, if you'll sit here. Would you like a

drink? I can have your meal prepared now." The woman gestured to a chair that looked more like a La-Z-Boy chair than a plane seat.

"A drink sounds good." Jenny was beyond confused. It had taken three weeks to prepare for her trip to Hawaii. She couldn't switch gears fast enough now that her entire travel itinerary had changed at the hands of an old, wealthy, but obviously eccentric woman.

# 2

Ric Karaka stepped onto the front porch of the large, old house and breathed in the morning air. He loved the smell of the island. It brought back memories, the first good ones he'd had, from after high school when he'd originally come to Lanai, one of the smaller Hawaiian islands. The fresh air, often mixed with the aroma of some nearby flowering plant or tree, had an erotic edge to it.

He didn't regret living on the banana plantation, although he was still getting accustomed to all the silence and space. It was a far cry from the inner city in L.A.

"Life goes on," he reminded himself, voicing the mantra he'd used for years as he stretched, then tested several of the floorboards on the old porch as he headed down the stairs. The first half of his life made hell dim in comparison, but Ric had always found the energy to push himself forward. "You never would have thought you'd be here, though, did you, old man?"

Ric was only thirty, but he didn't see any reason to try clinging to his youth. He hadn't started enjoying life, or learning how to move ahead in it, until he'd let go of his childhood. Not that years in foster homes, being used so a family who didn't want him could receive a government check every month, had been much of a childhood. Once he managed his emancipation at seventeen, Ric had finally taken charge of his own destiny.

Thirteen years later, he hadn't made any mistakes yet. The old banana plantation didn't look like much right now, but with funding, he'd turn the place around. Sweat and sore muscles didn't bother him when they came from hard work. He wasn't running from anyone anymore, and he knew who he was.

Ric's full name was Ricardo Karaka. It wasn't until he reached college, managing grants so he could attend UCLA, that he had learned anything about who he was and where he'd come from. He was the son of Julio Karaka and Maria Winston, two people who'd loved the hell out of each other but were ripped from life before they were really able to live it. Ric was all that was left of both of them. He didn't resent their dying, especially since he never knew either of them. And he didn't resent the state for taking him in and placing him in foster care.

Julio Karaka came from a family of farmers. The Karaka family dated back generations here on the island. The moment Ric had discovered that he'd hopped on a plane and flown to Lanai. The chances of him not being related to all of them, with such an odd last name, were slim to none. And he'd been right. There were still quite a few Karakas around on the island, although none of them farmed anymore. Meeting his father's side of the family helped explain his coal-black hair and dark skin that got even darker when he worked outside in the summer.

His mother, though, had been a blonde goddess. Ric remembered the first time he saw her picture. No wonder his father had fallen head over heels for the rebellious daughter of a billionaire.

It wasn't until he came to the island that he learned that

much about either of his parents. His grandparents, Pedro and Alicia Karaka, took him in for a while. But when they lost the banana plantation, there was barely enough food, or room, for the two of them in the small house they had moved into on the other side of the island. During the time he stayed with them, he had learned a lot about the hot, sultry romance between Julio and Maria.

Ric had politely listened to Alicia as she fanned herself and looked at him dreamily as she told him how Maria Winston had become smitten with her oldest son. Julio didn't care about her money, and Maria didn't blink an eye when her family cut her off for marrying a poor farmer's son. The Winstons never knew Julio and Maria had a son, since Julio's death had cut them off from Alicia.

Ric had managed the research and learned the details about his birth. Maria had been pregnant and alone. Her family had disowned her, although Ric would never know why she didn't turn to the Karakas. Maybe she believed they wanted nothing more to do with her. Possibly she'd been extremely depressed after her husband's untimely death. She could have been destitute, penniless. Whatever the reason, she gave birth to Ric in a hotel room all by herself. The motel maids found him crying in his dead mother's arms the next morning. His mother had lived in a home with several other women for a while while she was pregnant. According to the records that followed him through life, Maria's roommates said she knew she was having a boy and named him Ricardo. She had called him Little Ricky while he was in her womb. Ric never went by Ricky, but he got more than many orphans received. He knew his name.

All of that was ancient history. Ric survived, grew up, went to school, and managed a loan from the bank to buy back the Karakas' banana plantation. It got him a warm welcome from his father's side of the family, since the farm had been lost in a foreclosure. His grandparents and uncles weren't convinced he would make a good farmer and were even a bit more cautious when he told them he would turn it into a bed-and-breakfast. The Karakas were well known in the local community. Today they might be poor, but they were proud. When he shared with his grandparents and two of his uncles, Juan and Jose, his plan to renovate the old plantation house, their silence spoke volumes. They feared their newfound grandson and nephew would bring shame to their good name.

Ric turned as the screen door behind him opened, then shut with a bang. Colby, his bloodhound mix, sauntered to the edge of the porch and stared at the land in front of the house.

"They'll learn soon enough I don't discuss plans if they aren't solid," he said, reaching to scratch her head as she stared up at him with soft, brown eyes. Colby might not say much, but she was the best addition he'd made to the large, rambling old house so far. He watched her prance down the steps, then follow her nose as she started a spiraling pattern through the yard. "It's Karaka land. Can you smell that?"

Colby wagged her tail and continued her urgent sniffing until she found the right spot to take care of her morning business. He wasn't sure what had compelled him to take in the bloodhound mix when she'd shown up at his door shortly after he'd moved in. No one knew who she was or where she'd come from. Ric understood her plight.

Colby was an orphan, just as he'd been. She had no family, no home, no roots. Ric had lived on the streets long enough to know there was no such thing as coincidence. Colby's gift for tracking had brought her to the one house on the island that needed a family. Ric once believed he would find the perfect girl, have kids, and be the perfect father he never had. That dream was long gone. Ric and Colby were family, and together they would show his newfound family, and every one on the island, just how successful he could be.

Timing was everything. Ric knew how to keep his credit

score high enough to do business. And right now, times were hard. He'd qualified for the loan and convinced the family who bought it off the bank for next to nothing to sell it to him.

As one of his foster mothers used to brag when she'd come home from her Realtor job—ignoring him and the other foster kids and drinking with her husband—"Location, location, location."

His negligent foster parents had nurtured him more than they'd ever know. Ric stared off the front porch, down the long, one-lane driveway leading to the highway that circled the island, and at the endless ocean beyond. He had location nailed down. Some might see this old house and the untended land as an eyesore and a wasted investment.

There were still pineapple bushes growing on the property. Ric had no intention of turning it back into a farm, but, instead, a bed-and-breakfast. He might plant a few banana trees just for atmosphere. It was going to take a lot of hard work to turn the place around. Sweat labor would be his saving grace. That, and a solid investor.

He had the first, and by day's end, he'd have the latter.

Colby finished doing her business at the same time that someone pulled off the highway into his driveway. She bounded across the yard, baying loudly as her ears flopped, and she ran toward the old faded blue Buick Skylark. Ric made sure the door was locked and the screen door secure before following his dog to greet his grandparents. They knew he was going to meet Samantha Winston today, his maternal grandmother, with whom he'd been exchanging letters for the past few months. The last thing they would do was tie him up so he couldn't get business under way.

Ric was a realist. He prided himself on the fact. No one knew his private excitement to meet another family member— his mom's mother. He's barely slept a wink last night. When he had, it had been filled with heaving stories about his mom, stories that would bring him closer to the woman who died giving him life. He would soon know more about the woman he'd been clinging to during the first few hours of his life.

Anyone would think him weak with thoughts like that. Ric had been clear and to the point with the Karakas and Samantha Winston, his grandparents, concerning this meeting today. He wanted this meeting to discuss a business venture—the bed-and-breakfast. Samantha would hear the details in person. The Karakas already knew, and they thought he was crazy. Samantha wouldn't think he was crazy. She was a very successful businesswoman.

Ric had done the right thing, keeping the letters between him and Samantha business related. His mom's mother spoke the language of big business. Ric couldn't wait to meet her. He knew he got his ability to turn a dollar from her.

Pedro Karaka climbed out from the driver's side of his Buick and patted Colby's head as he walked around the front of the car, then opened the door for his wife, Alicia.

"Ricardo!" Alicia Karaka extended her arms, greeting Ric as if it were the first time they'd seen each other and not less than twenty-four hours since he'd been at their place on the other side of the island. "So today you take on the Winstons," she said, not waiting a minute before jumping into her reason for being there. "You remember what we told you last night, your grandfather and I. These are not good people. Keep your head high and remember you are a Karaka, good blood and good people." She reached him and clasped his face, squeezing it with her damp, arthritic hands as she grinned up at him.

"I'm half Winston, too," he reminded her, smiling down at her leathery face and twinkling dark eyes. There weren't many people on this planet capable of giving unconditional love so easily. Alicia Karaka was one of them.

"And half Karaka, which is why I'm not worried one bit," she said, laughing and giving his head a little shake before releasing him. "Now, what are you going to say?"

"Mother," Pedro Karaka complained under his breath, giving her a hard side glance before shifting his attention to Ric and looking apologetic.

"Shhh, shhh." Alicia didn't look at her husband but waved her hand at him dismissively.

Pedro ignored the gesture and the command to be quiet. "We came to wish him the best of luck," he said, sounding as if it weren't the first time he'd reminded his wife why they were stopping by Ric's place unannounced.

Another day Ric might have been amused. Alicia and Pedro were good people. Some might even claim he was blessed to have them as grandparents. But Ric saw them as a repeated reminder as to why he would never get married, why he'd quit the dream of his childhood to be a good father and husband someday. They spoke over each other, interrupted each other, and went off on tangents, losing focus as to what they were originally talking about.

Ric wouldn't ever get stuck in a mess like that. His grandparents had spent a lifetime together and had nothing to show for it. They were broke and lived in a shack.

"Of course we wish you good luck." Alicia ignored Colby when the dog walked between her and Ric. "And we want you to know how proud your papa would be if he were alive today."

Ric had heard a lot of that since he'd moved to the island almost a year ago. It wasn't the easiest thing for him to wrap his brain around. If Ric got his practicality from his father, then his dad wouldn't be proud until Ric accomplished his goals. He was simply moving forward, securing his success and his roots into place.

"Thank you, Grandmother." There wasn't anything else to

say. When she simply beamed up at him, Ric leaned forward and gave her a gentle hug.

Alicia wasn't going to have anything to do with that. She wrapped her arms around Ric and held on as if her life depended on it. His grandfather, Pedro, nodded as he watched his wife.

"Give us a call when you get home," he said, apparently deciding his wife had clung to Ric long enough and slowly began peeling her away from him. "Your grandmother will worry until you do."

Alicia made a clucking sound as she swiped her hand at Pedro, as if she would hit him several times for suggesting such a thing. A simple sidestep on his part and he avoided her efforts. She continued waving Pedro off as she turned to the car.

"Are you sure this is what you want to do?" Pedro asked, turning from his wife and pulling on his multicolored shirt. Once, the old man probably had hair as black and thick as Ric's, but strong streaks of silver dominated it now.

Pedro had asked as if there were other options. Ric tried to tell him this was standard practice in business. A venture this size didn't get off the ground without financing. He could go to the bank and take out another loan, hopefully. But he'd only paid a year on his mortgage so far, and as it was, the money he'd saved was quickly dwindling. If Samantha Winston financed this project, once the bed-and-breakfast was up and running, he'd be able to pay off the mortgage and pay her back with money left to live on. He'd crunched the numbers enough times to have them memorized.

"Everything will be fine." It was a line he'd learned from the foster mother he'd had through part of grade school. "Don't worry," he added. Then, again not sure what to do, he extended his hand. "I'll call you two once I'm done."

Pedro was old-school, and stubborn as hell. No one could get the old man to see any viewpoint other than his own. More

than once, Ric had explained why he was approaching Samantha Winston. He had no clue how Pedro ran his farm for all the
years he did when he appeared to be so staunchly against bor-
rowing money. And God forbid the old man understand a line
of credit.

"You would think after a year you'd understand the concept
of family, boy," Pedro said, ignoring the extended hand and instead taking Ric by the arm and walking with him toward the
driver's side of the car. "Sometimes I think you got every lick of
stubbornness your grandmother could pass down through her
blood. We're going to worry. We're going to support you. And
we're going to ask questions and butt our heads into your business on a very regular basis. I've been over this with you. Your
grandmother is living proof of this."

Ric watched Colby as she circled around Pedro, sniffing his
pockets with each turn. Pedro absently stroked the dog's head
but kept his stern, watery gaze on Ric. He wouldn't admit
Pedro had a point, especially when it wasn't the issue at the moment. He wanted Pedro to understand business, and Pedro
wanted him to understand the concept of family, something Ric
had never had prior to a year ago and what many people didn't
seem to give the same value to, at least as far as he'd seen. Ric
stood a better chance of explaining business to his grandfather
than the other way around.

"I understand," he lied, and the look Pedro gave him proved
he saw through the lie. Ric patted his grandfather on the shoulder and held the car door while Pedro got in. The old man slid
a large piece of jerky out of his pants pocket and tossed it to
Colby. "I'll be sure and let both of you know how things went
as soon as I'm done visiting with her."

"Don't make it all about business, boy," his grandfather
said, wagging his finger at Ric. "Take time to know your
blood."

Pedro and Alicia Karaka backed out of Ric's driveway, the old man taking it at a snail's pace. Ric waved after them for a moment, then turned to his dog, who was on the trail of some rodent and already heading across the field where neglected banana trees and rows of pineapple bushes grew.

"You ready, Colby?" he yelled.

Colby bayed loudly, one of her ears inside out, as she gave up on her hunt and came bounding toward Ric's truck. She pranced around in circles until Ric opened the passenger door for her. She leaped into the seat and immediately sat facing forward without giving him a second glance.

"All right, girl," Ric informed Colby as he climbed in, then revved the engine. "You're going to chill in the truck while I tend to some business. You know the drill."

Her response was to lean forward and sniff the glove box where her bone was kept, a reward for not chewing on his upholstery when Ric left her in the truck. He waited until his grandparents had pulled out onto the road, then made a U-turn in the driveway and headed for town.

Joe Seal, whom Ric had met right after moving to the island, moonlighted as a bellhop at the Four Seasons at Manele Bay, one of the two hotels on the island. He had his eyes open for Samantha Winston's arrival. Joe had called Ric the night before and confirmed that the Samantha Winston party had arrived as scheduled and, it appeared, with more servants that usual. Ric guessed she might have quite an entourage with her. This was the half of his family that was loaded.

Not that he had any desire to drain her dry. And he expected her to be wary, to not trust him, and to anticipate that he wanted her money. His story was too stereotypical. Long-lost relative shows up on the doorstep looking for handouts. It would be what he would think if the tables were turned. No one had ever given him a handout his entire life. Not so much as a meal. And that wasn't what he was asking for now. Corporations like Winston Enterprises invested their money in smaller companies all the time. No, Ric wasn't after a free ride.

Ric had given the old woman time to relax after her flight. Now it was time for her to know her grandson. He still would want to meet her even if he didn't need her to invest in his new business. And, truth be told, he admitted to himself as he gripped and released the steering wheel and realized he was already in town and hadn't even turned on the stereo, he would have been a hell of a lot more nervous meeting her if it weren't for his business plans. The banana plantation kept him focused, helped his mind stay where it belonged—on sensible, level-headed matters. Otherwise, he'd be stepping into unfamiliar territory, which was not something he liked doing.

Although somewhere around eighty years old, Samantha Winston still had an active hand in the huge line of restaurants and hotels her family owned around the world. She was owner and CEO of Winston Corporation. Shortly after arriving on the island, and meeting his grandparents and uncles, Ric had learned enough about his mother's side of the family to start researching. It hadn't been hard tracking down Samantha Winston. She owned several homes, and he learned from reading tabloids and *People* magazine, which did an extensive piece on her almost five years ago, that she lived in Minneapolis during the summer, Houston during the winter, New York during the spring, and Los Angeles in the fall. None of that appealed to him as much as studying her business portfolio. In her earlier years, Samantha Winston had taken her father's business and quadrupled its value.

A woman after his own heart.

Ric knew the moment he explained his plans to her, she would be more than willing to invest in him. He didn't need to play the long-lost relative. There was no point. He would speak as a shrewd businessman spoke to another shrewd business-person.

Ric wasn't an idiot. The bed-and-breakfast would make it. Samantha understood business, and she'd see what Ric saw—the perfect business in the ideal location.

The Four Seasons, which was one of two hotels on the island, was designed for the very wealthy. He'd grown used to the flashiness of the rich and famous, as well as the recluses, who were probably even wealthier and who came to Lanai to escape the paparazzi and other invasions of their privacy. He pulled into the hotel parking lot as a Rolls-Royce pulled out.

Ric waved at Joe Seal, who stood in his black hotel uniform in the parking lot, talking to a kid Ric didn't know. Ric parked his truck off to the side of the parking lot, opened the glove box, and took out the massive rawhide bone he'd purchased the day before after Colby had finished off her last one.

"Try and make this one last at least until I get back," he said, handing the bone over to Colby.

She accepted her bribe not to eat the truck's interior and looked at him with her jowls sticking out over the bone. Colby winked at him. Good enough answer, he hoped.

"Be good," he ordered, lowering both windows a few inches to give Colby fresh air, then hopped out of his truck, locked it, and headed across the parking lot toward Joe.

"Slow morning?" he asked, extending his hand and shaking Joe's.

"It's been off and on. The morning tourists are already out and about the island. It won't pick up again until this afternoon." Joe gave Ric an appraising look and rocked back on his heels. "So you're here to meet the old lady?" Joe asked, falling in alongside Ric as they started toward the entrance. "Your grandmother, huh?"

"It's time for her to get to know her charming grandson."

Ric wasn't ready to announce his intentions of trying to get her to finance converting the old banana plantation into a bed-and-breakfast.

"Well, she hasn't left the hotel today. I haven't seen her, but hope to. She's a good tipper." Joe grinned and scratched his short dark brown hair. He was a big guy, stocky but not heavy, and shorter than Ric. He was tan from working with his father-in-law and was, according to his wife, Susie, quite the stud. Ric didn't see it but wouldn't argue with Susie. "Fill me in on all the details later. If I don't go home with some kind of tidbit for my wife, she'll drown me with questions until she makes me call and ask for a total recap."

Ric snorted, knowing Joe wasn't exaggerating. The couple times Ric had been over to Joe's house, Susie had spent the entire time on the phone talking to someone about how she was not a gossip. "I'm sure I'll see you when I leave. You'll have to bring the kids out to the place when you get some time off."

"Whenever that might be," Joe grumbled, although he didn't look put out and rocked back on his heels again. Work was hard to find. Joe wouldn't complain about too many hours. "Let me know when you're ready to reroof that old house. I can't believe you're living out there the way it is now."

"I manage, and will do. Hopefully soon." He'd heard enough comments about his choice to live in the dilapidated plantation house. He was saving money by not paying a second mortgage or rent. Not to mention by living there he had discovered other things that needed fixing that he might not have noticed until after he'd opened his doors for business.

Ric waved at Joe over his shoulder as he strolled into the lobby. He had only been in the hotel a couple times, the last time to help lay carpet with a job he got with Joe several months ago. Just as the last time, Ric entered a different world as he walked across the lobby. He didn't want to be impressed, but breathtaking was the best way to describe the hotel. Although most of Lanai was breathtaking. After living in the inner city of Los Angeles all his life, he'd seen enough ugliness. Beauty, whether it be skin deep or to the bone, surrounding him every day sure made life seem a lot easier. It was a good thing Ric understood that anything that appeared easy was usually a hell of a lot harder than something that appeared complicated.

Melinda Sadey worked the front desk and had her eyes on Ric the moment he had arrived on the island. Although he'd flirted with her on a few occasions when he'd been to the bars, she wasn't his type. Melinda was somewhere between forty-five and fifty-five years old and preferred her men a bit on the younger side. Ric had no intention of ever touching the woman but didn't mind casually flirting until she gave him the numbers of the three rooms booked under Samantha Winston.

Room 201 was a large suite and reserved with very specific instructions. The other two rooms, 211 and 213, were smaller suites alongside each other down the hall from Samantha's room. Ric didn't care to speak with her entourage. He got out of the elevator on the second floor and walked to the end of the hallway to the large suite, then rapped firmly on the door.

After knocking a second time, Ric reluctantly approached the two other doors. He didn't want to speak to hired help, but possibly Samantha was in one of the rooms. He stepped to the nearest of the two and again knocked.

A thin, short-haired man, who was probably in his forties, answered the door at room 213. He didn't say anything but simply stared at Ric, as if it wasn't his job to speak and therefore he had no intention of doing so.

"Are you Marc Waters?" Ric asked, and knew by the wary look the man gave him that he was. "I'm here to see Samantha Winston," he added before Marc could say anything.

"That's not possible." Marc cocked his head and made it look like he tried looking down at Ric. His tone was rather nasally, stuck-up sounding. "Who are you and what do you want?"

"I just told you what I want," Ric said, keeping his own tone civil in spite of the urge to push past the man and see if Samantha was in the room. "And I'm Ricardo Karaka, her grandson."

Marc made a snorting noise and began shutting the door. "Nice try, but Ms. Winston doesn't have a grandson. If she did, I would know."

"I am her grandson." Ric didn't like doors being shut in his face. He held his hand out, stopping the door. "Her daughter was my mother."

"Ms. Winston's daughter is dead."

"I know. I killed her."

Marc Waters stared at Ric, apparently not having a snooty comeback for that comment. Ric cringed inwardly, aware of the possibility that Ms. Winston might very well be in the room, listening to the conversation. It wouldn't surprise Ric, from what he'd learned of the lady's personality through her letters, that she would screen callers, taking advantage of her presence not being known and gathering what she could about them before agreeing to meet them. She had mentioned once in her letters to him that a woman in business had to be ten times more shrewd than a man, and as she'd put it, especially in her time, when women weren't involved in business.

Ric pushed the door open so he could see into the hotel room. Marc Waters instinctively took a step backward. It sounded as if he yelped under his breath. His eyes grew large as he sucked in a breath. If the man thought Ric would get rough with him, that wasn't Ric's fault.

"I've exchanged quite a few letters with Ms. Winston this past year." He kept his voice low, almost whispering. "She didn't know I existed before that, and I wasn't aware I had family. She told me the dates she would be on the island, and I agreed to come meet her." He had no intention of getting rough with anyone. It wasn't his fault he stood six foot two and the man before him was possibly a bit over five and a half feet and one hundred fifty pounds dripping wet.

"Sir, I've already told you," Marc said, stepping back farther, then turning and almost running to a phone on a round table in the middle of the room. "Don't make me call security."

Ric stared at the imbecile facing him, waving the phone at him like a weapon. "Would you like the number?" Ric wasn't sure if the man was going to start crying or piss his pants.

Marc Waters humphed, straightened, and looked to his side, through open glass doors that led to the bedroom half of the suite. "All I need for you to do is leave, Mr. Karaka." The man pulled his attention from whoever was in the bedroom and boldly stepped toward Ric. "Ms. Winston isn't here. I can't change that for you."

"When will she return?"

"She isn't going to return because she never came here in the first place."

"Marc? What's wrong?" a woman asked, peering around the opened doors. Her question was unnecessary since if she'd been in that room the entire time, there was no way she'd missed Ric and Marc's conversation.

The woman had incredibly captivating hair. Golden highlights wrapped around darker auburn strands. It flowed past her shoulders in thick, heavy curls. She had it pulled back at her nape, but the hair tie constricting those locks wasn't strong enough to confine all of it. Loose strands contoured her face. Ric had never seen such beautiful hair on a woman.

She looked at him and her blue eyes brightened. Her lips were naturally red and moist. She pursed them, looking as if she would blow a kiss. His insides tightened. She was beyond ravishing. Her high cheekbones and cute, slender nose helped show off her intoxicating beauty. There was something about her, beyond the obvious sexual appeal, that made Ric's dick stir to life. If he stared a moment longer, desires way too dark for someone who was probably related to him would surface and fog his focused thinking. He needed to remember why he was here.

"Is something wrong, Marc?" she asked, rephrasing the question as she gave Ric an appraising once-over.

"Nothing!" Marc waved an impatient hand at her. "Go into the room and close the doors."

The woman tilted her head, looking amused when she shifted her attention to Marc.

Ric immediately wanted her attention back on him.

"I said now." Marc apparently needed reassurance he was the man to listen to in someone's eyes. His chest puffed out when the young lady disappeared behind the connecting doors and closed them behind her.

"We were supposed to get together today." It wasn't completely a lie. He'd told Samantha in his last letter to her, which he'd mailed just a couple weeks ago, that he would contact her once she arrived on the island. "There wasn't an exact time set for our meeting, though," he added. "Now what do you mean she never came in the first place?"

"Samantha Winston isn't on the island." Marc had retrieved his balls and stalked around Ric to the door, then opened it, making a gesture with his hand. "Leave a card with me and when we discuss matters with her next, I'll let her know you were here."

Ric turned slowly, the small man's words not sinking in. "She isn't coming to the island?"

"Samantha Winston decided not to travel at this time. Apparently meeting you didn't seem that important to her."

Marc's words cut deeper than if he'd stabbed Ric with a knife. It took more than a moment to master the rage that took over the rush of desire from a moment ago. Samantha Winston wasn't coming. She'd changed her mind and decided not to visit the island. The truth hit him in the face but was damn hard to accept. Samantha had said they would meet and hadn't struck him as a woman to go back on her word.

"It's time for you to leave, Mr. Karaka," Marc said sternly. "We'll make sure to tell Ms. Winston you stopped by."

It had been the letters. They were such an odd way of communicating. It had tricked Ric and he'd fallen into the trap. No one wrote letters. They e-mailed, texted, talked on the phone. The only letters that existed were junk mail. No one read them, just threw them away without a second look.

Samantha Winston's letters had given him the power to dream. She'd been inquisitive about his past, present, and future. Her perfect penmanship and the quality writing paper she'd used had added to the personality of her he'd created in his mind. Although he hadn't mentioned converting the old banana plantation into a bed-and-breakfast—he'd wanted to discuss that with her in person—the many other ventures he'd told her he'd undertaken over the years had impressed her. Samantha Winston had expressed her opinion of Ric. She'd thought him intelligent, levelheaded, and driven.

Without Samantha's backing, the bed-and-breakfast would take a lot longer to do. If the place didn't start making money within the next year—if not sooner—Ric would be forced to find a full-time job to make the mortgage. He wouldn't have time, or energy, to restore the house. He'd be stuck in a dead-end job.

He'd been one hell of a goddamn idiot.

His movements were stiff when he turned from Marc, left the hotel suite, and took the stairs instead of the elevator to the lobby. It wasn't enough to ease the rage growing inside him.

Ric wanted to hit something, pound it until it didn't exist anymore. He was a fool. The humiliation rose like bile in the back of his throat. Nothing had ever pissed him off more. Ric had banked on sealing the deal based on letters with Samantha. His grandfather was right; Ric didn't get family.

He ignored Melinda's singsong voice when she called out his name. The bright midmorning sunshine annoyed the hell out of him for the first time since he'd moved here. The only thing worse than dealing with an idiot was behaving like one.

"Ricardo! Wait!"

Ric spun around before reaching his truck, the anger on his face apparent enough that the young lady he'd damn near drooled over in the hotel suite slid to a stop. She looked at him, her face flushed, while her unique hair color captured the rays of the sun and added to her radiance.

The smallest amount of sanity crawled back into his brain. "It's Ric, and what?" he demanded.

"Samantha told me you would be one of the appointments."

"I'm flattered I'm not the only appointment she blew off."

She wasn't very tall. He could see her crooked part and how strands that were different shades were pulled back, crossing over each other and confined in her hair clasp. Her skin was creamy white, not tanned like most women he knew. Her sleeveless blouse was silk, her skirt probably also pricey. It was a bit odd that she was chasing him down instead of sending the skinny, obnoxious man to do it for her. He wondered how she was related to Samantha Winston.

Or maybe they weren't related. Possibly this pretty young thing was Samantha's employee. She just indicated she knew the old lady's schedule. Her bright, beautiful eyes looked up at him with interest and curiosity. But how much curiosity? She had the edge on him. She would know if they were related since she'd overheard him tell Marc Waters he was Samantha Winston's grandson. Ric stared into her blue eyes, accentuated with a golden brown shade of eye makeup. Eyeliner drew attention to her eyes, making them look larger. She wore a lot of makeup for an employee, but didn't behave like a rich girl raised with servants at her beck and call.

"My name is Jenny, Jenny Rogers." She stuck her hand out, her arm straight, and waited for him to take it. "You're Ricardo Karaka, or Ric. I overheard you when you first came into the room and spoke with Marc."

"And how are you related to Samantha?" he asked, wrapping his long fingers around her small, warm hand.

"I'm not." Her mouth was open to say more but she didn't.

Ric held her hand in his and brushed his thumb over her wrist. Her heartbeat trembled under his touch, beating rapidly when he held her hand a moment longer than he normally would when shaking a stranger's hand. She wasn't nervous, at least not to the point where her palm would be damp. He made her cautious, though.

"Why did you come after me?" he asked, keeping his voice low. He didn't see Joe at the moment, but if Ric was spotted carrying on a conversation with a hot lady no one knew, it would take moments to hit the island grapevine.

When he released her hand, Jenny clasped her fingers together. Maybe she was nervous. He was usually dead-on when deciphering the mood of another person. Something about this sexy lady, with her many different shades of auburn hair, was harder to reach. It was as if she were one person on the surface and an entirely different person deep down inside.

"Can we speak inside? Possibly in the lobby?" Jenny gestured with her hand.

He cocked his head, imagining what she might want to discuss with him. "What's wrong with right here?"

Jenny glanced at the ground, then shot furtive looks at the surrounding parked cars. His truck was just a couple cars away. Colby must have been content with her bone because she hadn't spotted him and started howling. Ric kept his gaze focused on Jenny's when she finished her scan of their surroundings and returned her attention to him.

"I'm supposed to attend all of the meetings and functions Samantha was going to attend while she was here," she said, then paused, staring at him.

"Okay . . . ," he said slowly. How the hell was she supposed to stand in for a man meeting his grandmother for the first time?

She wrinkled her nose when she tilted her head, as if she didn't understand his response. Since he simply accepted what she'd just told him, he didn't see any reason to elaborate. And he didn't mind just staring at her. Jenny Rogers was easily one of the sexiest women he'd ever laid eyes on. He wondered if her rather vanilla outfit was her natural attire, or if she dressed differently when not under the charge of the Winston entourage.

"What I mean is I'm seeing her appointments, then reporting back to her."

"What do you report to her?"

"My impressions mainly. That seems to be all she wants."

"I'm to be interviewed before I am allowed to meet my grandmother?"

"You're on her appointment list. If she was supposed to meet you, I guess you get me instead." Jenny glanced up at him and gave him a small smile. She looked down at her hands before he could hold on to her gaze. Was she blushing over the double meaning that could be read into her words? Was she really that innocent? She was still hot as hell with an interesting accent. He'd guess Minnesota but it wasn't strong the way some in that region spoke. He liked the way it sounded, though.

Hell, he was even attracted to her modest attire. The straight-cut gray skirt she wore ended just above her knees, and her sleeveless blouse was tucked into her skirt and showed off her slender waist. Her hips weren't too round, but she didn't appear too skinny either. Her creamy white skin wasn't pale, just natural looking.

Ric knew women. For years he'd made them his most fo-cused project. And at a young age, possibly younger than many men, he'd figured out the type of woman who most satisfied him. Upper-class, hesitant, brainwashed, demure ladies weren't it. Unless he saw something inside them, like something he saw in Jenny, hinting that a darker side existed.

There was a particular quality a woman possessed indicating she wasn't as vanilla as others. Ric had managed more than once to pull desires out of a lady she never knew existed within her. He didn't think that was the case with Jenny.

Jenny Rogers was an illusion, right down to her simple Mid-western name. She was doing her best to appear modest, well bred, polite, and sophisticated. She shot him quick, furtive glances, suggesting she was shy, uncomfortable in his presence. Yet he would swear on his mother's grave Jenny was putting on an act.

If that were the case, what else might she be playing?

"No thanks," he said, and turned from her. Ric reached his truck, reminding himself no matter what might lie under the polite, modest layers of this auburn beauty, the point still re-mained Samantha Winston wasn't here. He needed to think, redirect his course, and talking to a sultry goddess with myster-ies lying beneath her surface wouldn't help his case.

When Ric reached for the door handle, Colby sat up, her ears high on her wrinkled forehead, and assessed the situation. The moment Jenny approached his side, touching the side of his truck, Colby let out a baying howl. It was her protective bark, although Ric couldn't tell if she was protecting his truck or her bone.

Jenny didn't jump back or appear startled by the dog. "Oh, wow, a bloodhound," she breathed as if they were her favorite breed.

"Yup." He had half a mind to open the door and "accidentally" let Colby slip past him, just to see if he could break Jenny's soft-spoken, sophisticated act.

"Ric, Mr. Karaka," she said, dismissing Colby and focusing on him, this time not pulling her gaze from the side of his head. "I know you're disappointed. Samantha Winston had quite a few appointments set up for her time here." She hesitated, chewing her lower lip and obviously choosing her words carefully. "I understand your meeting was quite a bit more personal than her other appointments." Again she paused. "But if you're willing to talk to me, possibly share with me how you discovered Samantha Winston or maybe something about your past . . ."

He looked at her, knowing his expression was hard and his temper seethed beneath his barely contained composure. He wanted to pound his truck. He wanted to take off and tear around the island, releasing the steam and fury building inside him. And he didn't care if Jenny saw how quick tempered he could be. It didn't bother him if she witnessed some of his aggression, and it definitely wouldn't be all he could release. What he didn't expect was for her eyes to widen, her round, moist mouth to pucker when she sucked in a breath. There was no way she couldn't see how mad he was right now, but instead of cowering or politely dismissing him and returning to her perfect world of order and old money, she stood there and faced his fury.

Ric lowered his gaze slowly, curious if showing her more than his anger might make her back off. He let his attention travel hungrily down her body taking in her full, round breasts pressing against her sleeveless blouse. He couldn't see her bra although it was obvious she wore one. Her nipples were hard, even though it was warm outside. A loose strand of hair fell free from her clip and drooped around her face, curling against her long, slender neck. He was being a prick and he knew it, but damn her anyway for trying to appease him when she didn't have a clue how Samantha Winston not showing up destroyed plans he'd been foolish enough to believe he could pull off in the first place.

"You want to spend time with me and know me better?" he growled.

"You had an appointment with Samantha, and I'm supposed to see to all her meetings," she said, basically repeating herself as if the words were a mantra she was holding on to in order to maintain her civility.

"Meeting with you wouldn't be the same as meeting with an old lady who is a grandmother I've never met," he informed her, purposely lowering his voice and taking a step toward her.

Jenny stood her ground, tilting her head to hold his gaze. He saw the slender vein at the top of her collarbone pounding with her heartbeat. It was barely visible at the edge of her shirt but was tantalizing nonetheless. Ric imagined yanking the sleeveless shirt out of the way, possibly popping a few buttons off, and tasting her smooth, creamy flesh.

"I understand."

He seriously doubted she did. "I'll return at eight tonight. Be outside the hotel when I pull in by the front door," he ordered, forcing his attention from her and opening his car door. Ric pushed Colby back and climbed into his truck. "Oh, and wear something nice," he added, then closed his door before she could finally tell him to go to hell.

# 3

---

"I just got off the phone with Samantha," Marc announced, standing outside his suite as if he'd been there waiting for Jenny to return, which he probably had. His tone made it sound as if he'd tattled on her and was proud of it. "She is not happy with how you ran out of the hotel after that man."

Jenny had hoped to get into her suite and compose herself before having to deal with Marc. As it was, he marched into her suite right behind her, the door closing behind him as he continued with his tirade.

"Representing Samantha Winston requires grace and style," he snapped as he remained on her heels. "You don't chase *anyone* across the parking lot like a common . . ."

"Yes?" She made fists on either side of her waist, keeping her back to Marc, more so he wouldn't see how shaky she was. What had just happened out there? She walked around the well-polished table in the dining area of the large suite, next to the sliding-glass doors that led out to her private *lanai*, which she'd learned was the Hawaiian word for "porch." Papers were scattered across the table, all of them notes she'd taken since arriving so she wouldn't screw anything up. Apparently she'd forgotten to write down not to run after anyone like a common something or other, which she wasn't. Any more than this was a common task she'd been asked to perform.

"If you would only work with me a bit," Marc pleaded.

Someone knocked on the door and Jenny spun around.

Jenny's heart was still beating too hard from her confrontation with Ric Karaka in the parking lot. Now it took on a painful, erratic thump against her rib cage. It was because she was out of her element, she told herself. Men didn't get to her like this.

She stared across the living room, with its elegant furniture, including a china cabinet stocked with fancy plates Nana probably would have refused to eat off of and real crystal glasses. There were shelves built into the peach-colored walls. And Jenny had thought she'd died and gone to heaven when she'd just sat on the couch. It was more comfortable than her bed back home.

Jenny focused on the solid hotel room door. She forced herself to calm down. Mr. Karaka—Ric—wouldn't know this was her room. It wasn't under her name. All three rooms were reserved under Samantha's name.

Ric had knocked on Marc's hotel room door, looking for Samantha. Had he knocked on Marc's door after having knocked on this door and no one answered? Had Ric returned, and since Marc didn't answer his door, he'd then come to her suite?

Marc waved his hands in the air dramatically as he turned for the door, his paces measured and his back as straight as a ruler. He mumbled to himself, probably about how he was forced to work with the most inept woman he'd ever laid eyes on. Jenny would have to call Samantha as soon as she had a moment alone and not rely on Marc telling her what to do or not do. Samantha didn't need to hear about Jenny's performance from Marc. Jenny would share her side, too. He wasn't in her shoes trying to pull off this bizarre job and Jenny doubted he'd be able to pull it off any better than she.

When Marc opened the door, he immediately stepped to the side, waving in the chauffeur, Sean Earnwell, a tall, quiet man who looked like he could double as a bodyguard. "I'm at my wit's end, Sean," Marc announced, giving Jenny a scathing look. "Maybe you can reason with this woman." He said *woman* as if it were a bad word.

Sean was ying to Marc's yang. He sauntered in, all six foot, two inches of him, and winked at Jenny as if he could easily guess what the problem was. When Sean didn't smile, he was incredible intimidating looking. Sean had been nice to Jenny from the moment they'd met. She had liked him immediately.

"Is anyone else hungry?" Sean asked, as if Marc hadn't just said something. Sean still wore the tuxedo he'd dressed in when he'd driven Marc and Jenny to the hotel from the airport. He was Samantha's driver and had come along with them with the sole purpose of escorting her wherever she needed to go. Apparently Samantha didn't use public transportation or take cabs.

"Food!" Marc again gestured widely with both arms and paced toward Jenny.

For a moment she thought he might bulldoze into her. She held her ground, her hands still fisted at her sides. If anything, she was grateful for these two being here so she couldn't mull over Ric Karaka's behavior too much. The more she thought of how he'd behaved, undressing her with his eyes, with a sneer on his face, the angrier she got. He was pissed off that Samantha hadn't been there, which she'd understood. But he'd treated her like a . . . like a woman he could do what he wanted with.

It was suddenly too hot in the room, and food sounded like a good idea—anything to get out of there. Ric Karaka had rendered her speechless the moment she'd laid eyes on him in

Marc's room. She had fumbled her very first appointment. Marc's hostile nature toward Ric hadn't helped.

It was possible she was taken aback because Ric didn't look anything like what she'd expected. Not that she had created an image in her mind, but tall, dark, and sexy wasn't it.

He'd been very tall, dark skinned, and looked incredibly muscular. To say he had a rugged bad boy look about him was putting it mildly. When he'd learned Samantha wasn't there, he hadn't looked so disappointed as he had pissed. He had dark green eyes that had searched the suite like an angry predator who had just been threatened might look right before attacking.

Jenny gave herself a mental shake. Ric Karaka had treated her poorly and she was getting hot and bothered thinking about it.

She was *not* getting turned on thinking about him. He'd been rude, out of line, and bossy. All she had to think about was how she would knock him down to size and put him in his place when she saw him that night.

"Food is a perfect idea. Jenny has a luncheon date tomorrow with two engineers Samantha was supposed to meet with. Oh, this entire idea is simply preposterous." Marc pointed a finger at her and Sean. "And don't think I didn't make myself perfectly clear to Samantha, because I did. How Samantha expected this girl from Nowhereville to be able to handle her schedule is beyond me."

"What have you done wrong now?" Sean asked Jenny, grinning.

"Don't encourage her." Marc almost leaped in between her and Sean. "The three of us are going to dinner, and we're going to make sure Jenny knows how to eat."

"Knows how to eat?" she asked incredulously. "I assure you everyone in Nowhereville knows how to eat."

"Yes," Marc said adamantly, ignoring her comment as he stood in front of her, brushing his chin with his thumb and index finger and making *tisking* sounds. "And the first part of learning to eat properly is knowing how to dress for dinner."

She almost informed him she'd learned how to dress herself quite a few years ago, but she was quickly learning that any sarcastic comment only put Marc in a worse state.

"Fine. It's not as if there is a lot to choose from anyway," Jenny said, indicating her small wardrobe hanging in the closet. "But before you decide what I'm going to wear to dinner, get out and give me a few minutes of privacy."

"Excuse me?" Marc looked aghast as he quit brushing his chin and his jaw dropped.

"Give the girl some privacy." Sean knew when to jump in, and Jenny was eternally grateful. He took Marc by the arm, guiding him out of her suite as the smaller man protested loudly. "Don't make me hold him down too long," Sean said, winking at her before closing the suite door and leaving her, finally, with her own space and completely alone.

She traipsed into the large bedroom with its four-poster bed and sighed loudly. All of this was too much. Did Samantha really expect everyone she was scheduled to meet to be anything other than irate that they were to meet with Jenny instead?

Turning, she crawled up her bed, then collapsed, rolling to her side as she reached for the phone on the bedside table. Samantha had instructed her to use the hotel room phone instead of Jenny's cell phone, for which she was very grateful. Jenny would call her grandmother, too, when she had a moment. She would use her cell phone for that and would wait until it was after nine in the evening in Parkville. She and Nana shared cell phone minutes, and Jenny didn't want to waste long-distance minutes when it was free to call after nine.

It was already after three. She needed to call Samantha. There was a five-hour time difference between them, and Samantha probably didn't keep late hours. Jenny needed to clarify whatever Marc had told Samantha about Ric.

TEMPTATION ISLAND / 53

On the second ring, Samantha answered, her smooth, soft-spoken, cultured tone not depicting any accent at all. "Good afternoon, Jenny," she said in greeting.

"Hi, Samantha." It seemed weird calling a woman who was somewhere around eighty, according to Sean, by her first name. Samantha had insisted, though.

"Well I've already heard Marc's rant, my dear. I'm sure you're calling to give me your version of your first meeting with my grandson."

Jenny picked up on Samantha saying her *first meeting*. Which meant she intended for Jenny to meet with him again. She exhaled slowly, silently, willing herself to match Samantha's composed tone and began explaining her initial meeting and re-action.

"Needless to say, he was very disappointed to learn you weren't here," Jenny finished after reiterating the exchange between Marc and Ric.

"Needless to say?" Samantha queried. "Do you believe this man is so incredibly eager to spend time with family he's never known?"

Jenny ached to ask about the mother Ric claimed to have killed. It had been a horrible thing for him to say. Samantha would have picked up on it immediately, especially since Jenny was sure Marc would have relayed the rather crude comment to her while justifying his reasons for kicking Ric out.

Jenny chose her words carefully, not wishing to defend him. For some reason, she found herself stressing how this anger seemed deep rooted. She pointed out that he appeared very controlling by nature. He definitely wasn't easily intimidated. He intrigued her.

"I got the impression he doesn't like his schedule being interfered with," she said, and when Samantha remained quiet, Jenny pressed on, pleased with herself and believing she was somewhat accurate in her perception of the man's nature.

"Marc wasn't very polite, either, insisting Ric was lying since Marc knew nothing of a grandson."

Jenny wasn't sure why Marc didn't know about this appointment, but Samantha didn't enlighten her.

"I'm going to meet with him this evening at eight."

"You are?" Samantha sounded surprised. "I got the impression he stormed out of the hotel. How did you arrange for this rescheduled appointment?"

Jenny blinked. Marc hadn't told Samantha that she'd run out of the hotel room and across the parking lot to speak with Ric? That one threw her for a loop. Marc said Samantha wasn't happy with Jenny running after Ric. Had he lied, or was Samantha testing her somehow?

"I followed him to the parking lot," Jenny told her, not hesitating. "I wanted him to know I was aware of his appointment with you, since Marc told him otherwise."

"Did he, now?"

Jenny opened her mouth to respond but then rolled onto her back and stared at the speckled ceiling.

"He shared the story as he saw it."

Samantha's tone was so matter of fact, Jenny wasn't sure if the old lady was upset or not.

"I'm not sure if Marc saw me run across the parking lot to catch up with Ric, or if he guessed." *By how out of breath I was when I returned to her suite,* Jenny almost added.

"Did you run after him?"

"Yes," she said slowly. "I did."

"What compelled you?" There wasn't anything accusatory in Samantha's tone.

"Honestly, I don't know. Maybe I have a hard time watching people storm away in anger. Isn't it human nature to want everyone around you to be happy?"

"I wish it was," Samantha said wistfully. "So, my dear, you

confronted this young man in the parking lot. How did that conversation go?"

"He was . . ." She almost said *pissed*. Nana didn't approve of such words, and Jenny caught herself before speaking that way to Samantha. "He was angry."

"What was his anger based on?"

That was an odd question. Jenny wasn't following Samantha's line of thinking, which made it harder to answer the way she thought she should.

"Because he felt stood up," she said, snapping before she could stop herself. It was on the tip of her tongue to ask Samantha why she would do this to Ric. Samantha hadn't come across as heartless, and Jenny didn't understand why she was coming across this way now. "Do you doubt he is your grandson?"

"I already know that he is."

Jenny blinked. Her next question was out of her mouth before she could stop herself. "Then why didn't you let him know you weren't coming to Lanai?"

"If I had, then he would have been prepared to meet you. We want first impressions, Jenny. Which is exactly what you're giving me. I never would have known how missing me would upset him if we had handled things differently, would I?"

Jenny wanted to say it was a heartless thing to do. She gripped the phone, glaring at the ceiling until her eyes began burning. It wasn't her place to interfere with these two or with any of Samantha's appointments.

"I'm meeting with him at eight this evening," she again informed Samantha. "I'll give you a call in the morning to let you know how it goes."

"Very good. And I do believe you have a luncheon date tomorrow." She changed the subject, dismissing this grandson she'd never met as easily as she did the next topic once she'd prepped Jenny on who she was meeting. "Sean will drive you everywhere you need to go. This is always to your advantage, because he will be there if you need his help in any matter."

Jenny didn't mention Ric had said he would pick her up at the front of the hotel, but she ended the call, promising Samantha she'd call around the same time tomorrow. Samantha liked order. If something didn't happen the way she expected it, the older woman was immediately put out.

Damn. She'd known Samantha Winston only a couple days and had known Ric Karaka just a few hours and already they possessed similar personality traits. Throw them off track and both got upset.

"Which is the way a lot of people are," she reminded herself, sitting up on her bed and crossing her legs.

Jenny blamed the heavy air-conditioning throughout the hotel for causing her hair to curl unmanageably. After giving up on putting it up and taking one last look at herself in the mirror, and the outfit Mark had chosen for her, Jenny joined Marc and Sean for an early dinner. At least in her eyes it was an early dinner. Both men seemed famished, as if they had to wait forever to eat because of her.

The only way to make the meal tolerable was to play along with Marc and allow him to teach her "how to eat." Which apparently over the past twenty-five years of her life she'd been doing all wrong. By the end of the meal, Jenny finally passed Marc's inspection. She sat with her back as straight as his; had memorized which fork, knife, or spoon to use with each course of the meal; and had held her tongue when she wanted to ask if it wouldn't be a lot easier if they simply ordered finger food so she wouldn't embarrass anyone.

When she finally made it back to her room, it was after six. She just finished the longest meal she'd ever had and had barely eaten a thing. Fish had never been part of her diet, and it was all anyone seemed to eat here. Returning to the bathroom, she sighed in frustration at the tight curls twisting down her back. Her hair was hopeless.

It might have been best that she didn't have a lot of time to stress over her eight o'clock appointment with Ric, but she managed to do so anyway. After trying once again to twist her hair into a bun at the back of her head and allow the tight curls that were determined to be free to drape her shoulders, Jenny gave up. All she succeeded in doing was sending curls flying everywhere.

Marc had taken her shopping the moment they'd arrived on the island, having gone through her wardrobe in her suitcase while on the plane and all but fainting over what he insisted was the most inappropriate attire a young lady her age could wear. Jenny chose the khaki pleated shorts and a brown blouse she never would have given a second glance to while shopping. She had to admit after trying it on that it did bring out the color in her eyes. Marc had seemed happier after buying her new clothes than he had since. Jenny hated people not liking her, but she wasn't sure she'd ever be the person he wanted her to be.

She finished her outfit off with a wide forest-green belt, its muted color not standing out but adding just enough color for her not to drown in eternal brown. High-heeled sandals were the final touch. Nana wouldn't know what to think if she saw Jenny right now. Why dress casually in shorts if she was going to wear high-heeled sandals?

"No one, and I do mean no one, your age wears anything less than three-inch heels." Marc had come close to a wave of hysteria over that discussion and had fanned himself with his hand when she'd finally consented to open-toe sandals with barely a three-inch heel. The straps crisscrossed over the top of her feet and wrapped around her ankles.

Jenny gave herself a final spin in front of the full-length mirror, then sighed. She shouldn't be so worried about how she looked. This meeting was for Ric to impress her, not the other way around. Her agreement with Samantha, while here, was to gather first impressions, then reporting them without exaggerating. Even as she tried convincing herself that what Ric thought of her was irrelevant, she hurried to splash a bit of perfume on either side of her neck before glancing at the clock.

Just before eight, she headed out of her suite and almost ran into Sean.

"Very nice," he murmured, giving her an approving nod as he straightened, then clasped his hands behind his back.

Jenny stepped to the side, glancing down at the pleats in her shorts. At home, she wore cutoffs or gym shorts. The pleats did make her feel a bit dressed up, in spite of the fact they were shorts.

"Thank you." She beamed at Sean and turned toward the elevators. She wasn't going to risk the stairs in heels.

"Do you have an address?" Sean followed her into the elevator.

"No. Do you want me to ask him for one?" she asked once the elevator doors closed.

"It would be helpful."

The elevator moved with such solid, fast movements between floors that Jenny barely noticed they'd descended. She stepped out when Sean held the door for her and caught sight of the large grandfather clock ticking solemnly at the end of the hallway leading to the lobby. It chimed eight times.

"I guess there's no harm in that," she decided, falling into step alongside Sean when it became apparent he was escorting her to the door.

In all truth, she was flattered. Sean's normal business routine was interrupted along with Marc's when Samantha decided to have Jenny take her place. It was very chivalrous for him to escort her to Ric's truck. They reached the circular doors that led to the canopy outside, where a handful of cars idled. Jenny ignored the people loading or unloading luggage. Ric's truck stood out among the smaller cars, none of which were more than a few years old. Not to mention the several limousines taking up space at the front and rear of the large loading and unloading area.

Ric's truck was solid steel, an older-model Ford. It wasn't rusted but was far from the first-class vehicles surrounding it. Yet there was something formidable about the truck. Something that made all those nearby park a respectful distance from it. She didn't imagine it was out of disgust but more out of respect. Even sitting in his truck, Ric commanded attention. She might have chalked it all up to her imagination if she hadn't been distracted by Samantha's limousine parked right in front of it.

Sean wasn't being chivalrous and escorting her. He was walking with her because he planned on driving her.

"I told you over dinner, that Ric Karaka was picking me up." Jenny shifted out of the way of a hurried businessman, then stepped to the side of the front revolving door. A large decorative fern stood almost as tall as her and blocked her view of Ric. "He's parked outside in that pickup truck."

Sean leaned to the right, tilted his head, and looked rather obvious as he stared at Ric's truck. "I should take you."

She wasn't sure what he saw when he stared at Ric, but Jenny guessed he stared at a confident, aggressive man. That was what she saw. And it sent chills rushing up and down her spine.

Sean seemed to grow in size. She sensed the protector in him emerging, and it made her smile. Sean saw a threat, someone who might try and push his way into her world, and right now, he was charged with overseeing her world. That awareness made her weak in the knees. Jenny dared peer around the fern to where Ric sat in his truck, waiting.

He wasn't looking at the hotel but instead was staring straight ahead.

"I'll be fine, Sean," she said, patting his thick arm; then moving around him to the door.

"Here." Sean stuffed a small card into her hands.

Jenny looked down at it, then glanced up at him curiously.

"That's my personal cell number. Text me his exact address." Sean cleared his throat when she continued staring at him. "It's my job to know where you are at all times. No one is going to say I'm not doing my job right."

She patted his arm again. "I'll text you," she promised. "The last thing I want is to get you in trouble with your boss."

Sean grunted something, but she didn't catch it. Instead she pushed through the rotating doors and out into the warm evening. The breeze should have been comforting, with its slight smell of the ocean. Jenny looked at the waiting truck and Ric sitting inside. When he turned his head and looked at her, a wave of excitement gripped her. She definitely would not share the impression she got of him at that moment.

Before she reached the truck, Sean was at her side again. This time he pulled open the truck door, his attention on her and not Ric. Obviously Ric hadn't appeared to be ready to get out of the truck and open the door for her.

"I'll expect that address within the next ten minutes or so," he told her, but not so quietly that Ric couldn't hear him.

Jenny hesitated, not having expected him to so boldly appear in front of Ric and to insult him. "No problem," she muttered, taking his hand when he extended it, then holding on as she stepped up and into the passenger seat. Immediately she smelled Ric's aftershave and something a bit more rustic, not an aroma she would have expected on the island. It was a rugged smell, a mixture of leather, fresh-cut wood, and Irish Spring. So far, on Lanai, she hadn't had a lot of exposure to any man who looked like he did a lot of physical labor.

"Do you want my home address?" Ric asked, his slow drawl cool and relaxed.

Jenny shot a look at him, but he had leaned forward, giving Sean a hard stare. She turned her attention back to Sean, who still held the door, as if he hadn't yet decided this was safe territory for her.

"Yes," Sean said without hesitating.

Ric continued with his slow speech, reciting the address, then asking if he should write it down.

"Nope." Sean didn't elaborate, nor did he make a move to write it down. As a limousine driver, he had probably already plugged it into his internal GPS and tracked the location. "What time should I come pick her up?"

"I'll bring her back," Ric answered without hesitating.

Sean didn't hesitate either. "What time will that be?"

"When she's ready to return."

Jenny had tried keeping up but was feeling a bit dizzy from looking from one man to the other. She sighed, bringing a pause to the banter. When she gave Sean a warning look, then looked at Ric, exasperated, she found both men staring at her, looking anything but pleased.

She placed her hand on the door handle. "If it will make you feel better," she told Sean, deciding if she didn't take charge, this could go on indefinitely, "I'll call you when I'm ready to return."

Sean waited only a moment before nodding once. He'd returned to his silent nature.

After Sean closed the door, Jenny sat facing forward, saying nothing else. She took a moment to compose herself before looking at Ric. At the same time, it infuriated her to no end that this man, this alleged grandson of Samantha Winston, created a frenzy inside her she normally didn't experience. She needed composure. She needed to take control of this moment and maintain that control the entire time they were together. Something told her that if she didn't, there would be very little she would be able to share with Nana or Samantha about her evening, once she returned to the hotel.

Breathing in silently and promising herself she would maintain a professional air, Jenny looked at Ric and caught him studying her. Instantly, her heart started racing.

"I asked you to dress nice." His gaze traveled down her body, slowly, torturously.

"I *do* look nice," she stressed, managing to sound calm. If he was this pompous, she would have no problem maintaining control of the evening. All the physical good looks would fade if he was ugly on the inside.

He grunted. "Not for where I was going to take you. But I can show you the family's banana plantation. I wanted to give Samantha a tour, but since you're here instead . . ." he said, his words trailing off as he returned his attention to the road.

Jenny couldn't shake the sensation she'd just failed some test. The reason for this meeting was for *him* to impress *her.* She couldn't forget that for a second. If she was going to do as Samantha wished of her, she needed to probe a bit deeper and learn his motivation. If Ric were a game player, or just an asshole, the sooner he would quit doing a number on her equilibrium, the better.

"Where were you going to take me?"

"There's a club in town you might enjoy," he offered, his slow, deep baritone possessing a lazy drawl that was almost hypnotic. "I thought you might like a break from those two male servants tailing you."

"They aren't tailing me."

"Oh, really? So no one reprimanded you for chasing after me earlier?"

"I did not chase after you," she snapped, damning him for being so incredibly perceptive. "And thank you for thinking of taking me out, but it isn't necessary."

Something tugged at the corner of his mouth, as if his lips

might curve up in a smile. She wanted to know what he found so amusing.

"What's this banana plantation?" she asked, and folded her hands in her lap. She gave silent thanks for choosing her outfit. Going to a nightclub with Ric would not have been a good idea. "I thought Hawaii was known for pineapples, not bananas."

He shot her a side glance. "You'll see."

It took only a few minutes to leave Lanai City and take the highway around the island before Ric slowed his truck, then turned into a long, single-lane driveway. In spite of the island being so small, a mere thirteen miles wide and eighteen miles long, the moment they left the beachside hotel, the island transformed into a beautiful forest. The road turned rugged and uneven. Jenny grabbed the dash, which was the only thing she could find to hold on to. She did her best not to fall against Ric as they continued over the bad road. When floodlights lit up the rolling meadow in front of them, Jenny straightened, awestruck by the mansion sprawling out before them. She wasn't sure what she'd thought a banana plantation would look like, but this wasn't it.

Ric slowed when the driveway curved in front of the house, then stopped the truck in front of the steps leading up to the front porch. And it was the widest porch she'd ever seen. It went from one end of the house to the other and was deep enough someone could easily throw a party on it. She climbed out of the truck, realizing too late when Ric came around the truck that he looked as if he would have opened the door for her. Jenny stepped around him and imagined a family relaxing on the porch after the end of a long workday.

"Watch your step," Ric instructed behind her when they neared the porch steps.

Jenny tried picturing the house with fresh paint. The wooden structure was faded so badly she wasn't sure what color it used to be. The first step creaked under her weight, and Ric placed his hand in the middle of her back.

That shot her out of her revelry of the house. Immediately, heat she wasn't ready for spread through her insides. She sucked in a breath, took the next step, and her heel slid into the split wood.

"Oh, no," she wailed, reaching for support when her high-heeled sandal got stuck in the porch stair. She lost her balance, and her shoe.

Ric's arms snaked around her, pulling her against him. His hand had created heat inside her strong enough to distract her and make her trip, but so much hard muscle pressing against her as he lifted her up the stairs to the porch created a quickening in her gut that swelled too fast for her to catch her breath.

"The place needs work." His deep voice was too close to her ear.

"I noticed." Her voice was barely audible. Jenny's heart pounded in her chest as his strong, solid body remained pressed against hers.

Jenny didn't move, and Ric didn't say anything else. It seemed time stopped, and she wasn't sure how long he held her, the two of them standing on the extra-large porch with his arms wrapped around her and his face at the side of her head. If she turned and tilted her face just a bit, she would be able to kiss him.

Lord. What was she thinking?

She jumped when the front door shook. Ric let go of her as the bloodhound she'd seen earlier in his truck leaped at the inside of the door, greeting them with a big grin and her tongue hanging out the side of her mouth. Jenny somehow balanced herself on one foot as Ric reached behind them, pulled her sandal out of the broken stair, then placed it in front of her. His hand slid around hers in a firm grip, helping her balance until she'd slipped her foot into her shoe.

"Thank you," she mumbled.

"I've managed to fix one of the upstairs bedrooms, one of the bathrooms, and the kitchen," he explained, and let go of her hand. "Looks like I need to move the porch stairs up higher on the list. Are you okay?"

There was concern in his voice, and he looked worried as he studied her foot.

Jenny put her weight on it. "I'm fine," she told him.

Maybe he worried she might try suing him. Ric accepted her answer with a nod, and his dark, brooding expression returned.

Jenny focused on his backside as he fingered his keys until he found the one he wanted, then opened the screen door and unlocked the house. Part of her brain wondered at him locking up the house when there weren't any neighbors in sight. Lanai City had a population of under four thousand. It didn't strike her as a place where theft was a problem.

The larger part of her brain, though, drooled over his broad shoulders. He wore a T-shirt that stretched across roped muscle. His torso tapered into a narrow waist. She dropped her gaze to his dark blue jeans and noticed how they hugged his tight ass. His thighs were thick, his legs long, every inch of him a sculptured piece of perfection.

"Colby, behave," Ric instructed, his tone softening drastically. "We've got company. Use your manners," he continued fondly, scratching her head and tugging her loose skin as Colby sat loyally next to her master and stared up at him adoringly.

Jenny felt the quickening inside her unfold all over again as she watched his fingers stroke the dog. If she didn't get her act together soon, she'd never pull off this meeting. Samantha would wonder why Jenny wasn't able to give her a decent, detailed report of her meeting with Ric. And worse yet, Jenny worried Ric would detect her intense rush of raw, unleashed lust. She imagined him acting on it, taking her into his arms and crushing her against his virile body as he kissed her savagely.

"Hi there, Colby." Jenny's voice was raspy, and she cleared it.

As Ric continued petting his dog, Jenny managed to walk around him, needing space so she wouldn't forget why she was here.

Observe and report.

Jenny paused just inside the door, once again swept off her feet. This time it wasn't by a broken porch stair, or a perfect male body and hard-packed rippling muscles pressed against her.

She turned around slowly, taking in the incredibly large living room. The room took up the front half of the house. It was rectangular and held all kinds of possibilities for decorating and design. The walls were white and clean, although she guessed they hadn't been painted in years. She loved hardwood floors, and it was almost a crime to see how dull and dark the floors had become over the years from lack of attention. Other than a couch against the far wall, a flat-screen TV facing it, a coffee table, and a desk against the wall next to the TV, there was no other furniture in the room.

Jenny took in the large space, imagining all that could be done with it as she finished turning. She stopped, facing Ric with his dog sitting next to him, and caught the small smile on his face as he watched her.

"Want the full tour?" he asked, apparently not needing to ask what she thought so far.

Jenny was sure it was written all over her face. "Sure."

Colby must have translated her response as a welcome to be greeted, for she left Ric's side and bounded to Jenny. "Hey, girl," she said, reaching and preventing Colby from jumping on her just in time. The large dog wagged her tail vigorously and looked up with adoring brown eyes.

"Colby, behave," Ric said, his voice low.

Obviously he'd spent time with his dog, as the simple command lured the dog back to his side.

"Have you worked with her since she was a puppy?"

"Nope." Ric led the way out of the living room and down a wide hallway.

For a moment she thought he wouldn't elaborate. Somehow she needed to get him talking, to share more about himself. She was drooling over him again as her heels clicked against the bare floor. More than anything, she wanted to give Samantha a good review of the grandson she'd just discovered she had. She fought to come up with questions to start the conversation, but all that came to mind was, did he had a girlfriend? Or, worse yet, would he think her shallow if she suggested they have sex in one of the rooms of this large, old house? And if that didn't seal her fate, she could top it off by making him swear not to tell a soul they fucked each other, especially Samantha.

Nope, Jenny definitely couldn't ask him anything like that. Focusing her attention away from roped muscle stretched taut under his blue jeans, she stared at the dog.

Normal questions. She needed questions that would get him talking.

Did he have a girlfriend? Did he live here full-time? She glanced at a wide staircase that disappeared into darkness as they entered the kitchen.

"Shortly after I bought this place, Colby started coming around. She was homeless and alone." He walked across the kitchen and reached for a box of dog biscuits on top of the modern-looking refrigerator. Colby immediately started baying and jumping in circles. This time Ric didn't demand her obedience but lovingly gave her two biscuits. "That was a year ago. No one knew where she came from, and she and I got to be friends. We seem to get along okay."

Jenny laughed, which grabbed his attention. "I'd say you two get along very well," she said, grinning. "So you two live here?"

"She stays out of my way, so there's enough room." His green eyes lightened, growing clearer when the corner of his mouth tilted into a crooked smile.

Jenny was sure she'd melt. If she stood still another moment, her legs would turn to jelly, her muscles no longer capable of holding her. Already her insides were sweltering into molten lava. Turning abruptly before she began undressing him with her eyes—or, worse yet, her hands—she gestured in front of her.

"So tell me, did you completely remodel this kitchen? How much of it is original?"

# 4

"The cabinets have been completely replaced. When I bought the place, the existing cabinets were rotted worse than the front porch stairs." Ric took advantage of Jenny having her back to him. He loved her auburn hair and would swear the golden highlights that showed off her thick, heavy curls were natural. His fingers itched to drag into those bountiful locks, get tangled, and tug until her head fell back in full surrender.

"I love how spacious it is in here. Do you know the history of the house? Are all the rooms so big and spacious?"

She was obviously enamored with the house, which should thrill him. Every time he met her gaze, though, she diverted hers. It was going to be one of the biggest challenges of his life giving her a tour, being completely alone in the home and knowing they wouldn't be interrupted and keeping his hands to himself. After preventing her fall on the front porch, Ric wanted her in his arms again.

But he wanted to know more than that hot little body. It still bugged the crap out of him that Samantha, who had seemed so friendly and eager to share all she knew about the Winston family, his mother's family, would pull a stunt like this and send someone in her place to meet him. Obviously he'd pegged her wrong, and he'd always read people so well. He also couldn't help but wonder if there was a trick behind all of this. Call it years of surviving on the streets, but Jenny Rogers was too damn easy to read. Knowing he could probably have her naked within five minutes, if he tried, made it hard to concentrate.

"The house was built by my great-grandfather. It was in the Karaka family up until ten years ago, when they lost it to foreclosure. After coming to the island, I was able to convince the current owners to sell."

He pulled out one more dog biscuit, then put the box back on top of his refrigerator. Sliding the biscuit into his chest pocket, he patted it as he looked down at Colby. She stared at him hopefully, her eyes shifting from his face to his chest pocket. Ric patted the top of her head, aware of how she hadn't barked at Jenny once or spent too much time sniffing her out. Colby held true to her breeding and was an excellent judge of human character. Ric hadn't had many workers help him restore the place yet—there just wasn't the money to cover the payroll. Some of the day laborers he knew had questionable reputations. Ric had kept them in sight the entire time they worked for him. Colby had picked up on it immediately and wouldn't leave them alone either.

"All the bedrooms are upstairs. You can check them out for yourself."

He wanted her to look at him again. Jenny's bright blue eyes glowed with sensuality. Yet she was doing her best to maintain her distance and give all of her attention to the house. "I'll be curious to hear what you plan on telling my grandmother once I've shared everything with you."

Jenny shot him a quick look over her shoulder, her full red lips puckering. She was a sexual goddess. It had been more than a bit insulting to learn he needed to impress someone other than Samantha with the banana plantation. But after he'd left the hotel, his outrage calmed down a bit. Jenny was not just beautiful, dripping with sensuality, she was also an intense sexual creature doing her best to hide a natural heat simmering inside her. Ric suspected why she was avoiding looking at him, instead making a show of focusing on anything and everything but him.

Ric wasn't conceited—hell, he knew rejection better than most. It appeared, however, that Jenny might be as turned on by him as he was by her. What he wasn't as sure about was what to do about it. He wouldn't risk the banana plantation, and his future, for a couple of hours of incredible sex with one of the most beautiful women he'd ever laid eyes on.

Ric led her out of the kitchen, and down the hall, with Colby taking turns walking alongside him, then Jenny. Ric walked into the private den, a large room with high ceilings and long, narrow windows and heard himself repeat the words his grandparents had told him about his dead relatives. Was that why Jenny was here? Was Samantha testing his scruples?

"My great-grandfather and great-grandmother built this house together, with the help of their five sons. They had lived in the Philippines. My great-grandfather was well known for his banana plantation. His office, where he and his wife did all their bookkeeping, had windows overlooking his crops. When they moved the family to Hawaii, they built this office so he could see his banana trees." Ric watched Jenny run her finger along the length of the wooden desk he'd found at a rummage sale and put in here to make it appear more like an office. "I guess my great-grandfather moved here under protest, which is why there aren't any windows facing their staple crop, which was pineapples. As you thought, bananas aren't farmed in Hawaii."

"That's what I thought." she nodded, her back to him again as she stared out the middle window at the dismal-looking banana trees, although they weren't really trees, but really, really large plants.

Ric hadn't had the heart to have them cut down yet. "As much as he missed his homeland, my great-grandfather never returned, and the Karakas became one of the prominent pineapple plantation families on the island for many years."

Jenny turned around, brushing her hair behind her shoulder. "You sound proud."

He shrugged. "I didn't know any of those people. And until a year ago, I had no clue I had such a large family. It's just a good story."

Jenny searched his face, appearing truly fascinated. "So your grandfather was one of these sons?"

"Yup. He was the youngest, just five years old when his family built this house."

"Why do they call it the banana plantation if they grew pineapples?"

"Because my great-grandfather insisted on it." Ric had asked the same question and with pretty much the same baffled look on his face Jenny had right now. "Times were hard in the Philippines, and although my great-grandparents were very good farmers, they didn't own their land and paid a high price to their landlord out of each crop. My great-grandmother's family was from Lanai, and when the two of them were offered this land, free and clear of any mortgage, to live on, work off of, and raise their family, not even my stubborn great-grandfather could turn down the offer."

"What did the locals think of a pineapple farm being called a banana plantation?" she asked, grinning. Her blue eyes were bright in the sunlit room. She licked her lips, then absently twisted a loose curl of hair around her finger.

Ric swore she did both actions without any thought, which, if it was the case, made her an even more dangerous seductress. A woman who plotted and used her body to gain knowledge, or anything else out of life, was a hell of a lot more easily played than a lady who naturally possessed the ability to render a man speechless with her God-given beauty and skills. He continued studying her, needing to know her motivation and wondering if his gut was right when she came across so relaxed and comfortable, as if she truly had no hidden agenda.

Which he found a bit too hard to believe.

"I'm sure the same thing they think today." Ric held his hand out, wondering if she'd come to him with the simple gesture. "It's hilarious but after all these years accepted, especially with bananas struggling to grow on one side of the old house and pineapples on the other side."

Jenny stared at his hand, her expression sobering. She didn't move and began chewing her lower lip. "You said mortgage free." She cleared her throat. "How did they lose it to taxes?"

"Come on," he said, nodding toward the door instead of answering. His parents had defaulted on the loans they'd taken against the property. "Let's just say I didn't get my business skills from the Karaka side of the family."

"I hope all of the house's wonderful history isn't a thing of the past," Jenny said, leaving the den when he stood to the side of the doorway for her to exit first. "Hopefully, you'll have a lot of good years here."

"I hope so."

Jenny hesitated in the hallway, and Ric paused next to her. He experienced an overwhelming sensation to take one of the thick curls and wrap it around his finger as she'd done to herself. As he paused in the middle of the hall and she faced him, her back to the wall, he contemplated methods of seduction, of actions subtle enough she would either slip into his control or give away her cover by expertly dodging his efforts.

"The banana plantation's history is very much part of it today. That is the entire reason I bought the place," he informed her, then took her arm and turned her around so she faced the door, which was next to the door to the den. "It isn't a thing of the past, but rather is the strength of the place today. Because of its history, this huge, old house will continue to stand tall and strong. Very soon this place will once again make enough money to support all of the family who have relied on it over the years." He used his free hand to open the door. Colby bounded into the dark room ahead of them.

"Oh, really?" Jenny allowed him to guide her through the doorway, looking over her shoulder at him.

She seemed so intrigued by what he told her; she appeared less aware of him touching her.

"Yes," he said, suddenly fighting to maintain his composure when the two of them stood in the slightly smaller, much dimmer room.

Jenny's creamy white skin was so smooth and warm. Ric loosened his grip but didn't let go. The light switch was on the wall right next to him. He'd spent weeks redoing a lot of the wiring in the house. It would have taken less time if he'd brought in an electrician, but the house had so many code violations that he brought it up to standard on his own, fearing any licensed electrician would have refused to work on the old place. He'd been proud when all the wall lamps and ceiling fixtures in the house finally worked without flickering. But now, standing so close to Jenny, his fingers brushing over her soft skin, he was inclined to enjoy the intimate darkness for another moment before reluctantly letting it go.

"What room is this?" She spoke quieter than she had a moment before. She was affected by the dark room, too.

Ric looked down at her. She'd tilted her head and was searching his face. He prayed her fascination with his home was legitimate. But when he captured her gaze and her eyes were large and fixed on his, he knew he didn't miss the curiosity he saw there. Another moment passed. He let it go, watching the soft shade of pink rise in her cheeks. Jenny didn't back away from him. She didn't press the conversation or even demand he turn on the light, but just watched him. Maybe she wasn't an expert seductress. Her eyes grew darker until they were like deep, blue pools, glowing from some inner light he definitely wanted to explore. Jenny was most definitely interested in more than his home.

Ric let go of her arm and turned on the light. That was enough knowledge for now. His opinion of her wasn't completely formed, other than fucking her would be a damned good idea. He could make it happen if he handled things properly. He needed to decide how best to get Jenny to convince Samantha to finance his bed-and-breakfast. The jury wasn't out yet on what technique, seduction, or another approach would be his best means to an end. He couldn't forget for a moment that his only goal was to get the bed-and-breakfast up and running.

"The large den was my great-grandfather's room for handling the books and managing the plantation, but this room was my great-grandmother's." Ric would focus on the tour and learning what he could about Jenny for now. "My grandfather told me his mother would call him and his brothers into this room after breakfast and assign their chores for the day. She managed the family from this room. I want to furnish this room so it looks like a study again."

"Was she some kind of dictator?" Her voice was still quiet, even a bit raspy. She rubbed her hands together, then brushed them down the side of her shorts when she finally moved, her heels clicking on the bare floor as she followed him and stood in the middle of the room. "This house seems happy. I don't get the impression your great-grandparents would have been cruel."

Ric hadn't ever given a lot of thought to any feeling in the house. He looked around the bare room, at the plain walls, which were in dire need of fresh paint. "I didn't get that impression," he said, never knowing what to say when people tried giving personality to inanimate objects. If that was what it took for Jenny to fall in love with the place and his plan, she could give the house all the personality she wanted. "I've got a pretty good idea of how the room was once furnished according to my grandparents," he offered, approaching her as he moved to the door. "I plan on using it as a parlor, or even a room to handle business affairs, if needed."

Jenny was glancing around the room. "Before you furnish it, you will need to scrub the windows and clean it up." She grinned broadly when she returned her attention to him. "My grandmother would throw a fit if she saw those windows right now," she added, and laughed.

Something jerked deep inside him at the sound of her laughter. There were dimples in both cheeks when she flashed him her amused smile. The melodic sound of her laughter not only seemed to make the room brighter, but it also reached out and clenched his gut, twisting it as strange sensations tripped over each other inside him. Suddenly he wondered if manipulating her was the right thing to do. No one could fake the natural sincerity and open, relaxed personality Jenny displayed. If she was truly as real and unpretentious as she came across, it would put her and Ric very much out of each other's leagues. Ric knew how to handle users and players. He understood those in the game for their own benefit. He'd never hesitated in taking on a thief or a backstabber. Ric prided himself on never letting anyone take advantage of him. He knew very well how to handle any of the many types of bad people out there.

Jenny wasn't coming across as any of those people he'd studied all his life and mastered taking on and conquering until they submitted to his will. Ric wasn't a thief. He wasn't a con artist. He'd never stabbed anyone in the back. But he'd never backed down from a confrontation and knew more times than not, he thrived on beating the bad guy at his own game by sheer plotting and analyzing the person until he could best them with his intelligence and keen sense of observation.

Jenny might be what she appeared—honest and open. He would just have to match her level and make his moves carefully. A lady like Jenny would be crushed, hurt, if she believed she was being worked into behaving the way he wanted her to. He relaxed, crossed his arms, and gave her his best winning smile. If he was right—and he seldom read people wrong—he had one big mystery to figure out: Why had Samantha sent this beautiful lady in her stead?

"I'm sure I can find some cleaning supplies if you're interested."

She bit her lower lip, fighting the grin that managed to spread across her face. "That might be fun," she murmured.

God. He shook his head in more disbelief than he would let her see. She actually made cleaning sound fun. Seducing her as she bent over, then stretched to clean the long, narrow windows definitely sounded like a good time.

"Okay, upstairs," he announced, tucking away this new bit of knowledge. It would take some pondering on his part to best determine how to mold her into the sensual lover he was already imagining.

She took the stairs slowly, holding on to the banister. Ric had no problem holding back, climbing a few steps behind so her round ass was at eye level. It swayed delightfully in front of his face. If he wasn't incredibly capable of controlling his feelings and emotions, he'd have had a raging hard-on by the time they hit the second floor. As it was, he took in the khaki shorts, pleated so they didn't fit snug against her slender waist and narrow hips. They were far from short shorts, yet he still got an eyeful of her smooth, beautifully shaped thighs.

Jenny had thin, white legs. Another lady might try spraying on a tan or hitting tanning booths repeatedly until they'd successfully darkened and leathered their skin. Jenny appeared very comfortable with who she was and how she looked. And her complexion complemented her perfectly.

He let his gaze trickle down to her ankles and the high-heeled sandals she moved so gracefully in. Shorts and high heels. Yet another sign the woman, whose ass swayed temptingly in front of him, teetered between two lifestyles. The conservative, well-bred side was apparent. Ric spotted the pink polish on Jenny's toes that matched her fingernails. It was a flashy, bright splash of color that also gave away a side of her Ric decided he would like to know better.

"Wow," she breathed when she walked around the curving banister, brushing her fingertips over it and looking down the long, wide hallway. "How many bedrooms are there?"

"Technically, there could be ten bedrooms." He'd already broken down how he would handle guests in the bed-and-breakfast, but he wanted her to fall in love with the place before he told her his plans for it. "Several of them are suites with adjoining rooms, though, which makes for five rooms. Those on this floor are larger, with a sitting room off each bedroom, as well as a bathroom."

"Your great-grandparents must have had a lot of money." She was as impressed as he'd been after seeing the layout of the second floor.

"Not really. When the boys weren't doing chores or school-work, they were working to build this house."

"Slave drivers," she mumbled.

"The way my grandfather shares the story, I don't think it was a bad memory for him. If anything, he learned a lot during the years he and his brothers and father built room after room, adding the third floor. He sounded proud when he shared the story with me."

Jenny looked at him, nodded, but didn't say anything. She digested what he'd said, though. He saw it in her eyes. Ric wanted her to say something, but she didn't. He wanted to know her reaction to what he shared with her about the history of the old home. She would take her thoughts and reactions to all of this back to Samantha. Ric wanted to know what Jenny would say, and the level of enthusiasm she would use when saying it. If she didn't give a raving report, there would be no point in asking Samantha to back the bed-and-breakfast.

Ric showed her each room, remaining in the doorway as he watched Jenny saunter in, turn slowly, her eyes glowing as she continued singing the house's praises. He'd done a bit more work to the master bedroom, which he showed her last. Colby had given up on the tour and was sprawled out on his bed when they entered.

"Oh, my." Jenny didn't enter his bedroom as far as she had the others. For one, it was furnished, and although it was a spacious room—twelve feet deep and almost twenty feet long—Jenny paused when she reached his four-post bed where Colby now sat, wagging her tail over company joining her. Her heels quit making noise when she stepped onto the braided carpet his bed was on. "So all the bedrooms are the same size? This one looks bigger."

"Yup." Ric moved in next to her and extended his hand to Colby, who immediately leaped to the end of the bed, but one firm look from Ric and she sat, glancing at Jenny as she pushed her head against Ric's hand when he began petting her. "At least the bedrooms on this floor."

She looked shocked when she looked at him. "This floor?"

"There are more bedrooms on the third floor."

"Wow." She didn't pull away from his gaze. "Are there this many rooms upstairs?"

He shook his head, holding her attention. "The floor above us has five bedrooms, but they don't each have their own bath or sitting room."

"This place is huge," she whispered, sounding in awe.

"There's still a lot of work to do."

"I see that."

"What do you think so far?"

"Hmm?" she asked, diverting her gaze for the first time and glancing around. "I think it's beautiful. A lot of work, but beautiful."

"Is that what you're going to tell Samantha?"

She looked at him, searching his face as she puckered her lips. "I'm going to tell Samantha about you, not the house."

"What are you going to tell her about me?"

She cleared her throat and stepped backward, turning as she did and reaching for the tall bedpost at the end of the bed. She walked to the other end of the bed and brushed her fingertips down the length of that bedpost.

"Actually, I thought up some questions." She faced him, intentionally staring into his eyes, although the beautiful glow in hers had disappeared. Was it possible she didn't like this any more than he did? "If you don't mind."

"Shoot." He crossed his arms, staring at her. They faced each other, each standing at the opposite end of the large bed. She might be uncomfortable, but he hadn't asked for this either. Colby cocked her head and looked from one of them to the other.

"Oh. Well," she began, but hesitated, licked her lips, and fingered the bedpost. Her thick auburn hair she'd pulled back still managed to tumble over her shoulders. She shoved it behind her back, as if irritated by all its mass. "Here?" she asked finally, making a show of looking around his bedroom.

Ric did the same, taking in the extra-large bed, the dresser he'd found in town for a steal and that almost matched the bed. There was the large wardrobe that could serve to hang his clothes, but the walk-in closet worked nicely for the few pieces of clothing he owned. Instead, the heavy, old, nicely polished wardrobe held his extensive DVD collection. There was satellite TV, but Ric hadn't tried bringing that out to the banana plantation yet.

"The house is huge, but it's just me and Colby here right now." He shrugged. "Unless you'd rather go sit in an empty room. Did you have a preference?" He was joking but the way she took a step backward had him guessing she probably didn't get that.

"No. That isn't what I meant." She looked at the bed as if that would make it easier to read her mind.

Ric didn't have to read her mind. Her concerns were stamped clearly across her face. She stared at the incredibly large bed with a mixture of fear and excitement warming her cheeks.

"They aren't formal questions or anything," she added, taking another step away from the bed.

Ric looked down at the same time her heel stuck in between two of the braids in the rug. She teetered, her arms flying out at the same time he leaped around the bed and grabbed her.

"Shit!" she yelled, caught off guard when Ric swooped her into his arms. Then, in less than a second, every inch of her stiffened as she seemed to become aware of her body pressed against his. She twisted, pressing her hand against his chest. "Hey!"

"Be still," he grumbled, knowing he wouldn't drop her, but if she kept moving the way she was, she might get more of a greeting from his body than she was ready for at the moment.

Apparently she caught his meaning because she quit moving. In fact, she became very still. Her headband was useless at keeping her thick, long curls out of her face. She seemed folded in half, sinking into herself as she froze and stared at her knees.

"I don't know if you wore these heels to impress Samantha's crew or me," he began, pulling one shoe off her foot, dropping it, then grabbing the other. "But, believe me, I won't be impressed when you land on that hot little ass of yours and sprain your ankle."

He took the other shoe off, then dropped it where he had the first. Jenny still didn't move. Ric held her, standing next to his bed, with Colby at the edge of it, sniffing his shoulder and Jenny's hair. He envied the dog. Pressing his face into all those thick strands had a strong appeal to it.

"I have an image I'm supposed to maintain while representing Samantha," she mumbled defensively. "And I don't wear heels that often."

"I noticed."

Her bare feet were higher in the air than her knees. She had pretty toes, and the polish on them made them look even nicer. Maybe Jenny wasn't accustomed to wearing high heels, but she definitely knew how to look nice. Something told him she would be just as hot in cutoffs and a tank top, maybe even with a smudge of dirt on her adorable nose—from working alongside him on his house.

He blinked, moving his attention to her knees and then up her thighs to where they disappeared into her shorts. Wherever the thought of her working alongside him came from, it could just go right back to that unknown spot. The only time Ric had women in his life was when they were stretched out on top of or underneath him, naked, in bed.

"You can put me down now." Jenny didn't move. She didn't even look up at him but continued staring ahead with her hair partially draped over her face.

Ric let go of her legs, letting them fall to the ground, but kept his other arm in place around her shoulder. When she returned to an upright position, he kept her pressed against his body. Her shirt twisted and he looked down in time to get one hell of a view of mouthwatering cleavage. His dick danced to life in appreciation of what he saw and pressed against his jeans.

Jenny froze once again when his cock moved between them. She looked up at him. Ric had never seen a more intense shade of blue and damn near drowned in her lust-filled gaze.

"I don't know whether to thank you for saving my ankles from a sprain or to slap you at your crude attempt at seduction."

Ric raised one eyebrow. "Crude attempt?"

She pressed her hand against his chest and moved to slide out from the arm around her. Without her heels, she was several inches shorter, the top of her head barely coming to his nose.

"Yes," she said sharply. "Sweeping me off my feet wasn't necessary."

He gripped her jaw, keeping her head tilted where it was with her staring up at him. He'd never seen such enticing eyes with her shade of blue adjusting from light to dark based on her mood. It was something he could stare at for hours, entranced, as his words and actions turned them completely opaque or made them translucent.

"Miss Jenny Rogers," he drawled, bringing his mouth close enough to hers he caught her breath when it hitched and she focused on him without blinking or moving. "I promise when I seduce you, there will be nothing crude about it. And I firmly believe sweeping you off your feet will be very necessary, if not enjoyed by both of us."

# 5

Jenny sat at the computer desk in Ric's living room, staring across the length of it. She heard Ric moving around in the kitchen, whistling some catchy tune as he opened and closed cabinets. She could go in there, stand in the doorway and talk to him while he prepared drinks for them. His tough attitude seemed to make her feel even more rattled.

Her heart still raced from when she'd been in his arms. Every part of him was so solid. And when his dick had throbbed against his jeans, her insides had swelled in response. Ric was large and thick. She'd been acutely aware of every inch of his hard dick as her world had slowed in that melting, lust-embraced moment. Even now, after announcing she would rather talk to him downstairs, in his living room, it was still almost impossible to rein in the unbearable pressure that still throbbed inside her.

"Here we go." Ric sounded incredibly pleasant, and pleased with himself, as he came into the living room.

Jenny watched muscles flex against his well-worn jeans as he moved toward her across the long room.

"I guessed you probably prefer your beer in a glass." He carried a large tray, his long fingers wrapped around the handles at each end. It was made of wicker with a smooth wooden base on which he'd placed a variety of items. "And these are shrimp capellini. I made them myself and will be offended if you don't try them."

Jenny leaned forward, immediately intrigued. Ric hadn't struck her as the kind of man who would spend any more time in the kitchen than was necessary to grab items out of the cabinets and return to wherever he would be lounging. One glance at the long, plush-looking couch, and she guessed most of his time was spent right there, with the remote strategically planted at the edge of the coffee table.

"What's in it?" she asked, staring at the shrimp, which had basil leaves placed among it, giving it almost a gourmet look.

Ric seemed pleased that she asked. He sat on the end of the couch, right where she'd guessed was his *spot,* and placed the tray in the middle of the coffee table.

"Shrimp, of course," he said, then gave her a winning smile. "And cherry tomatoes, basil, and garlic." He scooped a few of the shrimp onto a small plate, then handed it to her. After doing the same to another plate, he set the dish down, then lifted her beer. "Although, if my local cuisine doesn't appeal to you"—he grabbed an unopened bag of pretzels off the tray and slid them along the coffee table closer to her—"I figured a girl from Minnesota would certainly appreciate some pretzels."

"Thank you." She held the glass of beer to her lips and felt the foam form around her mouth as she drank. When she licked it from her lips, Ric watched her, the hunger in his eyes so damned obvious it stole her of all coherent thought for a moment. The swelling inside her turned into a throbbing need between her legs as she felt her clit swell, pressing against her underwear and shorts. If she moved just a bit, adjusted herself so she could rub the all-too sensitive tiny part of her against the seam of her shorts, there wasn't a doubt in her mind Ric would be aware of the movement, and why she did it. Jenny forced herself not to budge.

"I've decided how we're going to do this," Ric began, leaning back on his couch and draping his long legs against the edge of the coffee table. "Ask me anything you wish. But after I answer each question, I get to ask you a question." He turned his attention from his plate of shrimp to her, capturing her gaze and holding it as he stared deep into her eyes. "Deal?"

"Deal," she agreed.

Ric smiled broadly and popped one of the shrimp into his mouth. "Good. Shoot."

He looked a bit too satisfied, which again made her heart race. She didn't know Ric. But he'd already made himself clear on a few points. One, he was going to flirt with her—heavily. She had a good guess how far he would take things, but thinking about that made it impossible to focus on anything else.

Two, it mattered a lot to him what she thought of his banana mansion. On this subject, she wasn't sure of his motivation. But she would find out.

Three, he was a good cook. It might not have been her first impression, but it was very close, since he'd fed her within hours of meeting her. That said something about a man. Not to mention how he served her. Bringing all the food in on a tray and using serving dishes and small white plates for the shrimp showed a man who cared about appearance and presentation. Ric knew how to entertain. She wondered if Samantha knew his background—probably.

Jenny leaned back in her chair, allowing the silence to continue for another minute as she ate one of her shrimp.

"Oh," she exclaimed, tasting the mixture of basil and garlic, accompanied by the fresh shrimp and the juice of the tomato. She placed her plate on her lap as she pressed her finger to her mouth.

"They're good, aren't they?" Ric asked.

She nodded, grinning. He continued smiling as he watched her eat and swallow. Jenny took another drink of her beer, licked the foam from her lips, then placed the beer on the coffee table.

"Okay. I have my first question." She needed to get them on topic. Jenny wasn't sure she'd ever met a man who could make her hot by just watching her eat food he'd prepared for her.

Ric slipped another shrimp into his mouth, taking only a moment to pull his attention from her before looking at her through thick, black lashes. As sensual as it had been being watched while she ate, watching Ric's jaw and Adam's apple move proved more provocative than she'd ever thought possible.

She looked away first, all too aware of need growing between her legs when she finally did shift as she placed her plate on the coffee table. "Why are you so in love with this home?"

Ric's smile faded. "That's your first question?"

She frowned. "You don't like the question?"

"I figured you would ask questions about me personally in order to give a better report to Samantha."

"I think explaining your fascination with this banana plantation—which other people might think of as merely a dilapidated old home—would say a lot about your nature."

Something shifted in Ric's expression. "It's not something I expect you would understand. I've found family I didn't know I had, but none of them would understand, either, because none of them were lost."

He pressed his lips together, controlling inner demons that twisted his expression. A muscle twitched in his jaw. His eyes narrowed, making it harder to see how green they were. She'd admired his thick, black lashes, but now they were walls, barriers that hid his emotions from her. Jenny got the oddest sensation she was seeing Ric Karaka for the first time, and he wasn't a happy person. She'd touched on something and opened her mouth to press, to dig deeper and pull those demons out of him.

Before she could speak, Ric held up his hand. The smile he'd given her quite a bit since her arrival returned, although something was missing from it.

"My turn."

"That's your answer?" she complained.

"We didn't determine guidelines on how extensive the answer should be. Do we want to do that now?"

She considered this.

"Or do we want to not put restrictions or regulations on our answers so we're both free to share what we wish?"

Jenny nodded, although she still hesitated. She might learn as much about him by what he didn't say, as well as what he did say. She just needed to give some thought as to why he answered the way he did to her first question.

"No restrictions or regulations on the answers," she conceded.

"Why did you agree to take Samantha's place on this trip?"

She hadn't been sure what questions he would ask her, but it made sense he would want answers to help justify her invasion into his family reunion.

Jenny almost said Samantha had been somewhat insistent. But she didn't want to upset Ric. In spite of his sex appeal and charm, there was a vulnerable side to him, which became more apparent when anything pertaining to his plans around Samantha was mentioned. She reached for her beer and took another drink, taking a moment to think of the best answer.

"I think when you meet Samantha, you'll find out she's one cool old lady," she began, intentionally keeping the answer light. Ric stared at her, showing no sign of commenting, nor indicating that her initial answer affected him one way or another. She plowed forward, keeping her answer accurate yet vague. It wasn't her place to create a rift or any resentment between Samantha and Ric. And she didn't want to be in the middle of these two. "At the airport they weren't letting people board my plane, and it was making everyone waiting very irritable. I won't say she felt sorry for me, because I didn't get that off her. It was something about her sudden determination once she made her mind up that I would do well coming in her place. And I admit, I was curious to be in her world for a few days."

"Her world? A few days?" Ric had been leaning forward and now straightened, his black eyebrow arching. "You don't work for her?"

She wagged her finger at him. "That's three more questions and it's my turn."

Ric didn't smile when she did but leaned back in his chair, crossing his arms and staring at her. If he was going to throw a fit over the rules he helped establish, they wouldn't be playing this game much longer.

"Where were you born?" she blurted out.

"Los Angeles," he said quickly, then moved to the edge of his seat. Suddenly he appeared the predator, ready to pounce and make his kill. "What is your world, Jenny Rogers?" he asked, his voice lowering to a sultry drawl.

Jenny got the strangest sensation she'd just walked into a trap. She didn't mind sharing things about herself with Ric, although the point of their meeting tonight was for her to learn about him. What sucked was she wanted to get to know him, but not because she needed to report to Samantha. Something about the disturbingly handsome man staring at her turned her on and created sensations inside her she wasn't sure she'd ever felt to this extent before.

"My world is Parkville, Minnesota, where I was born and raised," she offered, trying to remain relaxed when he seemed to be staring past her face and deep into her soul, straight to the point he'd ignited with a torrential fire that wasn't going out any time soon. "I graduated from high school there, and since then I've worked at a grocery store."

Ric nodded, and continued to do so when she didn't elaborate. He seemed content with her answer and didn't act as if anything she just said bothered him.

"What is your world, Ricardo Karaka?" she asked, smiling at him.

Ric's expression remained grave. "I don't have a world."

She tilted her head, watching him. When his face stayed stoic, something tightened inside her. Jenny put her beer on the coffee table and moved to the edge of her seat.

"Maybe it would be better if we didn't make a game out of this," she said softly.

His expression darkened as he pinned her with narrowed eyes that were now almost black with an emotion she would swear was close to extreme outrage. Instinctively, she gripped the armrests of her chair, holding his irate stare as her heart began pounding.

What demon existed inside this man? And what exactly had she said to unleash the fury she now saw on his face?

"Trust me, darling," he drawled, his low baritone still managing to send shivers of anticipation over her flesh even though she was suddenly acutely aware of how alone she was with him, this man who was a complete stranger not only to her, but also to Samantha and her employees. "I'm definitely not playing a game."

Marc had thrown a fit over Jenny going after Ric. Sean had showed a side of himself Jenny doubted he displayed often, trying to prevent her from taking off alone with Ric. Yet she'd ignored both of their warnings. Nana wouldn't be able to live with herself if something terrible happened to Jenny while so far away on a trip her grandmother would blame herself for Jenny taking. She managed to swallow around the lump lodged in her throat and not cower or show any defensive action when Ric continued to appear enraged before her.

"Good." She exhaled, forcing a smile on her face and even a small laugh. "You had me worried there for a moment."

"I'm here to create my world. Do you understand that?" he asked.

She didn't know what he was talking about. "Sure," she muttered.

Ric didn't look away from her. "Why did you chase after me earlier at the hotel?"

Jenny stared at him, unsure if they were still playing questions-and-answers. When Ric studied her, finally no longer looking her in the eye but letting his focus shift lower, until she was sure he was staring at her breasts, she decided either way, it was a question she needed to answer. If Ric believed she chased him down for any reason other than knowing Samantha would want answers, it would be best to clear the air right now.

"I didn't *chase* after you," she stressed, hopping up from the chair when Ric seemed intent on staring at her chest. He was making her nervous, and she wouldn't give him that power. Jenny needed to redirect this conversation and take charge. "Where I come from, we take our work seriously. I agreed to fly here instead of Samantha, attend all of her appointments, and give her my impressions."

"Oh, really."

Ric didn't stand but she noticed the roped muscle flex in his arm. He appeared ready to pounce.

She left the corner of the large living room, walking barefoot across the wooden floor toward the large window next to the front door. It offered a view of the front drive, the large front yard, and beyond the highway, the ocean. The front porch expanded past the window, making the view beyond it more picturesque.

Jenny kept her back to him and the room, focusing on the tranquil setting outside and using it to help calm her nerves. "You left in a hurry or I wouldn't have had to hurry as well." She heard her defensive tone but plowed on, determined he would not see her as the type of lady who ran after a guy just because she found him good-looking. "I made an agreement with Samantha, and when I tell someone I'm going to do something, I will do it."

"How commendable of you."

Jenny jumped in spite of herself. Ric was right behind her. His breath was in her hair as he spoke. She hadn't heard him move. Even though her flesh prickled with nervous anticipation and heat rushed over her creating a lustful blush that warmed her skin, she was proud of herself for sounding calm when she continued speaking.

"I'd like to think that's how most people would handle the situation," she said smoothly.

"How would most handle this situation? An old lady, who by all appearances seems to be quite wealthy, strikes a bargain in an airport, sends you on her private jet to an exquisite hotel on a remote island with all the amenities," he said, speaking just over her left shoulder. "All she asks in return is that you meet the people she planned on meeting, apologize for her absence, then report in to her later and tell her what you thought of the people you met. Did I miss anything?"

"That pretty much sums it up," she said, focusing on a gull as it glided across the sky, although she was much more aware of the inches of air between her backside and his muscular body.

If she swayed just a bit, they might brush against each other. Would he let it go at that and continue carrying on about her being on the island instead of Samantha, or would he keep their bodies together? Maybe he'd make her turn around and kiss her.

Jenny swore if her insides burned any hotter from the lust intensifying inside her, she very well might turn around and attack him. Then she'd never know what he might have done.

"So what would motivate a person to do as instructed and not take advantage of the situation?"

She inhaled and filled her lungs with the smell of him, of his aftershave mixed with soap and laundry detergent. The personal hygiene products he used all were familiar smells, but bundled up together and wrapped around all that brawn and intense nature they created a scent that could only be identified as Ric's own personal smell. It was rugged, alluring, dangerous, and rather addictive. She took another breath.

"There isn't much to take advantage of," she explained. "Samantha isn't asking much of me, and she's already offered more in return than I could think to ask for with the trip, the hotel room . . ." She let her words taper off when she almost added that she got to meet him.

"Isn't she? And there isn't?" It seemed his voice was closer to the side of her head. It was definitely softer, almost a whisper, yet his quiet tone was anything but soothing. At this rate, he would completely manipulate her senses.

Which would give him complete control.

That wasn't going to happen.

Jenny might not be the skilled seductress, but she wasn't stupid either. If she didn't grab the reins and take control of this conversation, of this moment, Ric would have her saying and doing anything he wanted. And as much as submitting to him had its carnal appeal, having his respect mattered more. Once she knew she had that, then she might consider the carnal appeal.

Jenny winced over her logic but wouldn't deny how strongly attracted she was to him. An odd thought hit her. Samantha probably had a picture of Ric. She might be an old lady but she was still a lady. Had it crossed her mind that Jenny might be attracted to Ric? Did Samantha have an inkling of how Ric might react to her? And if she did, how would she have gathered that knowledge? Was Ric a player and a successful seducer of many women?

Jenny slid away from the window and Ric, moving to the middle of the room. When she turned to face Ric, he was already moving in on her again. She held her head high, although he was quite a few inches taller than she, especially now that she was barefoot. The bigger they are, she reminded herself.

"No," she told him, which caused him to slow his advance. He paused, watching her. Jenny continued, her confidence building and the thick fog of lust in her brain slowly subsiding as she took Ric on. "Samantha isn't asking too much of me. I'm quite capable of forming an opinion of someone based on their actions and behavior," she informed him, "not to mention by what they're willing to say or not say."

"I'm glad to hear it." Once again he started walking toward her.

Jenny held her ground. "She's offering her full hospitality. There's nothing to take advantage of. Although I'm sure a person of lesser character might find some part of the bargain to abuse." She licked her lips, her mouth suddenly dry. Before he could close the distance between them, Jenny moved again, heading back to her glass of beer. She had half a mind to grab his bottle and down it instead of drinking beer from the glass and being forced to lick the foam from her lips. "You should be grateful your grandmother is such a good judge of character."

"I'll withhold my judgment of her until I have the pleasure of meeting her in person."

Jenny picked up her glass and drank but knew the moment he was behind her again. When he once again stalked her, closing in on her without making one floorboard creak under his large frame, heat flushed into her womb. Her heart once again began racing. But it was the images of him wrapping those muscular arms around her and preventing her from moving that successfully had her frozen where she stood.

At the same time, in spite of her fogged brain and images of him tossing her to the couch and coming down on top of her, a sobering thought brought her pause. She'd made a fatal error. By returning to the far corner of the large, basically empty living room, she'd placed herself in the corner. Ric now had her closed in.

"You'll like her," Jenny said, staring at the remaining beer in her glass.

Ric reached around her, and his long fingers moved over hers as he took the beer from her. "Are you sure?"

His hand was warm and dry, yet managed to scald her flesh when he pressed his palm against the back of her hand. When he lifted the glass away from her, Jenny began rubbing her palm and fingers, against her shorts. There wasn't any doubt in her mind Ric was seducing her. As easily as she accepted this truth, at the same time she struggled with the reasons behind his seduction.

"Of course I'm not sure," she said, proud when she still sounded calm. He'd definitely managed to raise her body temperature off the scale. The only thing she was sure of at that moment was how dangerously close she was to throwing caution to the wind. "Why did you bring me out here?"

Ric didn't say anything, and she applauded herself for throwing him off guard. It was a dangerous step, but she dared turn around. He stared down at her with green eyes so dark they stole her breath. Once again, there were mere inches of air between their bodies. She was growing even more aroused facing him, which she knew would happen. Especially when she was sure if she leaned in and kissed him, Ric would immediately take control, devour her mouth, and possibly rip her clothes from her body and make love to her. She almost staggered on her bare feet just imagining it happening.

"I wanted to show you the banana plantation."

"Why?" she pressed. If she kept him on the edge, forced him to continue responding to questions as his lust tore away at him, she would remain at the helm.

"Because I wanted you to fall in love with it. I wanted you to see what I see here and share that with Samantha," he bellowed.

She was disappointed when he turned away from her and dragged his fingers through his dark hair. "I put too much weight on my meeting with my grandmother," he said, and walked to the front door.

Colby appeared out of nowhere the second he touched the doorknob. Her tail wagged vigorously, the dog unconcerned by the sudden tension in the air. Jenny watched him pull open the front door. The moment he disappeared outside, her temper flared. She ran after him, barefoot, and bounded onto the front porch as the evening air, thick with the smell of the sea, closed in around her.

"What?" she hissed when she didn't see him right away.

Jenny hesitated for only a moment at the porch stairs, spotted the weak board, then leaped over it as she raced into the yard. Ric was headed around the side of the house, his long legs putting distance between them. She wasn't as fast, but she was determined.

"Stop!" she yelled, running around the side of the house. "Ric, wait!"

He stopped, spinning around, and for an instant she thought he'd take off again, putting even more distance between them. The demons she saw tormenting him earlier once again hardened his expression. Ric had managed to move around to the side of the house with the pineapple field spreading away into the darkness. If she hadn't been so focused on him, and the rage she felt coming off him, she might have asked why the pineapple trees looked like bushes. Instead, she came to a stop a few feet from him and studied his irate expression.

"What just happened?" she asked, confused.

Her headband had slipped to the back of her head when she'd taken off after him, and Jenny yanked it out of her hair, no longer caring if she looked nice. Her thick, long hair fanned over her shoulders, and she reached behind her to pull it straight behind her back, then moved to reposition the headband.

Jenny didn't get a chance to put the headband back in her hair.

Ric moved quickly. He cleared the distance between them, damn near knocking the wind out of her when he made impact. Ric wrapped his arms around her, yanking her against all that hard-packed muscle. He lifted her off the ground, keeping her body pressed against his as he captured her mouth with his.

All the heat swelling inside her exploded into an array of fireworks that popped and sparkled before her eyes. Jenny swore her world shifted at that moment. She gasped and Ric impaled her with his tongue. She tasted the beer and shrimp on his breath but was aroused even more by the skills he possessed. His tongue eased around hers, creating a wicked dance she managed to follow as his arms tightened around her.

Jenny wasn't sure when her hands moved to his shoulders, but she held on, feeling all his roped muscle flex under her grip. Ric was incredibly strong. The physical side of him matched his dominating personality. She'd been confused when he ran, but as he tortured her mouth with a passion she managed to match, she realized Ric hadn't been trying to escape but rather wanted to prevent her from seeing how tormented he was.

They began a rhythm, his tongue swirling around hers and Jenny matching his movements as their frantic kiss slowed into a sultry, hot, passionate embrace. Ric continued kissing her, but his muscles relaxed. Jenny was drowning in him, every inch of her throbbing with a need for more of him, but at the same time, she'd be content to simply kiss him for the rest of the night. As torturous as their actions were, they were also intensely satisfying.

Ric growled when he ended their erotic dance of the tongues and nipped her lower lip. He began a wet, hot path of kisses along her jawbone, pressing enough with his mouth that her head fell back. The moment she exposed her neck to him, he pounced as if he were just offered an even better gift than what he'd just taken.

His hands slid over her ass. Those long fingers of his stretched over her shorts, then tucked under them, pulling on the material until the seam rubbed against her clit. White heat exploded inside her, releasing a searing need. What had started as a throbbing between her legs quickly became a pulsing wave so strong she ached to come.

Release was right there. Ric's fingers pressed into her upper thighs, so close to the source of her heat but not quite there. Her world began teetering, and she wondered if they would make love right there, standing in the yard with too many clothes on. She wasn't sure she would last until they were naked and lying with each other.

"Sweetheart, you're so hot," Ric whispered against her neck as his fingers moved farther under her shorts. "I can feel how you're smoldering for me," he growled.

"Ric." Her mind wasn't anywhere close to being in a state where she could form words. "Ric," she repeated, buried far under her fog of lust.

"It's okay, sweetheart," he whispered.

Jenny wasn't a virgin, but something told her he was a lot less of a virgin than she was. His skills didn't come from watching "how to" videos on YouTube.

Despite being wrapped in the thick cloak of passion that still had every inch of her craving the next step of foreplay, Jenny had a moment of clarity.

Giving in to her attraction to Ric might be the biggest mistake she'd ever made in her life. One of those mind-boggling atrocities that would never allow her to return to her life as she knew it. She'd been massaging his shoulders, but her fingers stilled. Ric's tongue was tracing a path along her collarbone. He managed to stretch her open simply by moving his fingers under her shorts. He was so close to reaching her entrance, to moving inside her.

His cock did a wicked dance between them. His dick was as hard as stone, long and swollen. It might even be at the point of no return.

Was she at that point, too?

Damn. She really wanted to have sex with Ric. But doing so might very well jeopardize her entire stay here on Lanai, which would mean she'd fuck him, then never see him again.

"Wait." The word barely made it past her lips.

"I know," he muttered, and adjusted her in his arms.

"What?" she asked, feeling an urgency to regain control of her thoughts.

Ric climbed the porch stairs before Jenny realized he'd started walking. He was carrying her back into the house. When they passed through the living room, he shifted her so he cradled her against his chest and she stared at her bare feet, bobbing in the air as her legs hung over his arm.

"Ric," she managed when he'd climbed the stairs.

It was amazing how easily he held her—as if she weighed nothing. Soon he was down the hallway and in his bedroom. Ric wasn't breathing hard; his heart didn't beat any harder than it had when they'd been outside. It dawned on her she didn't know what he did for a living, but she'd guess it must be something physical.

"Stop," she gasped when he tossed her onto the bed.

Ric stood at the edge of the bed, tearing his shirt off. She stared at his ripped body, complete with dark skin and a spray of tight, black curls stretching over bulging muscles. In a matter of seconds, he'd fulfilled several of her fantasies.

"Why are we doing this?" she blurted out, balling her hands into fists and pressing them into the bedspread on either side of her as she stared up at his perfectly chiseled face.

Ric's fingers were on the top button of his jeans. His short hair was slightly tousled, and in the dimly lit room, his green eyes were smoldering orbs of dominating power. In her deepest, darkest fantasies, Jenny had always imagined this aggressive, dominant man overpowering her, fulfilling every dark fantasy she'd ever dreamed of until her body was so sated she floated in blissful satisfaction.

Sometimes dreams were just that.

"Because it's what we both want," Ric said, his voice deep and gravelly.

"What do we both want? Sex?" She wouldn't deny it. More than anything she wanted to fuck him.

"Don't reach the regret stage yet, sweetheart," he said, leaving the top button of his jeans undone as he crawled onto the bed toward her. "You want to come so badly right now it will fog your sense of thinking about it clearly."

Jenny didn't stop him when he dragged his fingers through her hair and tugged until she tilted her head to the side. He cradled her in his hand as he leaned forward. Their faces were inches from each other, but he didn't try to kiss her. Instead, those smoldering eyes of his bored into her psyche, branding the look on his face deep into her memory.

"The regret of not fucking each other will be stronger than the remorse both of us will dwell on after we've had mind-blowing sex."

She stared at him, allowing his words to sink into her brain. "You're saying if we don't have sex, we'll be too distracted by not having done so that it will make any further communication between us incredibly difficult to handle."

"Difficult, but not impossible." He tugged on her hair, pulling her face closer to his.

Jenny wasn't sure she had the strength to fight him. He continued bringing her closer to him until she was forced to move her hands in order to keep her balance. She didn't look away from him when he reached for her shorts and freed the button above her zipper.

"I really should hate your guts," he whispered, his mouth so close to hers his lips brushed over hers as he spoke.

But his words made her pause. She tried straightening but Ric used that moment to kiss her hard enough that her lips stung. He knocked her off balance, and she fell to her side. Ric didn't let go of her hair and kept her steady as he unzipped her shorts and moved his hands down her shaved mound to her soaked pussy. His fingers eased inside her, filling her until he pressed against that spot that craved his attention most.

Jenny arched her back off the bed, reaching over her head and gripping Ric's wrist as he continued holding her hair. He wasn't pulling on it but more like tangling his fingers in it. She used his wrist to hold on, to keep her world from toppling over.

How long had it been since a man had touched her like this? Had a man ever touched her like this?

"Ric," she hissed as white lights flashed before her eyes.

"Do you want to come?"

His words traveled toward her through a thick haze of desire and hesitation. If she let go, she'd have the orgasm of her life. She was positive of the fact. But letting go and giving in to her bodily needs would be terrible, right? Jenny was here to learn who Ric was, to hear him share with her what he wanted her to know.

"Do you, darling?" Ric's voice was closer now.

She blinked, fighting to focus as his fingers began moving in and out of her. They stroked her tormented inner walls, soothing and adding to the torturous need still growing to intolerable levels.

"I just don't think . . . ," she began, but hesitated. She wasn't sure they should do this, but she couldn't get the words out to stop it.

What he was doing felt so damn good. She wanted this. Hell, she craved it from the deepest, darkest depths of her soul.

Ric managed to free his fingers from her hair and gripped both of her hands in his. He kept her hands over her head, although his grip was relaxed around her. She blinked again, knowing in spite of how desperately she might have craved an experience just like this, Ric was wrong. She wouldn't be less distracted if they had mind-blowing sex.

"We can't . . . ," she continued, yet again her worlds trailed off.

"Okay." He responded to the words she didn't say.

She wasn't sure if a second passed, or possibly a few minutes, but Jenny realized his fingers continued stroking her. It would take nothing to let her eyes roll back in her head and release the dam, which barely managed to hold back the torrential orgasm building inside her.

Ric spoke her name on a breath. "Jenny."

Her lids fluttered open and she stared up at him. His face was a sculptured image of concentration, hard lines and set angles revealing how much effort he put into pleasing her and refraining from his own pleasure.

Suddenly she wanted to reach for him. When she tried moving her hands, his grip tightened, latching down around her wrists and restraining her. A dangerous glow appeared in his sensual green eyes.

"Do you want to come?"

"Yes," she whispered, unable to hold back any longer. "Yes," she repeated, although it wasn't necessary.

The moment she said yes the first time, Ric thrust deep inside her, impaling her with his fingers and hitting an exact spot needed to ignite her release. Jenny howled, her body jerking and coming off the bed. He thrust again.

"Oh!" she howled, crying out from pure pleasure.

"Come, sweetheart," Ric whispered, his lips over hers.

She blinked but couldn't focus, especially when he continued moving in and out of her, his movements aggressive and determined. Jenny couldn't focus with his face so close, and when she started to cry out again, he captured it and made love to her mouth as he reached that special spot one last time. Jenny soared into an orgasmic state of bliss, her climax coming on so hard and with so much energy it almost made her black out.

# 6

Jenny stepped into the dining room and smiled at the host when he moved around his podium and was immediately at her side, as if he'd been waiting for her arrival.

"Miss Rogers," he said gallantly, nodding.

Jenny looked at him, curious as to how he knew her name.

"Your table is this way. Mr. Sagawa and Mr. Pritchard have already arrived."

"Thank you."

"Joshua. My name is Joshua, Miss Rogers," the host offered, and gestured with his hand for her to follow him.

"Thank you, Joshua." She was ill-prepared for this meeting but would pull it off somehow. She'd managed to get this far through the day.

Marc and Sean hadn't said a word to her about her time with Ric the night before. She was more grateful than they'd ever know. Ric had either decided she was too much of a tease or he needed to be alone after making her come so he could masturbate and take care of what she hadn't. Either way, he'd brought her back to the hotel, unwilling for her to call Sean and wait for him to come pick her up.

She brushed her hands down the silk, sleeveless dress she'd decided to wear. It was a godsend that Samantha had been asleep by the time she had returned to the hotel the night before. Jenny hadn't been forced to discuss her evening with anyone, which was an incredible blessing since she wasn't sure she could express in words what happened without anyone she told immediately making arrangements to have her hauled straight back to Parkville, Minnesota.

"Miss Rogers, may I present Mr. Sagawa and Mr. Pritchard," Joshua announced solemnly when they reached a spacious circular table in the far corner of the dining room. Open glass doors allowed a wonderful breeze in from the ocean.

"Miss Rogers," Mr. Sagawa said smoothly. He was a man somewhere in his forties or fifties, with the same olive skin Ric had and equally thick black hair. Fine lines of silver gave him a distinguished look. "It is an absolute pleasure to meet you, my dear."

He stood, along with Mr. Pritchard. Joshua pulled her chair from under the table and held on to the back of it after she took her seat.

"Likewise, Miss Rogers. This is a wonderful treat." Mr. Pritchard, who sat opposite Mr. Sagawa, looked as if he hadn't smiled most of his adult life. His vocal inflection belied the solemn, almost dreary gray eyes that met her gaze as he spoke. "I've been a good friend of Samantha Winston's for many years. This is a marvelous idea on her part. I must say," he added, although didn't add what it was he must say.

Joshua finished seating Jenny and came around to her side, focusing only on her as a waiter appeared, towel on arm, and aptly maneuvered his way around the table as he began pouring a fruity-looking drink into crystal glasses.

"We have an award-winning swordfish dish as our main en-trée today," Joshua explained to her. He went over the menu without offering to let her see one.

When it became apparent that Jenny was to choose what all three of them would eat based on Joshua's explanations, she re-membered some advice Nana had given her during one of her small panic attacks after arriving on the island. It was better to admit she wasn't prepared to handle a situation than to pretend she knew something she didn't and make a fool out of herself.

Jenny quit looking at Joshua and glanced at Mr. Sagawa. He was watching her intently, his black eyes friendly enough. He smiled, showing off white teeth. She glanced at Mr. Pritchard. He had his hands folded on the edge of the table as he sat stiff and erect in his chair and stared out at the ocean. It took him a minute to pull himself from his thoughts and notice she was watching him.

"I'm not an expert on island cuisine," she admitted, and knew how right Nana had been the moment some of the ten-sion slipped away with her confession. "I'm very open to sug-gestions from either of you."

Mr. Sagawa opened his mouth to speak, his relaxed expres-sion making him an easy ally. It was Mr. Pritchard who spoke first, though.

"The swordfish sounds wonderful, Joshua," he decided.

Joshua looked at the older man, then nodded to the waiter. "Mrs. Winston always orders the fruity cocktail," he said, smil-ing and thanking the waiter under his breath when the younger man finished filling all three glasses with the chilled drink. "It's what she has named this particular drink, which she made me promise would be present with your meal," he added, beaming at Jenny. "Mrs. Winston will be anxious to hear your thoughts on the drink."

"I look forward to trying it," Jenny said, watching condensation begin to form on the thin crystal glass. "And, Mr. Pritchard, we shall try the swordfish."

Mr. Pritchard didn't return her smile this time, or look amused as he had when she first sat down. She caught the two men exchanging looks and wondered what faux pas she'd committed. The waiter offered suggestions for their meal, and Joshua added his opinion on appetizers and side dishes. When Mr. Pritchard again tried deciding for all of them, Joshua would give him a glance, then confer with Jenny. She finalized their meal choices, convinced at the end of the ordeal that with a restaurant this nice, all the entrées were probably delicious.

After they were left alone at their table, Jenny leaned back in the high-backed chair and smiled at both men. No one sat at any of the tables around them, and the ocean view spilled in through both sets of open doors. This truly was paradise, she thought as she brought the chilled crystal glass to her lips and sipped.

"Oh, my," she exclaimed, swallowing the strong alcoholic drink.

"Mrs. Winston loves a good, stiff drink in the early afternoon," Mr. Pritchard announced as if he were proud.

Jennie nodded, feeling the alcohol burn all the way down her esophagus. She placed the crystal glass next to her plate. "It is very good, but I'm not a big drinker and want to keep my thoughts clear through our lunch."

"Maybe sipping it is best," Mr. Sagawa suggested, grinning.

"Exactly." She gave him a broad grin and tried relaxing in the chair. It was very comfortable. The ocean outside was a rich blue, complementing the light blue sky. Everything around them was tidy, and perfect for a carefree meal. But Jenny wasn't sure she'd be able to relax again until she returned home. "Now, please, gentlemen, tell me what you planned on discussing during our meal."

Mr. Pritchard lifted his fruity cocktail to his lips and sipped, barely wetting his mouth from what Jenny could tell. He cleared his throat, apparently taking the floor although he took his time responding as he placed the glass on the table, then adjusted the collar of his starched white button-down shirt. He might very well have been the only man on the island wearing a shirt like that.

"Mrs. Winston was very excited to meet with us today. She, in fact, assured us she would give us most of her time." Mr. Pritchard turned his head slowly and narrowed his eyes at her, making his gray orbs look like that of a raptor, ready to extend its talons and swoop down for a kill.

Jenny found his stare unnerving and picked her glass up and took a drink before reminding herself how loaded it was with alcohol, possibly more than one kind. It didn't burn as much going down this time, though, and she tasted more of the fruit juices added. It really was quite good.

She looked at Mr. Sagawa. "What were you going to meet with her about?"

Mr. Sagawa answered her question a bit faster than before, apparently realizing it would be the only way to have a turn speaking. "Mrs. Winston is considering financing a business venture we are planning to start on Lanai."

"What kind of business venture?"

Their waiter showed up at their table, carrying a platter that he held in one hand while skillfully moving the centerpiece on their table. He set the platter within reach of all three of them, then placed silverware in front of each person. Jenny stared at the calamari on the plate before her.

"This is a spicy chili sauce," Mr. Sagawa told her, using a small spoon to dish sauce onto his plate. "It is absolutely delicious."

Jenny managed a smile, accepting the calamari as she held

out her plate. Squid—she was going to eat squid. Her stomach clenched. She wasn't eager at all to expand her horizons.

"You were telling me about this business venture?" she reminded the two gentlemen, steering the attention from her as she studied the deep-fried calamari on her plate. Maybe it wouldn't taste bad.

"Yes. Mrs. Winston always enjoyed good visuals. I'm sure you'll completely agree with us after seeing what we brought." Mr. Pritchard nodded to Mr. Sagawa, who put down his fork and leaned to his side and lifted a flat, poster-sized leather case she hadn't noticed sitting beside him until now. When the young waiter returned to the table to check on their drinks, Mr. Pritchard turned to him. "Please bring the easel now."

Jenny nibbled a piece of the calamari dipped in the chili sauce while watching both men advise the waiter where to put the easel. The calamari actually wasn't as bad as she'd feared it would be. It wasn't comparable to eating slimy rubber as Nana had warned her. Jenny needed to remain more open-minded about seafood instead of basing her food decisions on how sea creatures appeared in movies. After all, shrimp were to die for, and they were nothing more than large, ugly spiders in the ocean.

Mr. Sagawa scooped another bite of calamari, covered in sauce, into his mouth, winked at her, then abandoned his food and chair to stand at the end of the table. She found herself wondering his age as he began pulling poster boards from his leather case and putting them in order so they leaned next to the easel. The waiter appeared again, with another waitress accompanying him, and they placed their main entrées at each table setting. Jenny stared at the swordfish and a side of mixed vegetables that appeared to be sautéed in a wine sauce. Fortunately she wasn't too hungry, although she ordered herself to try at least a bite of everything on her plate.

"Miss Rogers." Mr. Sagawa stole her attention from the food in front of her. "To begin with, I want you to have a good visual of the island."

Mr. Pritchard watched her as well, for the first time appearing rather pleased after glancing at the poster on the easel, a picture of the island.

"Here is Lanai City," Mr. Sagawa began. "And as you may or may not know, the remainder of the island is almost all privately owned. Right here," he continued, gesturing to a section of the island before swapping the poster out for the next one and sliding it onto the easel, "this is the section of land we're planning on acquiring."

The posters were very nicely done. This second one was a blown-up view of the section of the island in question. The topographical view showed the beach, the level land, and where the mountains began. Lanai offered almost every type of terrain a person might enjoy.

Mr. Sagawa removed the second poster and aptly placed a third one in its place. "With Mrs. Winston's financial backing," he said, flashing her a winning smile, "the resort will go here. We'll have a golf course and swimming pools. The resort, which will be named the Samantha Winston Private Resort," he said, again smiling as if he already knew how pleased this would make Samantha, "will be the most exquisite escape for those in need of a private paradise unlike any offered on all the islands."

"Or anywhere in the world," Mr. Pritchard added, nodding solemnly. "Your job is a very serious one, Miss Rogers," he informed her, turning away from Mr. Sagawa and facing Jenny. "We need financial approval by the morning in order to proceed on schedule."

"By the morning," Jenny said, understanding sinking in. They wanted her to convince Samantha to give these men the money for a resort they would name after her. Would Samantha even care about such a thing?

"That is very crucial."

"I'll see what I can do."

"No." Mr. Pritchard shook his head, staring hard at Jenny with narrowed gray eyes. "You will get her to agree. If Mrs. Winston were here, she would be signing her name to this project before lunch was over. I don't know what transpired for you to be here in her place, but since you are, it is imperative you present our project to her in such a way so she will understand how lucrative the Samantha Winston Private Resort will be. Falling behind schedule, even for one day, will cost more money than you will ever make in a year."

Jenny stiffened, getting the overwhelming sensation Mr. Pritchard blamed her for Samantha not being here. She'd definitely just been insulted. And he was bullying her over money. Mr. Pritchard needed her to get what he wanted, and she didn't think insulting her was the smartest move in getting his financial approval. It crossed her mind to ask why the two of them didn't finance the project themselves. Did their credit suck? Or was the project simply way out of their financial league? Her papa had said don't bite off more than you can chew. She hated that expression. Papa had used it way too often for every imaginable scenario. It came to mind now, but Jenny didn't say anything. She held her tongue and her temper.

"And, Miss Rogers"—Mr. Sagawa slid into his chair, facing her—"Having you as a lunch date has been very refreshing."

"Thank you," she said, managing a smile..

Mr. Sagawa and Mr. Pritchard were as opposite as day and night. Mr. Pritchard implied he knew Samantha very well, but if he did, why not call her? Jenny needed to pay attention to everything and everyone around her. These men weren't going to bully or charm her into any promise she couldn't keep.

Mr. Sagawa reached inside his suit pocket and pulled out a small, flat box—the kind that held jewelry. His grin was relaxed as he handed it to her.

"We're putting pressure on you, and it's obvious by the look on your face this isn't your area of expertise. Mr. Pritchard and I are confident in your ability to lean Samantha Winston in our favor. From what we've heard, she is very fond of you."

Jenny almost asked what they'd heard about her, and from whom, but Mr. Sagawa held out the box. "This is a gesture of our appreciation. Tomorrow when you confirm Mrs. Winston loves the thought of the resort, we will celebrate further."

She took the box and stared at it for a moment before opening it. Jenny wasn't able to hide her surprise as she stared at the beautiful necklace inside.

"Oh, my," she whispered, and delicately touched the blue jewels throughout the silver necklace.

"They are real," Mr. Pritchard announced stiffly. "And very expensive."

"I wasn't thinking about how much it cost," she said defensively, shooting him a hard look. Jenny knew how important it was to represent Samantha to her best ability, but Mr. Pritchard was getting on her nerves. "I'll let you know what Samantha says as soon as I know."

Jenny sat in her suite, her head still spinning, after leaving Mr. Pritchard and Mr. Sagawa. She relaxed in one of the chairs on the patio, with her bare feet propped up on the ledge. A pale blue sky spread out before her, and she breathed in the salty air. Lanai was beautiful, the absolute epitome of paradise. The extremely wealthy and the famous would pay a pretty penny to enjoy this paradise. This hotel suite could serve as part of that getaway. But a resort based on the drawings Sagawa and Pritchard showed her would be heavenly.

Her brain got muddled with all the facts when she tried laying them out. This was an island existing only for those who could afford it. Entrepreneurs and businessmen like Mr. Pritchard and Mr. Sagawa would become very wealthy men off the rich and famous. Yet they wouldn't earn a dime without the aid of one of those already rich exclusives. It was as if one couldn't exist without the other, and yet they too often loathed and used each other.

Jenny sighed, leaned forward, and let her feet fall to the textured patio floor. She rested her elbows on her knees and her chin in her hands. "I guess I'll call Samantha and get it over with." If she simply laid out the facts, and her honest opinions of her lunch date, which was what she was supposed to do, Samantha would never agree to finance the resort.

Glancing over her shoulder, she focused on the digital clock by the bed in her suite. She had an hour before Samantha would call it a night. And she couldn't wait to call at the last minute. But she had an idea.

Fifteen minutes later, Sean was pulling out of the hotel parking lot. Jenny moved to the edge of the seat, then slid to the middle. He insisted she ride in the back, even when it was just the two of them. Jenny complained that it made her feel like a child not old enough to sit up front with the adults, but Sean had been stubborn about it.

So she did the next best thing and leaned forward to rest her arms on the back of the front seat. "Do you know where we're going?" Jenny had shown him the plans Mr. Pritchard and Mr. Sagawa had left with her. She hadn't shown him the sapphire necklace they'd given her, though. It was a bribe and one she had no intention of keeping. She would give it back to them the next time she saw them.

"Yes, ma'am."

Jenny made a face at him. Sean was in full chauffeur mode, unwilling to lower his shield for a moment and treat her like a normal person.

"I hope so," she muttered, thinking that challenging him might make him talk to her.

Sean didn't blink an eye at her comment but remained relaxed, with his hands at ten and two as he drove along the highway next to the ocean. Since he wouldn't talk to her, Jenny slid back, still dumbfounded over Samantha's limousine not having seat belts in the backseat. Apparently she'd had them removed, complaining that they were uncomfortable to sit on.

Jenny stared out at the ocean. She'd been to a few of the Great Lakes growing up and had always heard people compare them to the ocean, but there was no comparison. Even if she couldn't see the other side of the lake, she knew it wasn't too far past where her eyes could see. The ocean was an entirely different story.

It made sense now that there was a shade known as ocean blue, because no other shade compared to it. Jenny had fallen in love with the view the moment she'd first seen it. And whenever she left the hotel, no matter the angle or location where she saw the ocean, she was mesmerized all over again.

"I believe the land in question begins around here."

Sean pulled her out of her love affair with the view, and she shifted her attention to the other tinted window as she slid across the seat.

"Are you sure?" she asked, staring at the house as they drove past it.

"Yes, ma'am, quite sure. It begins here and is all you see as we round this curve up here. I do believe there is a place to pull off the road if you'd like to get out and have a better look."

"Yes. Thank you."

Sean pulled off the road next to a sign that announced a scenic view. Jenny wasn't sure how anyone decided which view was better than others. There wasn't a bad view anywhere on the island. He parked and slid out from behind the wheel, moving briskly around the back of the car and frowning when Jenny opened the rear passenger door and let herself out. She made a face at him and grinned when his expression turned solemn.

"Doesn't this land belong to someone?"

"I do believe all of it is privately owned."

"Hmm," she said in response, wondering if Mr. Pritchard and Mr. Sagawa were that convinced the locals would sell their land so two investors could turn it into a play area for the rich and famous. "I don't see any for-sale signs." She'd walked to the edge of the paved parking area. "There aren't signs that say, 'Private property, trespassers will be shot,' either."

"No, ma'am."

Jenny rolled her eyes, exasperated with Sean's mechanical behavior, but then decided if he was going to treat her as if she were better than him, she could play the part, too.

"Go wait in the car for me. I won't be too long." When Sean began protesting as she lifted her leg over the short, metal barrier dividing the road side parking from the private land, Jenny waved her hand in his direction, dismissing him.

It helped being on the part of the island where the Samantha Winston Private Resort might be. Jenny imagined the tall grass mowed, or maybe they would keep its natural appearance. Something told her they wouldn't, though. Mr. Pritchard and Mr. Sagawa didn't strike her as men who cared a lot about natural environment. They would have this field mowed, possibly with a paved walk through it so those who wished to be one with nature wouldn't have to get messed up while doing it.

Jenny remembered a field a few blocks from her junior high. For several years, that field had been her world after school. Parkville was an old town, and it was one of many that never became a thriving metropolis but had managed during the couple centuries since its inception to stay alive. The field had once been the site of a warehouse. The warehouse was long gone, but if you knew where to look, you could see the basement to the warehouse, which was still there.

She and her friends had discovered the hole in the ground, hidden by a metal manhole cover. Manhole covers didn't belong in fields, which had bested their curiosity. At first Jenny had been terrified of jumping down into a hole that disappeared into inky blackness. She'd been just as afraid of being left behind, especially when the best-looking guys in her grade were already jumping into the unknown. Remaining behind where she was safe quickly lost its appeal.

As she walked, Jenny moved a rock on the ground with her shoe, wondering what might have been on this land at one time. She had learned many things during those early teenage years, about trust, about boys, and about the different types of boys out there. That forgotten basement had helped move her out of her childhood and into full-blown adolescence. Yet she'd also received a better history lesson than she ever would have in a classroom.

In that old, dingy basement, which during those years was almost like their secret clubhouse, there had been forgotten pictures and calendars on the walls. Old furniture had been stacked up against walls and left for waste when the building was torn down. She and her friends snatched all the flashlights and batteries they'd been able to round up and had moved the furniture, turning that old, decrepit basement into a place that held so many of her memories.

Jenny wondered about the house they'd passed when Sean first announced they were at the land that might very well be converted into a resort. Would it be torn down, memories of the place lodged in someone's brain but forgotten by most? How many other houses were on the land Mr. Pritchard and Mr. Sagawa had decided would be the best location to build the resort?

She continued walking through knee-high grass and neared a clump of bushlike trees heavily laden with large flowers that had an amazing fragrance. Mr. Pritchard and Mr. Sagawa might keep these bushes or trees or whatever they were considered. Their scent was incredible. She studied the large flower, committing it to memory so later she could look it up and figure out what it was called.

Maybe this clump of plants had once been part of a beautiful garden that was now a large field. Jenny told herself it was the way of life. Families would grow up and share adventures, secrets, tragedies and happiness in a small part of the world. Eventually that world would be tilled under to make way for a new set of memories to be created. Even though converting the land made sense in her brain, she wasn't able to turn it into a pleasant thought. All she saw were old memories being bulldozed under to make way for someone else's experience.

Another thought hit her as she made her way around the delicious-smelling plants. What would happen if whoever owned this land didn't want to sell? Was it Mr. Pritchard and Mr. Sagawa's job to convince them to sell? Could the locals be forced into selling their land?

She paused on the other side of the flowering plants and stared at the back side of a large, rambling home. The land was flat on either side of the house, and rows of sickly looking trees grew on one side while swordlike leaves sprouted from the bushes on the other side.

"Oh, God," she whispered when she realized she stared at Ric's banana plantation.

"Is there a problem?"

Jenny almost shrieked at the sight of the very large shotgun Ric was holding as he stared at her.

"Ric!" she gasped.

"You look surprised to see me." His words were cold, and his face showed her he was *not* surprised to see her. "Are you going to tell me what you're doing here? And the truth!" he hissed, glaring down at her as he held the gun, pointing it to the ground by his side. "Did you agree to come out here on behalf of your two lunch dates?" he sneered.

Jenny stared at him in disbelief. "How do you know about my lunch date?" she asked.

Ric didn't say anything but gave her a look that suggested she was stupid to ask such a question. Well, she wasn't stupid, and he was acting very strange when he'd been on fire the night before.

"I came here on behalf of myself," she informed him, straightening. "And I had no idea this was your land—if it is your land," she added. But when his expression remained hard as stone, she continued, willing to let him have it for scaring her to death with that gun, then acting as if he hadn't kissed her senseless the night before. "I saw your banana plantation for the first time just now. What's wrong?"

"Why are you here?" he demanded, ignoring her question. The man she met last night was gone. But the tormented anger she'd caught glimpses of before they'd had sex was present in full force.

It was a fierce stab to the gut, and Jenny didn't understand why he was acting this way. Instead of answering, she focused on the large shotgun he gripped in his hand.

"Are you going to shoot me?" she demanded. She could answer questions with questions, too. Her grandfather had taught her a few things when he had taken her hunting as a child.

"Nope." Ric swung the shotgun like a baton, then let his fingers slide away from the trigger. "But you are going to tell me what you're doing here."

"I have no problem with that." She fisted her hands on her hips and gave him what she hoped was the same hard look he was giving her. "But I do have a problem with you being an ass because you found me here. Like I would do anything to hurt your land."

She was somewhat satisfied when she saw his expression soften. He was a very different version of the sex god she'd been with the night before, though. The man standing in front of her was hard, dangerous-looking, yet still virile. Whatever demons haunted this man were out in full force tonight.

"Why are you here, Jenny?" he asked again, his voice softer but those sultry green eyes still probing, searching for something deep inside her. It was as if he already didn't trust whatever answer she might give and searched for the truth himself.

"Because I wanted to see the land that my *lunch dates* had discussed," she said, stressing "lunch dates." "They were two businessmen who thought they were going to see Samantha just as you had."

"And what made them mention this land?"

Jenny frowned, then shook her head. "I think you already know the answer to that since you seem to know my lunch dates might send me out here."

"Did they?"

"No," she insisted, almost yelling.

"Okay." Ric didn't seem put out by her growing frustration.

"Why are you so upset?" she demanded, sticking to the same tone and not caring at that moment if snapping at him caused his dark side to come forth even further. He was out of line. And if this was the way Ric Karaka behaved normally, it was no wonder he was all alone in that big, old rambling house.

Ric blinked, then adjusted his grip on his shotgun as he paced past her. When he turned, facing her with his back to the road, Jenny gave silent thanks Sean hadn't decided to traipse across the field to find her.

"Have you talked to Samantha about me yet?"

Jenny swore she could see his brain working overtime, processing information and deciding how best to use it. She didn't have a clue what he was trying to work through in his mind, though, and it was aggravating the crap out of her.

"No," she said, sighing. "And I need to do that soon."

"Why haven't you called her?"

"It was too late when I returned to my suite last night, and this morning I decided to wait until after my lunch date so I could give her all the information she wanted at once."

"What were you going to tell her about me?"

It wasn't a fair question, but his facial expression offered no indication he cared one way or another. Regardless of what unpleasant game he had devised, Jenny wouldn't play.

"Up until a few minutes ago, I was going to tell Samantha she could look forward to meeting her grandson," she told him.

Her implication didn't seem to faze him. "Sounds like you need to take time to know someone better before you start singing their praises."

"What is wrong with you?" She threw her hands up in desperation. "Why have you changed so drastically from last night?"

"Did you like that man?" he asked, lowering his voice as he stepped toward her.

Jenny backed away from him.

"And today you find me an asshole?"

"Tell me what's wrong," she insisted, digging in her heels and refusing to continue backing up as he stalked her.

"You met with two men today who wish to turn all of this into a playground for the extremely wealthy."

She wasn't going to worry right now how he knew that. It was obvious he had been filled in on all the details of her lunch, possibly by the waiters or the host. It wouldn't surprise her if Ric knew most of the staff at the hotel. He seemed the type of man who would secure his connections, and if he didn't normally act the way he was right now, he was probably liked by all the local community. When she didn't say anything, he continued.

"These men have flown here to the island, ready to take on the locals and seize all this land. All they need is Samantha's go-ahead. From what I heard earlier, they have a local bank that might possibly work with them if they have the backing of someone like my grandmother." He paused, staring at her.

"Okay," she said slowly, unsure where he was going with this.

His green eyes flared with emotions so intense Jenny swore she saw sparks fly around his pupils. "Did you wonder at all why I bought and am living in this incredibly huge, dilapidated old home?"

"You told me," she said, waving at the house. "It belonged to your great-grandparents. Family means a lot to you," she finished, shifting her attention to the sprawling old home. "It's not really dilapidated," she added, speaking softly. And she meant it. The banana plantation not only was cleverly named, it was built to endure the test of time.

"It's going to be worse than dilapidated if the men you had lunch with get their way. Why did you come out here?"

"I thought it would be easier to talk to Samantha about all of this if I had a solid visual in my head. I wanted to see exactly where the land was that Mr. Pritchard and Mr. Sagawa were talking about."

"They plan on taking over the entire island, Jenny," Ric told her, his baritone deep and warning. "Other than Lanai City, and parts of the island maintained by the state, this island is privately owned. Families who've lived here for years, who have established roots, who have worked hard to have what they do will be bought out with a tempting amount of cash, then cast off the island."

"Cast off?"

"Cast off, darling," he growled, taking another step closer.

The sun reflected off his raven-black hair. He looked even darker in the white polo shirt he wore. His khaki shorts ended at midthigh, showing off his long, muscular legs. "Once everyone who currently lives in the path of this exquisite resort sells their land, their homes, all they'll be able to do is take their cash and leave the island. There won't be anywhere else for them to live."

"Hopefully they'll think that through before they agree to sell."

Ric suddenly grabbed her, pressing his long fingers along the length of her jaw and tilting her head back. "No one is going to sell their land," he snarled.

There had only been a few times in Jenny's life when she'd seen the sky in such incredibly turbulent shades of blues and greens. It was always minutes before a life-threatening storm would wreak chaos across the land. Ric's eyes were that shade of green, a color that promised danger and destruction too intense to be controlled.

Her heart pounded painfully against her ribs, and she grabbed his wrist, barely able to wrap her fingers around it. "Ric, don't hurt me."

He didn't shove her but let go of her so quickly Jenny lost her footing and stumbled backward. She held her arms out to maintain her balance, and Ric grabbed her hand. He gave it a fierce squeeze and shook it so her entire body rattled, which made her teeth clatter together.

"I would never hurt you," he growled. "But I pray you possess enough insight to see when a man does possess the ability to hurt you."

"What?" When she tried slipping her hand from his, Ric tightened his grip.

"Those men you enjoyed your expensive lunch with while staring at some of the most breathtaking scenery on this planet are the ones who will hurt you." Ric lowered his voice as he tugged Jenny closer. He looked down at her, close enough to kiss her, as he continued dishing out a dangerous warning. "They plan on destroying this entire island. Does it matter to you if so many families are pressured into selling their homes, giving up all they have and very likely being bullied until they do so?"

"I don't have any say over anyone on this island," she complained, twisting her hand in his, although her efforts to free herself were futile. She gave up trying and relaxed her sweaty palm in his larger hand. "If you don't want the resort to happen, don't sell the banana plantation."

"Come with me." Ric turned, keeping a hold of her hand as he started across the land with long, determined strides.

It was all Jenny could do to keep up. If she stepped on an uneven bit of land, Ric prevented her from falling by tightening his grip on her. At one point, she stepped into an indentation in the earth, almost twisting her ankle. Ric was attentive, in spite of practically dragging her as he took them to his house. He kept her from falling to the side and damn near lifted her off the ground.

"Where are we going?" she demanded, holding her free hand out to balance herself.

"I want to show you something."

When they reached the side of the house, Jenny wanted to look over her shoulder, wondering if she should call Sean's cell to let him know she was fine, except Ric didn't let go of her and continued around the side of his house.

"You were wondering how I knew who you had lunch with and what was discussed," Ric continued.

"I figure you have friends who work at the hotel," she said.

"Are you curious what made me seek out the details behind your lunch date?"

Jenny hadn't thought it through that far yet. The first thing that came to mind, though, was that he was protective and possessive. It could also mean with all the demons inside him already, he didn't know how to trust.

"Let me show you what motivated me to learn who your lunch dates were." Ric led them to the other side of the front of the house. "If it weren't for this, I would have waited to hear you share whatever information you wanted to share about your lunch. I doubt I would have cared if you didn't mention your lunch date at all."

Jenny wondered if he said this so she wouldn't see him as obsessive or controlling. Ric was intelligent enough to know that no woman would find such behavior in a man appealing.

He stopped without warning, and she stumbled into his backside, recovering quickly when he let go of her hand and stepped around him. He reached for her again at the same time Jenny saw what he'd dragged her to the side of the banana plantation to show her.

"Oh my God," she gasped, and stared at the banana trees. They had already been in dismal condition but were now hacked away so that almost half of them lay on the ground, fallen on top of each other. "When did this happen?"

"A few hours ago."

She walked around Ric, moving closer to the trees. Jenny didn't try counting how many trees had been cut down, but whoever desecrated Ric's property did a good job of axing them down. It would take a fair amount of work to clear the fallen trees out of there.

"I'm sorry," she whispered, remembering that his great-grandparents had brought over their particular line of bananas and had planted them when they'd moved in.

Ric took her arm again, this time gently. The way his fingers brushed down her arm immediately caused her body to react. Her insides quickened, and heat rose from between her legs, immediately causing her pussy and breasts to swell with need. What kind of fool was turned on by someone who manhandled her, and who possibly didn't think that much of her, not to mention obviously had a lot of unresolved issues?

He moved closer, holding her arm just below her elbow and pulling her against him until his mouth was at the side of her head. "I'm not going to sell my land," he whispered into her ear.

"Okay," she said slowly, shifting as she spoke so she faced him. It hadn't crossed her mind that he would, and as she stared into his hardened, determined expression, she began understanding the severity of the situation. "They're going to try and force you out of your home," she said, not making it a question as much as an understanding of the disturbing truth.

"They'll lose this battle, not me," he growled, his voice rumbling from his chest as he stared down at her.

Gravel popped behind him just as Ric lowered his mouth to hers. Jenny froze, stiffening, when she heard the car pull up behind Ric. His lips were on hers, moving to kiss her, at the same time she sensed him tighten his grip on his shotgun. Instead of releasing Jenny, Ric kept her tucked in next to him as he raised his head to see who was there.

Which was why it took Jenny a moment to recognize the limousine when it parked in the driveway. She had a better view, though, of the second car when it slowed on the highway and turned in as well.

"Son of a bitch," Ric snarled, his body turning from warm flesh to cold steel as he pushed her backward. "Go inside, Jenny. Don't argue with me. Go inside now."

# 7

Ric had half a mind to aim and shoot out a tire. Paul Pritchard was one of the biggest assholes and most corrupt businessman Ric had ever known. And he'd known his share of crooks in ties over the years.

"Who's behind Sean?" Jenny asked, sounding relaxed and curious, and not listening to him.

"Get in the house," he stressed.

The moment Pritchard and Sagawa got out of the car and looked at Jenny, they wouldn't be the pleasant older men she'd had lunch with earlier. Ric didn't want her insulted to her face for being with him. And both men would do that—ridicule her for her choice in men. They would then promise her Samantha would hear about her lack of scruples. Ric wouldn't tolerate either one of those pricks insulting Jenny. He didn't want her humiliated and chastised to her face, and he didn't want her to witness him shutting the two pricks up, using whatever means necessary.

"But . . . ," she began, confused more than annoyed.

She could get as pissed with him as she wanted. As long as she was inside.

"Jenny, argue with me later. I'm serious." He grabbed her jaw, forcing her to give him all of her attention and quit looking at his unexpected, and unwelcome, company. "I'll explain later, but right now turn around, head into the house, and stay inside until I come get you. Do it now."

She stared at him wide-eyed, not blinking, until a car door opened and closed behind him. Ric let her go but then turned her around and gave her a gentle shove toward the porch.

"Watch out for that step," he told her, and watched when she hurried on to the porch, managing not to slip on the stair this time. She opened his screen door and front door, then closed both behind her when she disappeared inside without looking over her shoulder once.

"Fucking her won't help your case," Pritchard sneered, the cold, flat tone in his voice giving away his identity before Ric even turned around. Never had he known a man whose basic core seemed created out of pure evil.

Ric turned around slowly, itching to slide his finger into the trigger of his shotgun. He met Pritchard's squinty eyes and waited until the jerk quit looking past him at his porch and stared at Ric. Responding to Pritchard would only fuel the fire that fed the man's evil.

"What do you want?" Ric asked, moving his gun and holding it in front of him with both hands.

"I heard there was some damage done to your property," Pritchard said, jumping right into whatever plot he'd devised before coming there. "I just wanted to make sure it hadn't depreciated the value of this land. I'll make you a fair offer, Karaka, and even personally explain any of the business aspects of selling this dump that you might not understand," he added, his voice turning sweeter than honey as he squinted at Ric.

"I doubt you know what a fair offer is," Ric said under his breath, but spoke louder when he held up his gun. "Get off my land, Pritchard."

The asshole had the nerve to laugh at Ric's shotgun, as if he believed it nothing more than a toy. "I know you want to turn this dump into a bed-and-breakfast, which only proves you're as much of an idiot as your father's family is. It doesn't surprise me a bit that Mrs. Winston didn't want to waste her time meeting you. Do you really think she's going to buy into your fabricated story about being her grandson?"

When Pritchard smiled, it looked as if it were painful for him. His skin stretched taut over protruding cheekbones as he slid his hands into his pants pockets and rocked back on his heels.

The asshole wanted to push Ric to his limit, get him so pissed off he would do something stupid. Pritchard wasn't as smart as he thought he was, though. Ric wouldn't be pushed; he'd had years of experience in appearing calm and unimpressed during continual waves of ridicule and lies.

"What makes you think I'm the one she didn't want to meet?" Ric asked, sliding his finger against the trigger of his shotgun. He got more satisfaction than he thought he would when Pritchard turned his attention to the act and pulled his hands out of his pocket. "Now, I told you to leave. If I have to call the sheriff and report a trespasser, I'll make good use of the man's time and press charges for vandalizing my trees as well."

Pritchard snorted. "You go ahead and do just that. Waste your time if you want. All I have to say is destroying those half-dead banana trees will probably raise the value of this property instead of diminish it. But I'd think twice about trying to convince the old lady to back you and your little bed-and-breakfast venture. And don't think for a minute that sleeping with her sexy protégée will secure your deal. Miss Rogers is a small-town nobody, easily bought and sold. She's a mere moment of entertainment to the old lady and will be cast aside long before any deal is set in stone. Trust me on that one. Mrs. Winston won't waste another moment with the small-town hussy once she learns Miss Rogers's opinion on matters can be bought with a few choice trinkets, or a tumble in the sack."

Ric noticed Sean had cracked the passenger window. He was pretty sure he knew why Sean remained in the limousine. His presence was enough to show he knew where Jenny was and would sit there until he took her home. But Ric would bet the chauffeur was very loyal to his employer. Pritchard's cruel insults would only result in slitting the old man's throat.

"Don't underestimate her," Ric said, every inch of him tense as he fought to keep his cool and not lose it on the lowlife bastard. "And if I have to tell you to get off my land one more time, you'll be walking back to town." He raised his shotgun and aimed it at Pritchard's front tire.

"You're going to sell this place to me. It won't be worth your time living in it when you can't do anything with it," Pritchard announced, turning and heading back to his car. The passenger door opened for him before he reached it, although it was impossible to see through the windshield with the angle of the sun reflecting off it. "Give up on your bed-and-breakfast, Karaka," Pritchard yelled, using his passenger door as a shield and waving his finger at Ric. "No one is going to spend their good money on a Karaka. Your family didn't even know what kind of fruit to farm."

Ric fought the urge to shoot the man's finger off his hand. Pritchard slid inside the car, which backed up, turned around in Ric's yard, and accelerated down the driveway to the highway. Ric shook, fighting to lower his weapon instead of aiming and firing. He didn't shift his attention to the idling limousine still in his driveway until Pritchard had turned onto the highway and disappeared from Ric's view.

There wasn't anything to say to Jenny's limousine driver. The man was paid to sit and wait in the car, so he would do just that. Ric wouldn't tell him to leave. Already the guy got an earful of insults toward his employer. Ric had no intention of giving the guy anything to complain about to Samantha, other than possibly spending too much time with Jenny. Ric didn't see that as a character defect on his part. If anything, Samantha should appreciate that her grandson had good taste in women.

He turned to his porch and climbed the old stairs carefully. He'd planned on replacing the broken stair today until he'd spotted someone on the back side of his property. Ric had grabbed his shotgun and hauled ass across the undeveloped meadow, circling around until he got close enough to see it was Jenny. The outrage he'd felt when he believed that she'd teamed up with Pritchard and Sagawa and was assessing his land fueled his fury to the point of blindness. Ric saw now that Jenny's arrival on his property was purely out of curiosity. It wouldn't take too much to show her what creeps those two men were.

Ric entered his home and closed the front door behind him, locking it and then listening for a moment when he didn't see Jenny. The house was quiet, almost too quiet. He smelled Jenny's perfume, though, and swore his body was drawn to it as he walked across the living room and down the hall, pausing at the stairs leading upstairs for only a moment before turning to his kitchen.

Jenny ended a call when he entered the kitchen and slid her phone into her pocket. She quit leaning against his kitchen counter and stared at him. "When were you going to tell me your true intentions for this place?" she asked, her tone cold as she looked around the kitchen.

"Did you hear everything that was said outside?" He should have guessed she would have remained close to the front door or window, struggling to eavesdrop out of curiosity, not to mention maybe she'd been concerned for him. Although at the moment she looked anything but compassionate.

Jenny glared at him. "I heard enough," she snapped.

"Who were you on the phone with?" Ric noted she wasn't storming out on him. Maybe she was too mad to move. If she thought he was holding information from her or wanted to fuck her just to get closer to his grandmother, she'd sorely misjudged him.

"Samantha."

Ric nodded, moving to the refrigerator, deciding a cold beer sounded better than anything at the moment. He pulled out two bottles, ripped the cap off one of them with his teeth, and handed it to her. Jenny stared at him for a moment, her expression not changing, until finally she grabbed it from him. He had a feeling they might both need several.

"I'm sorry you had to hear any of what was said out there," he said after taking a long drink of his beer. The cold brew felt real good going down. As much as a solid buzz might help numb his outrage, it also might make Jenny even more furious with him when he dragged her upstairs. In spite of her anger, she looked hot as hell in her shorts and open-necked blouse.

"Are you? Weren't you trying to convince me Mr. Pritchard was a prick?" She gulped at her beer, tilting the bottle and downing a fair amount of it, then wiped her mouth with the back of her hand. "Or was it the part about your interest in converting this old place into a bed-and-breakfast that you didn't want me to hear?"

She drank more of the beer until her bottle was barely half full. When she burped, she slapped her hand over her mouth and Ric wondered if he was seeing her true colors or if she was so angry she was drinking the beer when it wasn't something she would normally do. Ric was just starting to get to know her, but watching her, even as her temper continued to flare, he had to admit he was more than intrigued. And it was a hell of a lot more than her incredible sex appeal.

He had been so mad when he thought she was working with Pritchard. But her outrage now, her fury over someone trying to use her, showed more of her true nature. Jenny was a good person. No one would take advantage of or abuse Jenny without her putting up a fight.

"I've been very anxious to tell you about my plans for this place," he said, keeping his tone soft, gentle, not only for her but also in his effort to subdue his emotions and think rationally. All he wanted to do was close the distance between them and unbutton her shirt. More than anything, he wanted to replace that beer bottle with his dick and watch her wrap her lips around him. But even more than sex, he wanted her to understand why he'd handled things the way he did. "This place is an investment," he added, focusing on her mouth when she brought the beer to her lips again.

"I thought you bought it because it was a major piece of family heritage." She sounded accusatory, as if she were catching him in a lie.

Ric wouldn't dwell on what she might have told Samantha. Jenny was pissed. And she had every right to be. But not at him. He hadn't told her about the bed-and-breakfast right away. His reasons were sound, though, and he'd stand by them.

"That is why I bought it," he explained. "That family heritage will be the theme of the bed-and-breakfast. People love history, and this place is loaded with it."

"Why didn't you tell me you wanted this for a bed-and-breakfast?"

"I wanted you to see how great the place is. I wanted you to fall in love with the place, and then I planned to explain my renovation plan and turning it into a bed-and-breakfast. It was how I planned to do things with Samantha, so it's how I did things with you."

"You knew I was calling Samantha after our first meeting." She wagged her finger at him before drinking more of her beer. "I came here with good intentions, excited and thrilled to have won a free vacation, then equally happy when Samantha saved the day and allowed me to come here. I'm seeing a part of the world I never would have seen otherwise, and I'm fulfilling Nana's dream." When she started to take another drink and realized she'd finished her beer, she set the empty bottle down on the counter and started out of the kitchen. "I told Samantha how you and Mr. Pritchard and Mr. Sagawa all presented yourselves as wonderful men, when none of you were," she announced over her shoulder, her tennis shoes making soft padding sounds when she stormed through his house.

Ric grabbed two more bottles out of the refrigerator, set his empty next to hers on the counter, then hurried after Jenny.

"And what did she say to that?" he asked, catching up to her in the living room, then coming around her so he faced her before she reached the front door.

Once again he screwed the bottle cap off with his teeth and handed her the first beer. Jenny took it, then walked over to the coffee table in the corner of his large living room and set it down. She crossed her arms when she faced him, which pushed her breasts together and allowed for a nice show of cleavage.

"What do you want out of all this?"

Her question startled him, and he stopped before he reached her, staring at her slightly flushed face. She tilted her head, causing long, thick, slightly tousled curls to tumble over her shoulder.

"Out of all of what?" he asked, needing to be very sure he understood her question before attempting to answer.

"That's what Samantha said, to find out what you want."

"I see." Ric knew all too well how unfair life was. He should have foreseen how Samantha would believe that, no matter how friendly or unhindered their letters were, Ric wanted money. "What do *you* think I'm trying to gain?"

Jenny threw her hands up in the air as she made a face. "How the hell am I supposed to know when you aren't even being level with me?" she said, yelling at him.

Ric remembered how Sean had his window slightly cracked in the limousine. He didn't doubt for a moment that the chauffeur would come bounding up onto that porch if he thought Jenny might be in danger.

He moved in on her, watching her eyes grow larger as he cleared the distance between them. She might be upset, but Jenny wasn't unaffected by his nearness any more than he was with hers. Ric reached the edge of the couch and set his full beer on the end table; then he tried grabbing the thick curl that was nearly twisted around her arm.

"Don't," she whispered, striking out at him.

There was no fire in her command, though, no intensity as there had been earlier when she'd revealed her temper. Before she could slap his hand away, he dodged the effort and grabbed her wrist.

"Not once have I said anything to you that wasn't completely the truth," he said, speaking equally as softly as he tugged slightly on her wrist. "I grew up without anything, many times not even a home. If that made me tough around the edges, shrewd when it comes to seeing a good investment, then so be it. I won't apologize for that."

Jenny stared at the hand holding her wrist and didn't try resisting when he brought her closer.

"Be pissed at me if you want, sweetheart. It won't stop me from fighting to know family that is mine or from doing what it takes to turn this old home into a thriving business." He pulled again until her hand was against his chest. Then, reaching for her, he dragged his free hand through all that thick auburn hair until he forced her head back so she'd look at him. "And it's not going to stop me from wanting you," he whispered.

Jenny cried out when he nipped at her lower lip and moaned

when he impaled her mouth with his tongue. Letting go of her hand, he moved both of his down her back, pressing her against him. Her hands were on his shoulders, digging in, pinching his flesh with her fingernails. But she wasn't trying to free herself.

Ric wouldn't force himself on her. Regardless of how instantly hard he was, his blood boiling with need, if Jenny resisted him, he possessed enough control to let her go. But she wasn't resisting.

He cupped her ass, enthralled with how perfectly shaped it was and how he could feel her heat through her shorts. When he lifted her, Jenny wrapped her legs around him, bringing them even closer together. The control he believed he possessed teetered dangerously when he moved blindly, heading for the couch.

He placed her on the back of it, letting her sit with her legs still pressed against his, and moved his hands between them.

"You might want to unbutton your shirt so you don't lose any buttons," he said against her mouth, his voice tight and raspy.

Every movement he made seemed constricted, his insides flooded with a craving for Jenny he could no longer hide. His cock swelled, full and throbbing against his jeans, and as desperately as he wanted her out of her clothes, he needed out of his as well.

Jenny lowered her head, looking down between them when she moved her hands to her shirt. "Do you have a condom?" she asked, her voice soft, tantalizing.

But his blood pressure soared at the question. She wanted him inside her. And, damn, that was exactly where he wanted to be.

"Upstairs." He backed away from her reluctantly, afraid to leave her for fear she'd change her mind. Ric told himself it was a smart move; he never had sex without condoms, and if there was any hesitation on her part, now was her chance to make sure this was what she wanted. "I'll be right back," he said, brushing her cheek with his fingers as he forced himself to walk away from her.

Jenny didn't suggest going upstairs with him. She simply nodded and brushed hair away from her face. As he took the stairs three at a time, enduring the pain from his swollen cock and hurrying to his bedroom, he didn't hear her move. Ric wanted her right where he left her when he returned to the living room.

He reached the side of his bed, yanked open the drawer of his nightstand, and grabbed a couple condoms, then hurried back downstairs. If she'd left the couch, preparing to leave, or had walked out the front door, he would have let her go. It would quite possibly be one of the harder tasks he would have endured in his life, but he wouldn't chase her down and drag her back to him. And he wouldn't try changing her mind. Making those promises to himself, he headed back down to his living room, forcing himself to slow down and breathe. Having a bit of blood back in his brain would make it a lot easier to behave and not scare the crap out of her when he stripped any remaining clothes from her.

Ric damn near choked on his next breath when he entered the living room and Jenny wasn't on the couch. He fought the urge to howl and tear after her, even as he saw her at his front door. Jenny wasn't opening the door but stood facing it. Obviously there wasn't enough blood in his brain, because it took him a moment to understand she was peering out the small window on his front door while securing the lock and speaking on her cell phone.

Jenny pulled her phone from her ear when she turned and faced him. "I told Sean to return to the hotel," she said, then chewed her lower lip and suddenly looked incredibly shy.

Ric imagined the chauffeur hadn't been too thrilled with those instructions. Which was just too damn bad. He moved to her, slipping the condoms into his pocket, then cupping her face. He drowned in her inquisitive eyes. Her flesh was on fire, and his hands felt cool against her cheeks.

"Good decision," he said, then tasted her again. "I never meant to mislead you."

He had been manipulating the situation, but not with the intention of hurting her, or Samantha. "I'm not like Pritchard and Sagawa."

Jenny lowered her arms and arched her body against his, leaning her head back to allow him easier access while devouring her. God! She was perfect in every way. Jenny was hot, sexually charged, and obviously not worried about what anyone said when it came to making decisions for herself. She could have ducked and run after hearing Pritchard accuse him of trying to sleep with her to gain what he wanted. Knowing Jenny would send the chauffeur away, probably knowing he also overheard Pritchard's crude accusations, raised Ric's opinion of her.

"I wouldn't be here if I thought you were," she breathed.

Jenny's heavy curls tried wrapping around his wrists as he gripped her shoulders, then ran his hands down her arms to her lower back. Her breathing quickened as his hands moved. She performed a wicked dance with her tongue around his, moving slow, almost lazily, as she tantalized and teased him with a sultry sway of her hips.

When he grabbed her ass, spreading his fingers and reaching to the curve where her ass met her inner thighs, Jenny moaned into his mouth. He pushed her against his erection, fighting to maintain coherency when the last bit of blood drained from his brain and into his cock. The pressure and tightening of his balls robbed his ability to breathe. Jenny tried sashaying her hips against him, knowing damn good and well she was pushing him to the edge.

Ric lifted her, feeling her breasts smash against his chest as their mouths became lost in each other, and she gasped for breath near his ear.

"The couch, Ric," she managed, breathless. "I want you to fuck me doggy style."

"On your hands and knees, my dear?" Ric obliged, moving stiffly with every inch of her pressed against him.

Jenny wrapped her legs around his hips and draped her arms over his shoulders. "Yes, with you behind me," she insisted.

"An incredibly erotic position," he pointed out, and let her slide down his body when he stood at the edge of the couch with the coffee table next to him. "And also very impersonal. Are we going to fuck each other's brains out?"

His crude question didn't faze her. The moment she stood in front of him, inches from his body, she began stripping. Within seconds, she stood before him in matching lace panties and bra.

"We want each other." Jenny reached for his shirt and began tugging it up his torso. "The physical attraction is growing stronger every time we're together. You know as well as I do that fucking each other will help eliminate the demands our bodies are making. Maybe once we've satisfied each other, our brains will be clearer and we'll remember to tell each other details that each of us might need to know."

"You've got this all figured out, do you?" Ric helped her out, pulling his shirt over his head and tossing it toward the other side of his coffee table.

Jenny had already moved to his jeans. Her knuckles pressed against his stomach as she undid the top button, then eased the zipper down. Immediately the tight pressure against his cock eased up a bit, allowing his dick to dance with eager anticipation.

"Oh, my," she whispered, tucking her thumbs inside his jeans and pushing them down his hips. Jenny snagged his boxers and took them down with his jeans.

"You might want to take my shoes off first, unless you wish to trap and immobilize me."

Jenny blushed when she shot a quick look at his face. "Now there's an idea." Her voice was huskier, breathy, and sounded hot as hell.

Ric also saw Jenny was doing her best to come across as brazen and confident, but her trembling fingers and flushed cheeks told a whole other story. Not that he had a problem with her sudden aggressive nature.

Jenny let go of his jeans, leaving them low on his hips. She stared down between them, possibly focusing on his unzipped jeans or imagining what he might look like once he was fully undressed. With her hair draped over her shoulders, his view of her breasts, covered only by her lace bra, was hidden. But he saw her flat tummy, the curve of her hips, and the red twisted threads of her thong that rose high on each of her hip bones.

"It's going to be a challenge getting your shoes off if you're just going to stand there." She took her time raising her attention to his face.

He hid a smile. Jenny had been staring down between them trying to figure out how to continue undressing him and had come to a dilemma she couldn't figure out. She placed her hands flat against his chest, her touch causing his flesh to sizzle.

"I'm sure we could make the task a lot simpler for you." Ric pressed his hands over hers, trapping her against his chest, and moved closer to the couch.

When he collapsed backward, the couch jumped in protest at the sudden impact and the coffee table slid to the side when he bumped it. Their two bottles of beer, both of them still full, foamed up and over the top.

Ric didn't care if they spilled over. The shocked look on Jenny's face, the way her breasts bounced and almost freed themselves from their lace confinements, and especially how her hair fanned away from her, flowing freely when she crashed down on top of him, would have been worth losing every drop of beer he had in the house.

"Crap!" Jenny shrieked, her eyes wide when she fell down on top of him.

Ric grinned, stretching out on the couch and moving his hands before she came to her senses and stopped him. He cupped her ass, spreading her open while his arms kept her firmly centered on top of him.

"The hell with the shoes," he grumbled, nipping at her lower lip when she was close enough to kiss him.

"So you do want your jeans trapping your legs when I shove them down to your ankles?" she whispered, lowering her head and kissing him.

Ric captured her lip again, scraping it with his teeth so that her breath caught and she tensed on top of him. Her nipples turned into hard pebbles, brushing against his chest.

"I'm not too worried about it," he said, and brought his hand up to the back of her head when she wouldn't willingly kiss him. Pressing down as he grabbed her hair in his hand, Ric kept her where he wanted her and ravished her mouth.

She moaned, finally surrendering and relaxing on top of him. The dominating female who'd damn near undressed him changed into a hesitant lover. Her fingernails scratched his scalp as she cupped each side of his head. When she stretched her legs, managing to slide one between his and the couch while her other leg draped off the couch, she enabled Ric access to her hot pussy, covered by the thin slip of lace.

Ric tugged on her thong, causing the lace to rub against her. Again her breath quickened and she tensed on top of him. A thousand questions rushed through his tormented brain. He wanted to know when she last had had sex, if there was a boyfriend back on the mainland, how often she had sex, and what her favorite position was.

She wanted it doggy style, and he had no problem giving her what she asked for. But he wasn't convinced it was her position of choice. Jenny was trying to satisfy her urges—and admittedly they were his urges, too—and at the same time prevent anything from developing between them. He would have to agree with her there. It would be too damn easy to become involved with this hot, sensual beauty.

Jenny quit kissing him and pulled her head up far enough to stare at him. Her lips were moist, swollen, and as captivating as her flushed cheeks and her heavily hooded gaze.

"This is making me crazy," she admitted, and thrust her hips against him, pressing into his hard cock.

Ric caught her meaning, knowing he'd been throbbing and pulsing between them as they kissed. Without any effort, he kicked off first one of his tennis shoes, then the other. Jenny's eyes widened. Her mouth took on the shape of a small circle when he easily came to a sitting position, forcing her to straddle him.

"I don't think I could handle you crazy," he drawled, moving his hands to her shoulders and sliding the red straps of her bra down her arms.

His cock thrust upward between them, eagerly stretching toward her pussy. The lace covering her entrance scraped the tip of his dick, and his eyes damn near rolled back in his head. He let go of her bra straps, leaving them hanging down her arms, before he ripped the piece of lingerie from her body.

Jenny shrieked, but her surprised expression disappeared and she regained her confidence as she began moving on his lap. She thrust her pussy against his cock, then rocked backward. An absolutely wicked grin appeared on her face. If she thought she had the upper hand with this position, that she could torture him until he was out of his head with need, she would soon learn how easily he could regain control.

"I know you can't," she purred, resting her hands on his

shoulders as she came up on him, pressing her lace-covered pussy against the length of his shaft as she captured his dick between their bodies.

"Do you think you're going to get away with torturing me?" he growled.

"I am torturing you," she said, her fingers digging into his shoulders when she rode up against him again, hissing through her teeth when she pressed herself against his dick.

Her lace thong was the only thing stopping him from sliding deep inside her. He pushed his cock against her heat, testing the panties. Ric held on to her gaze when her eyes widened.

"I'm pretty sure the torture is going to be mutual, sweetheart."

"Do you want it that bad?"

Jenny didn't come across as being a skilled seductress. Ric wondered if she saw how good she was at pushing him with her suggestive comments. Fire ignited inside him, consuming him with a ravishing need to have her. The smug look on her face, as if knowing she possessed the only thing that would make him sane again, fed his fire even more.

Ric rose to his feet, causing his dick to almost enter her when he kept her in his arms.

"Oh, God," she cried out, lowering her legs and trying to free herself.

Ric turned and laid her on the couch. She pushed away from him, scurrying to a sitting position and pulling her legs up. Jenny wrapped her arms around her legs and stared up at him, still wide-eyed. He'd caught her in her own game, and getting a bit rough proved she was desperately out of her league.

"Stay where you are." He shoved out of his jeans, then leaned down and pulled the condoms out of his pocket.

Jenny didn't move but didn't lower her legs either. Her gaze dropped to his dick, and she licked her lips. She wanted to be the seductress she tried being. He had no problem letting her play the role if that was what she wanted.

She didn't pull her attention from his dick until he came down over her. Then her gaze shot to his face.

Ric didn't hesitate. He grabbed her legs, pulling her so she once again lay down on the couch. The moment he had her positioned where he wanted her, he lowered his face between her legs and kissed her clit through the thin material of her thong.

"Ric," she gasped, her hands moving to her head. She dragged her fingers through her hair, pulling it away from her face.

"Yes, sweetheart," he murmured, in awe at the sight of her pussy when he dragged her red thong down her legs. "Damn," he growled. "You're absolutely perfect."

He couldn't wait. His cock throbbed painfully and weighed more than he could ever remember as he adjusted himself on the other side of the couch.

"Oh, my, Ric." Jenny relaxed, exhaling as she did and spreading her legs for him as she purred. "You don't know—"

Her words were cut off when Ric lowered his mouth to her moist heat. For a moment he forgot he wanted to watch her expression when he impaled her with his tongue. He breathed in her scent, which was rich and intoxicating. He traced a line around her swollen clit, and his balls hardened so painfully he could barely breathe. Every inch of him tightened, the need for her robbing his vision. His heart thumped so loudly in his chest he couldn't hear anything else. His skin was on fire. Wherever he touched her, or when she brushed against him, his skin zapped, tensing him up even further. Every one of his senses was working on overdrive, preventing him from focusing on anything but Jenny and what she was doing to him.

But as he began a wondrous exploration of her pussy, drinking in her thick cream and dipping into her scalding heat, the fog in his brain lifted long enough and he remembered to focus on Jenny's face. He was glad he shifted his gaze up her body.

Jenny's breathing came hard and fast. Her breasts were full, round, more than a handful. And her nipples begged for attention.

He'd fantasized about this moment. "Look how ripe you are." Ric adjusted himself, kneeling on the floor by the couch and pushing the coffee table to make room for his legs. He dragged his fingers over her tummy, again lowering his mouth and lapping at the thick cream soaking her shaved flesh. "You're on fire, sweetheart."

"Yes," she breathed, panting harder when he ran his fingers along the underside of her breast.

"Do you still want it doggy style?"

For a moment she looked at him as if she didn't understand the question. When a slow smile crossed her face and her lashes fluttered over her eyes, something exploded in his chest, a white heat so exhilarating and painful he was barely able to breathe.

"In a minute," she said, closing her eyes but reaching for him blindly, as if to grab his head and keep him positioned where she wanted him.

Ric obliged, chuckling. As much as he ached to experience her moist heat wrapped around his dick, it would be worth the wait to have her come before he entered her.

And she was close. So damn close. The moment he pressed his lips to her clit, then sucked the swollen flesh into his mouth, Jenny's entire body jerked off the couch.

"Damn! Shit!" she howled, lashing her head from side to side as she clawed for him, stretching her arms and dragging her fingernails over his scalp.

Ric reached for her wrists, grabbed one arm, and pressed her hand into her tummy. "Hold still," he ordered, then continued his journey down to her entrance. A fresh pool of her cream rested just inside the entrance of her pussy. Ric lapped it up like a man parched with thirst.

Once again she jerked, this time moaning and grinding her hips into his face. Ric let go of her hands and gripped her legs, pressing against her inner thighs and stretching her open farther as he feasted on her pending orgasm.

"Crap! Ric, I can't—"

"Hush," he said, not bothering to lift his face this time. Her legs trembled against his hands. Ric felt her constrict against his tongue when he impaled her, pulling more cream out as he stroked her inner walls.

If he hadn't been keeping her in place, she probably would have leaped off the couch.

"You're fighting it," he told her, aware of her growing effort to pull away from him as he pushed her closer to the edge.

"No. I want it," she gasped.

"Then relax. You're there, darling. Come for me."

"But I can't . . ."

Again she didn't finish her sentence. Ric continued coaxing her, sensing the moment she would explode. Jenny wasn't comfortable letting her orgasm happen. She fought it, continuing to buck against him and shaking her head as her hands fluttered between his head and hers.

The moment she peaked, a smooth sheen of perspiration erupted over her flesh. Her legs, her tummy, every inch of her was moist, but her pussy erupted. Ric drowned in her orgasm, in her rich, sensual scent, in the extreme constriction of her pussy, and the release of a riper, stronger cream that he couldn't get enough of.

His dick swelled, his heart pounded hard enough it hurt, and every muscle in his body tensed, yet he didn't want the moment to end. There had been women in his past who'd come all over him. It was always something he'd been very proud of when accomplished. All men loved knowing they were responsible for making a woman come harder than she'd ever come before.

When Jenny finally let go and her orgasm ripped through her, Ric swore he felt it tear at his insides as well. Instead of feeling proud, his ego stroked, a rush of humility washed over him. Ric stroked her feverish pussy with his tongue as he ran his hand up her leg, over her stomach, soothing her as her orgasm rode out its course.

He swore when he looked up at Jenny. Her face glowed with happiness.

# 8

Jenny couldn't catch her breath. Never in her life had she come so hard. Her heart raced so fast she wouldn't be surprised if her blood pressure was off the chart. Her pussy throbbed and was so soaked she felt her juices dripping down her inner thighs. When she managed to focus and glanced down at Ric, her heart came to a screeching stop. Suddenly she was gasping too hard and fast, trying to remember how to breathe.

"Get up." Ric's voice was rough, gravelly, and his eyes were so dark they reminded her of a dangerous, torrential storm ready to cut loose.

Muscles rippled in his chest when he reached for her, taking her hand and pulling her to a sitting position. Her hair fell in damp strands down her back, and she imagined she looked as if she'd been run through the ringer as she stared back at him, unable to pull her gaze from his.

He kissed her savagely, letting go of her hand and grabbing the side of her head as he impaled her mouth with his tongue. Jenny groaned, reaching for him and pressing her hand against his chest as she tilted her head and opened for him. Ric was one hell of a lover. He seemed to know her body better than she did. She would be addicted to him in seconds if she wasn't careful. But she didn't want to be careful.

"Come here." As easily as he'd instigated their kiss, Ric ended it, straightening and brushing his bare chest against her incredibly sensitive nipples.

She sucked in a hissing breath, the coarse, tight curls across his broad chest torturing her with sensations she barely had time to acknowledge before Ric was pulling her toward him.

"Against the couch, darling," he drawled, sliding his hands under her arms, then turning her away from him. "That's it, my dear. Spread your legs."

He positioned her, with Jenny facing the back of the couch, her hands pressed against the top of it as she knelt on the cushions. Ric cupped her ass, moving his fingers between her legs as he stood behind her.

"Oh," she moaned when he slipped his fingers inside her soaked pussy. It felt too good.

Already the pressure inside her swelled unbearably.

"Close enough to doggy style to please my lady?" Ric drawled from behind her.

She nodded, staring out the window at the large yard that stretched to the highway, with the ocean beyond it. Not that she focused on the view. She wouldn't have been able to if she'd tried. Every bit of her was tuned in to Ric behind her.

Jenny had mentioned the doggy-style position because it was less intimate, just as he guessed. She wanted to fuck Ric as much as he wanted to do her. That much was obvious. But getting involved with him, allowing any emotions at all to come into play, would be the biggest mistake of her life. The reasons why were so numerous, not to mention obvious, it was pointless listing them.

Now, however, after coming as hard as she had, it was as if Ric controlled every inch of her body. She was acutely aware of his every movement, the package tearing when he opened the condom, his hands moving between them when he put it on. She closed her eyes, imagining him sliding it over his hard cock. Jenny gripped the top of the couch, digging her fingernails into the fabric.

Ric gripped her waist, and she opened her eyes, her breath catching. He'd put it on faster than she had him doing it in her mind.

"Do you know how long I've fantasized about this?" He leaned forward, whispering at the side of her head.

Her breathing was ragged, and her hair drifted across her cheek when she turned her head. "We haven't known each other that long," she said, wondering if he'd imagined what fucking her would be like since the first time they'd met.

"So you probably don't want to know how many times I've fantasized about you," he whispered, leaning over her until his cheek brushed against hers.

"Uh-huh," she murmured, closing her eyes and kissing him.

Ric pressed against her entrance, and as she opened her mouth, moving her lips against his, he thrust deep inside of her. Jenny howled at the same time he released a low, commanding growl that affected every inch of her.

She swore she punctured holes in his couch as she dug in, holding on for dear life when he filled her. He was thick, a lot thicker than she'd thought he would be. He stretched her, creating sensations that tumbled over sensations as he moved deep inside her soaked pussy.

Jenny arched into him, the pressure damn near unbearable, yet she craved more of him. There was no logic to the emotions she experienced or the feelings rushing through her body. Ric hit a spot she didn't know she had, creating a rush of intense waves of raw, unleashed pleasure that flowed throughout her body. When she cried out again, ready for the dam of pressure inside her to break, Ric began thrusting, impaling her over and over as he pulled her up underneath him. He wrapped his arms around her, cupping both her breasts, and fucked her hard.

He had her pinned so neatly up against him, with her back flush against his chest and his chin resting on her shoulder, there was no way she could adjust her position when he increased momentum. And he was targeting a spot so tender and vulnerable, it pushed her over the edge with a rush of heat that exploded around her.

"Goddamn," she wailed, and swore the couch fell out from underneath her.

For a moment, Jenny wasn't sure if her eyes were open, or closed. Her world spun around her, and her legs might have slipped off the couch had Ric not been holding on to her, keeping her in position as well as preventing her from slipping over the edge to a place where she'd never return.

Even as her orgasm flowed through her, with every muscle inside her convulsing, Ric didn't slow down.

"That's it, sweetheart," he whispered. "Give me all you've got."

Like she had a choice. There were a few men in her past, none of whom had made a lasting impression, but she didn't have regrets. Not one of them had done what Ric seemed to do so naturally. He wasn't performing some incredible feat. They were fucking in the simplest of terms, primal and raw and without preamble. Yet he'd sent her twirling out of control with damn near his first thrust.

Jenny felt the pressure growing again as soon as her first orgasm passed. She didn't need to tell him to keep going or to do her in a certain way. Ric slowed the moment she caught her breath, yet remained swollen and filling her completely. But when she opened her eyes and found she could focus, he picked up the pace.

"Ric," she gasped.

"Jenny," he growled, then grabbed her jaw and turned her head to the side.

His kiss was savage, demanding, and his lovemaking fierce. She never would have thought such rough, unbridled sex would get her so damn wet, yet orgasm after orgasm tore at her insides. Jenny would have believed this could last forever, their positioning so perfect and the sensations each better than the one before. What she didn't expect was how Ric swelled, stretching her farther. He also seemed to grow, reaching even deeper inside her, tapping at the core of her womb.

It was more than she could handle.

Yanking her mouth from his, she howled, the cry of passion tearing at her throat. He reached the depths of her desire one last time, then bucked against her, his body growing as hard as stone.

A low growl started deep inside him, one so savage she felt it vibrate through her body as he released and convulsed. His cock jerked against her pussy walls as his hands slid over her moist body.

"Damn, woman," he grumbled, remaining stiff as a board for a long time even after he slowed, then stopped and remained buried deep inside her. "You drained me."

Jenny rested her chest against the top of the couch, knowing she was just as spent. In a moment she'd figure out how to reassemble herself. And then she'd worry how she would pull off returning to the hotel without it being obvious she'd just had the best sex of her life.

Hopefully it would be a very long moment. Ric slid out of her but kept her against him as he pulled the two of them to the couch. When he stretched out, adjusting her so she was flat on

152 / Lorie O'Clare

top of him, his arms wrapped around her like a protective blanket. Jenny decided she could lie there forever and relaxed, aware of how she suddenly didn't care what time she returned to the hotel—or if she did.

The next morning, Jenny was restless and exhausted. It was an odd mix that left her unwilling to go back to bed, yet unable to get anything done. After standing in front of the sliding-glass doors in her suite and staring at raindrops that bounced off the floor of her deck, she decided it was the rain's fault she was on edge. A night filled with dreams of Ric didn't help. They were just dreams, she repeatedly told herself, and hearing words of endearment or spending long, lazy days with him were not going to ever happen.

It was barely seven a.m., which explained her exhaustion, and already she'd showered and dressed. Marc wouldn't come around to harass her about her next appointment for a couple hours, but for some reason, spending time alone in her hotel suite didn't sound good. Nana wasn't answering her phone, although Jenny wasn't sure what she would say. There was no way she could spill the details about her night to her grandmother. Nana firmly believed in lasting relationships and the necessary steps to accomplish them. Nana had never understood and wouldn't discuss premarital sex.

Jenny tried joining the busy breakfast crowd, but after sitting at a table alone for a few minutes, she took her coffee cup and nodded to the waitress as she headed out to the veranda. There weren't any guests outside, in spite of the bamboo roof that kept the rain from soaking the airy cotton dress she'd opted for that morning.

"Feeling antsy this morning?" The waitress arrived a moment after Jenny sat and put a place setting in front of her.

"Yes, I am," she admitted, offering an apologetic smile, then placing her coffee cup down so the waitress could refill it.

"Well, I assure you, the islands seldom see hurricanes," the waitress offered, laughing easily.

Jenny shot her a surprised look that the young woman mistook as relief. She laughed again and clasped her hands in front of her waist. "Enjoy the rain. It really is beautiful. I bet you can't say that about a rainstorm anywhere else," she beamed, behaving the way most natives did, showing unending pride for their island.

"That's good to hear." Jenny looked away from the waitress and watched large drops slap against the trees' leaves, then splattering everywhere.

"What can I get you for breakfast, my dear?"

Jenny wasn't sure she could eat but ordered fresh fruit and a croissant, then continued staring at raindrops as they soaked the beautiful flowers surrounding the veranda. She wondered what Ric was doing and tortured herself even further when she imagined him possibly still sleeping.

He was the type of guy who would sleep in the nude with his blanket partially draped over his muscular body. She could picture his face, all stress and the watchful predator look always in his expression erased. Jenny imagined his relaxed, peaceful face, his eyes closed, and all that roped muscle still.

She let out a longing sigh, clearing her vision and once again staring at the colorful flowers doused with rainwater. It was only sprinkling now, and a cool breeze off the ocean flowed around her. The waitress had a point. Jenny had experienced all kinds of rainstorms, and this definitely was as close to a perfect rain as she'd ever seen.

Even so, the beauty around her didn't wash away the image in her mind of Ric. He was the definition of a perfect man. She'd been impressed prior to last night, but after making love to him, there were no doubts. Ric was so physical. She loved that. He was confident and never once hesitated. There wasn't a moment of awkwardness or doubt during sex. Ric knew exactly what to do, how to do it, and even knew her body better than she could have described to him. Remembering how he hit the spot deep inside of her and pushed her damn near over the edge with his initial thrust might have made her swoon, if swooning was something she did.

Instead she heaved out another sigh, reached for her coffee, and drank greedily. It was hot and burned her esophagus, but it succeeded in stopping the quickening in her womb.

"Lord," she whispered, and rested her forehead in her hand. Closing her eyes didn't work. The image of Ric, naked, was right there.

Jenny leaned back and was thankful for the distraction when her waitress appeared next to her with food in hand.

"Will there be anything else?" she asked after placing ornately sliced fresh fruit nicely arranged on one plate and Jenny's croissant on another plate. "More coffee?"

"Please." Jenny again put her cup down and reached for the miniature bowl with whipped butter in it.

"Miss Jenny Rogers?"

Jenny looked up at an elderly gentleman, then frowned at the cordless phone in his hand.

"There is a phone call for you."

She accepted the phone, her heart skipping a beat as she guessed Ric might be calling her. The waitress and elderly gentleman left without preamble, giving her privacy, which she had out on the veranda. No one else was sitting there.

"Hello?" she asked, hoping her voice sounded soft and sultry and not anxious.

"Jenny, sweetheart. There you are." Nana's voice cracked through the static on the line.

"Nana." She straightened, again focusing on her food. "Is everything okay?"

"How are you doing, dear? How is Hawaii?" Either Nana didn't hear her, which was very possible since the connection sucked, or she didn't want to talk about herself and only wanted to hear about Jenny's adventures.

"I'm doing fine," she said, speaking loudly, then struggled for what to say next. She wouldn't call her visit out here an adventure, although some might. It was more like a challenging string of events. "Everything is great. I'm watching it rain right now. How are you doing, Nana?"

"Well, I'm okay," she said, but there was something in her tone.

Jenny felt panic seize her insides. For a moment she imagined Nana had somehow found out she had sex with Ric. It wasn't that Jenny wasn't a consenting adult. She knew she was fully capable of making her own decisions and didn't regret a minute of the night before. But sucking in a breath, sticking her chin out, and adjusting her grip on the phone didn't ease the worry building inside her.

Jenny was all Nana had. They were all each other had. She wouldn't do anything to hurt Nana, not ever. Which was why she never intended on letting Nana know about Ric. Yet there was something in her tone.

"What's wrong?" Jenny demanded.

"Nothing, dear. Nothing I want you worrying about. You're having the adventure of a lifetime, and that's all I want to hear about right now."

Nothing she wanted Jenny to worry about? Those were automatic trigger words to make anyone worry.

"Nana," Jenny complained.

"Jennifer Julian," her grandmother said, using that tone she reserved for when she wouldn't budge on a subject. That tone, mixed with Nana using Jenny's middle name, meant business. "All that matters right now is that you're having the time of your life. You're doing something I never got to do, and nothing is going to ruin that, not for you or me."

Jenny sighed, although not too loud. Fortunately, the connection wasn't so great that Nana didn't hear it. "I'm having a wonderful time," she offered.

"Oh, my, I knew it." In spite of the static, there was something lacking in Nana's tone.

There wasn't any pushing Nana, though. That German stubbornness ran thick through her blood, and it never wavered. Jenny told her grandmother about her lunch meeting with Mr. Pritchard and Mr. Sagawa. She shared with her how she took a ride and looked at the land in question and left out only the part about running into Ric and staying with him.

"Well, good grief," Nana said, sounding worn out. "What is this Samantha Winston all about having you attend a lunch meeting like that?"

"She wants me to give her my impressions," Jenny explained, but didn't elaborate. She'd already told Nana why she was there. When Nana didn't say anything, Jenny frowned, pressing the receiver to her ear and putting her hand over her other ear to hear better. "Nana, are you there?"

"What, honey? Oh, yes. I think I'm going to lie down for a while. I love you, sweetheart."

"Are you sure you're okay?"

"I'm just tired."

After hanging up the phone with Nana, Jenny nibbled at her breakfast while staring out at the incredible view. Her stomach was still tied in knots. It bothered her that Nana might be incredibly lonely and unwilling to let Jenny know how much she missed her. And here she was gallivanting around paradise and making love to a beautiful man. Suddenly she felt sick to her stomach.

The phone was still next to her, and she decided to get her call to Samantha out of the way. The old woman would have instructions and advice for her luncheon meeting today, and it was as good a time as any to learn what they were. Her mind was in turmoil as she continued worrying about Nana. At the same time, Ric wouldn't stay out of her thoughts either.

Jenny dialed Samantha's number, spoke to the operator briefly as she charged the call to her room, then leaned back and stared at the croissant she'd successfully mutilated instead of eating.

"How is my young protégée doing this afternoon?" Samantha sounded suspiciously cheerful, unlike her usual somber all-business tone. Even her laughter sounded sincere. "Oh, wait, I meant morning for you, my dear. I hear you're enjoying a lovely rain there this morning?"

Jenny wondered who she'd already talked to and guessed it was Marc. Then she wondered if something he'd told her had put her in exceptionally good spirits, and if so, what?

"I'm sitting out on the veranda right now, eating breakfast. And, yes, it is a lovely rain." She tried matching Samantha's happy tone. "My grandmother just called and they brought the phone out to me," she explained. "I just hung up and thought I'd call you."

"Good. They are taking care of you properly. The staff at that hotel is exceptionally accommodating. Now, then, today's luncheon." She sounded more like herself now, cutting straight through idle chitchat and moving on to business. "This is a ladies luncheon. You're an honorary guest."

She continued explaining about the women who met once a month for lunch and that Samantha was part of their club. Jenny caught bits and pieces about the elite organization and how the ladies were very active in their community. When she shifted her gaze to the front of the hotel, she caught parts of the parking lot through the vast array of foliage decorating the lawns.

Ric stood next to his truck, talking to a man. They were too far away to see their faces, but the man pointed his finger in

Ric's face. Jenny's tummy started churning. She watched as Ric seemed to grow in size, apparent even at this distance. Then he lunged at the man; Jenny watched in horror as the man who'd been wagging his finger at Ric toppled backward, and her view was suddenly blocked by several very tall, straight-edged bushes.

"Is that a problem?" Samantha asked.

Jenny had no idea what she'd just been asked. "No. No. Of course not."

She stood, walking around her table. She still couldn't see Ric or the man who'd been in his face.

"They are a wonderful group of ladies, and I just know they are going to love your speech."

Speech? What speech?

Jenny froze, suddenly looking down and focusing on her call. "I can't wait," she mumbled, and for the life of her couldn't remember what Samantha had just said. She'd been too preoccupied watching Ric.

Samantha laughed. "I wish I was there for this part. You'll be a breath of fresh air to that group of ladies. I just know it. I have a feeling they will all be contacting me after the luncheon is over." She sounded rather pleased with herself over her prediction.

"I hope I don't let you down."

"Let me down?"

There was a pause, and Jenny searched the available spots around the palm trees and bushes, straining to catch a glimpse of Ric again. His truck was still parked. She could see it.

"What's wrong, Jenny?"

Jenny opened her mouth to tell her, then snapped it shut. The last thing she could tell Samantha was that her grandson had just been threatened in the parking lot. Ric appeared to have taken the matter into his own hands. Whatever the man had said had pissed the hell out of Ric. Who was the man who'd pointed his finger in Ric's face?

"Nothing." But she'd paused too long, and Samantha would press. In a way, she and Nana were very much the same. "It's Nana, my grandmother."

"Is everything okay, sweetheart?" Samantha almost sounded motherly.

"I'm sure everything is fine. She just didn't seem the same when I spoke with her just now. She told me she was fine but I'm just not sure. I think she might miss me."

"Oh, that's not good."

"I'll give her a call again later today and visit with her more, after the luncheon."

"Good thinking."

Jenny focused on the conversation, saying what she needed to say to get Samantha off the line. As soon as she hung up, Jenny hurried through the dining room, then the main lobby. One advantage of being on Samantha Winston's account was not waiting for the bill. All the employees knew she was here on behalf of Ms. Winston and bowed to her every need.

No one said anything as she hurried across the lobby to the revolving doors. Once in the parking lot, she forced herself to slow down. It was just like the first day she'd met Ric, with her chasing after him. The only difference was this time she was running frantically, needing to know what she'd just seen and that Ric was all right.

Jenny stopped, turning around slowly, becoming aware of one of the bellhops watching her curiously as he stood under the veranda by the main revolving doors. She realized she needed to make a show of knowing where she was headed, or she'd appear a complete fool. Turning away from the hotel, she continued marching across the parking lot, deciding quickly she would take a walk just so she'd appear normal.

There was no sign of Ric. What had she seen? She walked past his truck, which set off his dog inside the cab. Jenny heard her thumping her tail as Jenny walked behind the truck. She didn't see Ric, or anyone else for that matter, as she neared the edge of the parking lot.

"Where are you going?"

Jenny shrieked, jumping around to face whoever was suddenly behind her, and grabbed her chest.

Ric cocked one eyebrow, looking down at her curiously. She caught her breath quickly and glared at him. No way would he play all this off innocently as if nothing had just happened. He didn't even look pissed.

"I saw you," she said, daring him to deny anything had just happened.

"Saw me?" He was really good at looking innocent. "Where?"

"There." She pointed past him toward his truck. "With another man. It looked like he was threatening you."

"And you raced out here to protect me?"

Damn. Now he looked amused.

Jenny opened her mouth to answer but then decided she'd be the one asking the questions. "Who was that man pointing his finger in your face?" she demanded, putting her hands on her hips and facing him, which meant tilting her head back and glaring up at him, since he'd moved closer into her space.

Ric shrugged and ran his hand down the side of her head, pressing her hair back into place. "There are some eccentric people at this hotel. He thought I cut him off when I entered the parking lot."

Jenny stared into his dark, forest-green eyes, really searching them and seeing the lie he told. Something hardened in her heart, the pain of it almost unbearable.

"If that's the case," she said, her voice shaking as emotions she didn't want to deal with surfaced and threatened to boil over, "then you're one hell of a brute for lunging after someone for being wound too tight."

He wouldn't see her cry. There wasn't any way she'd lose

her dignity when all she did was hurry to make sure he was okay. But he simply stood there, his body so close to hers. The smell of his aftershave and soap wrapped around her, seeming to drag her closer like a magnet. She had to get out of there, or she'd die of embarrassment when the tears that burned her eyes started falling.

Jenny shoved her way past him, almost stumbling when she started running back to the hotel.

"Jenny." His gravelly voice might have stopped her in her tracks if his hand, suddenly wrapped around her arm, hadn't already done it.

"What?" she snapped, trying to free herself.

When he didn't let go, she slapped her free hand against his chest to brace herself. Hard muscle flexed against her touch. And the strong, solid beat of his heart sent hers racing.

How could she be falling for someone who was so blatantly lying to her?

Ric stared into her eyes and cursed. She struggled again to free herself.

"Just let me go," she insisted.

He looked past her, shifting his attention to the hotel, and released her arm. Jenny couldn't move. Once again he was too close. Instead she glanced in the direction he did, and that's when she saw him. Just past the bellhop, alongside a long, narrow limousine, stood a man watching them. She sensed Ric stiffen more than saw him.

"Why is he watching us?" Chills prickled down her spine, and she forced her attention on Ric instead of on the man staring at both of them.

Ric continued glaring at the men. "That's the man you saw."

"The one you lunged at for cutting him off? Yes. What did he say to piss you off?"

She watched him as he slowly pulled his attention from the

man and looked down at her. Jenny held her ground, knowing she'd just challenged him by suggesting he'd lied to her and that she knew it.

"Come on." He grabbed her again, this time nearly dragging her across the parking lot to his truck.

"What?" she gasped, then felt herself lifted into his truck, with his hand cupping her ass, and plopped down on the seat next to his bloodhound. "Hey!" she cried out, dodging the dog's wet tongue as Ric hurried around to the other side.

"Colby, behave," Ric ordered as he slid into the driver's side.

Colby plopped down between the two of them, looking straight ahead, obeying the simple command better than any dog Jenny had ever seen before.

"Wow," she muttered, staring at the dog's profile.

"Tell her she did a good job," Ric suggested. "She won't maul you again. I promise."

Colby thumped her tail as if she understood what Ric just said about her.

"Good girl," Jenny whispered, and stroked the dog's ear.

Colby looked at her with deep brown eyes full of admiration and, as promised, remained sitting.

Jenny fell back in her seat, then bumped against the door when Ric put the truck in gear and swung it around so fast she was barely able to grab her seat belt. She managed to see the man who'd been watching them dart around his limousine and climb inside before Ric pulled out of the parking lot.

"Wait a minute!" She pushed against Colby's rear to fasten her belt but also looked frantically around them. "I can't leave the hotel. Where are we going?"

"Hold on tight!"

Jenny wasn't sure if Ric meant her or Colby. But when he slid around the next corner, forcing the old truck to pull off maneuvers it wasn't designed to make, the bloodhound slid to the floor of the truck, then curled around Jenny's feet. Her legs were damp from the light rain, she realized, as was the rest of her, and dog hair clung to her skin as she gripped the "oh shit" handle above the door.

Ric spun around another corner, and her fingers burned as she gripped the cracked leather. She still ended up leaning toward Ric. He held out his hand to help brace her, and his forearm pressed against her breast. A moment later his hand was on the gear shift and his dark green eyes darted back and forth between his rearview mirror and side mirror.

"What is going on?" Jenny wailed, aggravated and more than a bit nervous. "Where are we going?"

"As soon as I know we don't have a tail, I'll know," Ric explained, which wasn't an explanation at all.

He'd knocked Jenny from the passenger side door almost into his lap more than a few times, and the seat belt cut into her painfully before he pulled the truck onto a dirt road and slowed in between a thick grove of palm trees.

"A tail?" She looked over her shoulder through the window behind them but saw nothing other than the end of the narrow dirt road and the highway. "What the hell is going on?" she shouted.

Ric put the truck in park and twisted in his seat while unbuckling his seat belt. He didn't answer until he was completely satisfied there wasn't anyone outside.

"I don't do threats," he answered simply, his green eyes turbulent when he looked at her.

She almost slapped his hand away when he reached for her seat belt and unbuckled it. Ric was behaving so strangely and her head was spinning, not only from being knocked around in the truck but also from the range of emotions that had toppled over each other since she'd gotten out of bed this morning. All of it was too much. And Ric still wasn't making any sense.

"I didn't threaten you," she reminded him.

"I know." His tone had softened. When he let go of her seat belt, it slid around her into its place and he grabbed her hand. "Come here. I want to talk to you."

"Ric," she protested.

He opened his door and jumped out. Colby bounded out of the truck after him. Jenny didn't blame the dog for wanting out after a ride like that. But her complaints fell on deaf ears as Ric pulled her across the seat and out the driver's side door.

"I need to return to the—" She didn't get to finish her sentence.

The moment her feet hit the ground, Ric wrapped his arms around her, pulling her to him as he pushed the truck door closed behind her. His mouth found hers with demands more aggressive than his driving. Jenny was suddenly pressed back against the cold, damp metal of the truck, her head pushed back, and Ric kissed her so savagely she forgot she was trying to resist.

Ric's entire body was as hard as steel. His arms were all muscle, crushing her against him. If he was a bit too rough, Jenny didn't notice the pain. She was swept away by his almost animalistic behavior.

Damn. There must be something in the island air. She was falling for a man who wasn't truthful with her and who behaved like a Neanderthal. The intensity of his kiss was close to something out of one of those historical romances she loved to read.

Jenny didn't realize he'd lifted her off her feet until he ended the kiss and rested his forehead against hers.

"I'm sorry I lied to you."

Oh, hell. "Why did you?" She wasn't sure she'd be able to stand if he did let her down.

"The man you saw in the parking lot is a lawyer, Randy

Hickam. He told me if I didn't sell the banana plantation, he would create a dispute over the property and tie it up in court for so long I'd never be able to make a bed-and-breakfast out of the place." His eyes flared with emotions so raw the energy surging from him zapped her insides. "And he ordered me to stay away from you."

# 9
---

"Is that when you lunged at him?" Jenny's bright blue eyes were moist from tears that stubbornly refused to fall.

Ric cupped her ass and pressed against her, using his body and his truck to sandwich her. They were almost at eye level. Her high cheekbones and slender, perfectly adorable nose gave her a rather regal look. He decided it was her full, pouty lips that he liked the most. And at the moment, they were moist, slightly swollen from kissing him, and parted as she breathed through her mouth.

"Yup," he admitted, praying the pain he sensed inside her wasn't from her learning how quick of a temper he had. "I told you I don't do threats. We're on my land now, which gives me the upper hand if he tries harassing us again."

"I see." She pressed against his chest. "Put me down, Ric. The truck is wet."

Letting her slide down his body tortured not only him. Jenny's breath caught and she gasped when his hard cock throbbed against her. Her hips brushed across his bulging crotch. Ric took a step backward, watching her carefully when she fussed over her dress and walked to the back of his truck. He didn't sense anger, but her mood was definitely conflicted. She better not think she was walking back to the hotel, because that wasn't going to happen.

He followed her to the back of the truck and released the latch, then let down the tailgate. "There's a blanket in the truck. We're going to talk."

"That might be a good idea." Suddenly she was composed and sullen.

Ric pulled out the folded blanket from behind his seat and spread it over the damp metal. Before Jenny could say anything, he lifted her so she could sit. Her legs hung off the edge of the tailgate, and she crossed her ankles, her back as straight as a board as she stared at him.

"I'm not going to pretend I'm someone I'm not," he began, facing her. "I told Hickam what I thought of his threats several times."

"And it was the fact that he threatened you that made you lunge at him."

Her expression turned guarded as she watched him. Ric studied her a moment, then understanding hit. "*What* he threatened mattered more," he informed her under his breath, and moved closer.

Jenny's eyes widened as she tilted her head, but she held her composure. "What exactly did he say?" she asked, her voice almost a whisper.

"Just what I told you." He took a long, thick strand of her auburn hair and watched as it tried curling around his palm. "I was ordered to stay away from you, and that isn't going to happen."

"Because you don't do threats," she stated flatly, nodding her head once.

Ric wrapped her hair around his fist until his hand cupped the side of her head. Then tilting her head back, he moved in, brushing his lips over hers before stating what she should have been able to figure out by now.

"Because I don't want to stay away from you," he grumbled, then nibbled her lower lip.

"Wait a minute." She scurried away from him, backing up into the bed of the truck. "You're not going to start making out with me if someone might be looking for us right now."

"Are you suggesting I'd be ashamed to have them see me with you?"

"I'm suggesting if someone I don't even know is telling you to stay away from me, it doesn't have anything to do with me." She shot a wary look around the truck. "They're using me to gain something from you."

"You're right." Ric hoisted himself onto the truck bed. His weight made it rock, and Jenny grasped for the side of the truck, looking frantic for a moment as she braced herself. "I'm sitting on a gold mine, and not only did they steal my idea, but they also think that creating a pretentious resort will come close to what the banana plantation will be once it's up and running."

"So don't let them stop you." Jenny looked toward the banana plantation, although she couldn't see it through the trees. "If you want to turn it into a bed-and-breakfast, then do it. How did they steal your idea?"

"I plan on it." Ric grabbed the blanket Jenny had abandoned. "I've talked to a lot of people about this project for a year. All I've needed is the funding."

"Then why did you let him upset you?" Jenny's clothes clung to her like a second skin but she didn't seem to notice. She'd backed herself up to the cab, and unless she jumped off the side, she wasn't going anywhere. Jenny planted herself on the edge of the truck, sitting and gripping the side with her hands. "Do you think they will try to physically stop you?"

Ric laid the blanket down on the bed and moved some tools out of the way. He sat down, resting his back against the cab, and studied her for a moment. It was time to tell her his full plans. She would approve or not, but without knowing, his actions were confusing her. He wasn't sure where he was going with Jenny, or if they were going anywhere. But it mattered that he showed her she could trust him. She was asking, and all he could do was believe her interest in the banana plantation was as sincere as the interest in him he'd seen in her eyes over the past days.

"I know they will try. They're already trying," he began, and started coiling clothesline as he explained. "When I thought Samantha was coming to the island, I planned on showing the banana plantation to her. I had hoped she would fall in love with the place and see the potential in it that I do. Jenny, that old structure will turn one hell of a profit once it's fixed up. But I need financial backing." He looked up and caught her watching him untangle and wrap the rope in small circles. "I'd planned on asking Samantha to back the project, but I wasn't going to ask until I knew she loved it and saw it for the gold mine that it is."

Her gaze met his. "And now Mr. Pritchard and Mr. Sagawa want the same thing from her." Jenny shook her head. "I'm sure glad I'm not super rich."

Ric forced himself not to hurl the rope from the truck. Instead, he dropped it at his side, then leaned back on his elbows and stared at the sky, fighting to remain calm. A car drove by on the highway. Jenny glanced in that direction, but he didn't turn to look. No one would bother them here, not on his land.

"I qualified for the mortgage and bought it for a fraction of its true worth." He had her attention again but continued staring at the tops of the palm trees reaching toward the dull blue sky overhead. It had stopped raining, but they were both damp. The humidity tightened Jenny's curls. Material clung to her firm, round breasts. If he looked at her for more than a minute, he wouldn't remember a damn thing he was saying.

"I've owned the place a year, and although I make enough to support myself, I don't make enough to impress the bank so that they'll finance this venture. Trust me, if there was any way I could support this project without asking for help from a family member—especially one I don't even know yet—I'd do it."

"I believe you."

"Do you?" He watched her as Jenny's gaze traveled down his body and up again to stare him in the eyes.

"Yes. You seem very focused on what you want, and I believe you'd do whatever was necessary to gain it, especially if you feel it will benefit you in the end."

He wasn't sure she'd just praised him. If anything, her flat tone made her awareness of his nature seem more pragmatic. She stated facts without an ounce of compassion or feeling slipping through. Ric continued watching her, wondering what shut her down so fast.

"Come here."

Jenny shook her head, although the action was barely noticeable. "No," she said, her voice a rough whisper.

Now he saw her pain. What exactly caused it? Was it knowing he had planned on asking Samantha for money? And if so, why would that bother her so deeply?

"Yes."

"I need to get back to the hotel. I have a luncheon today and need to give a speech."

Ric pushed himself up and reached for her, grabbing her hand before she could pull away. "Come here," he said, again emphasizing where he wanted her as he tugged, using just enough strength to force her off the side of the truck.

"Damn it," she complained when she slipped on wet metal.

Ric wrapped his arm around her waist, breaking her fall. Jenny collapsed on top of him but pushed immediately, squirming out of his embrace and trying to back up.

"I don't think so," he muttered in a husky voice, adjusting his hold on her and pulling her against him.

Her breasts smashed against him as the strap to the cotton dress she wore slipped off her shoulder. She was so incredibly sexy. Her defiance and sudden attempt at being indifferent added to her appeal.

"Now we're really going to talk," he informed her, and adjusted her stiff body against him, ignoring her nonverbal protests when she wouldn't bend to his demands. He wrapped his arms around her until she was curved against him. "You're going to explain, without mincing words, why you're pushing me away."

"I'm hardly pushing you away," she said dryly, and drummed her fingers against his chest to prove her point. "I'd say there isn't an inch of space between us, wouldn't you?"

"Drop the sarcasm, darling." He almost informed her it was hot as hell but was pretty sure she would start squirming all over again if he did. And much more squirming on her part and she'd lose that dress as quickly as he'd lose his desire to talk.

Jenny sighed. Ric waited it out, holding her firmly but not hurting her. He was pretty sure she was feeling anything but pain. A long moment passed and she began relaxing. When he was pretty sure she wouldn't bolt like a scared doe, Ric shook out the blanket, then pulled her down onto it. Jenny didn't touch him, but stretched out next to him. Ric lay down, this time going flat on his back. He grabbed the duffel bag from amidst his tools and supplies he always carried on the truck and eased it under his head. It served as a decent pillow.

"Tell me what you're thinking," he encouraged her.

"Fine." She still made a show of being put out. "You want me to talk, here it is. I'm disappointed in you."

He was jumping ahead of her in his thoughts, speculating about what he'd done to set her off and how she would react now that she believed something existed in him she hadn't known was there before. One thing he was certain of: she hadn't picked up on his true colors. As much as he'd love to believe that coming to the island, getting to know family he never knew existed, and buying a ranch that he came home to every night had changed him, the truth was often quite a bit more subtle. Ric was still the hardened delinquent who had raised himself and methodically plotted his path through life so that he'd prosper and possess what he needed to survive. Nowhere in there was the compassion required to care about someone.

Yet he felt . . . something. Her words stung unlike anything he'd ever experienced before.

Jenny shifted, propping herself on both her elbows and resting on her tummy next to him. "No curiosity at all as to why you've disappointed me?" she asked quietly, her brow wrinkled as she searched his face.

"You're going to tell me." He sounded callous, but it covered unpleasant emotions that made his throat tighten. How was she able to make him feel this way?

She grunted and puckered her mouth, surveying him and remaining quiet.

Ric preferred to stare at the sky than watch pain cloud her pretty eyes. Jenny was watching him.

Ric didn't like her looking at him the way she was. "You want me to guess?"

"You already know." She appraised him with a disgruntled look on her face.

"I see."

Her eyes were exceptionally blue, and her hair was twice as curly as normal. It was clouding up again, but there was enough sun to accentuate the golden highlights in her auburn hair.

Ric rested a hand on his chest and counted his heartbeats as he returned his attention to the sky and a large, heavy-looking cloud slowly moving into place with the others above them.

There was no way he'd guess at what disappointed her. At the same time, he wasn't the kind of man who gloss-coated some false, flashy image. He wasn't ashamed of not being perfect.

"You've come to the conclusion that there are different types of businessmen—some who threaten, manipulate, even bribe you with precious gifts. And there are others who pull you in to the project until you feel the inspiration in each room. These businessmen help you breathe the passion behind the project, possibly even seduce," he added, and dared to reach for one of her tight, long curls. She didn't swat his hand away from her—a good sign. "Yet before long you experience the disappointment you claim to have now."

"And why is that?"

"Because both types are pricks."

The hard defiance was gone. Jenny looked more confused, and for a moment he thought she might deny it, defend him to himself. When she tried getting up, he grabbed her, this time moving her so she was pinned underneath him. Her breathing became quicker, forcing her breasts to press against her dress and her nipples to pucker with greedy need.

"Get off of me."

"No," he whispered, and grabbed her hands before she could shove at him or slap him. He wasn't sure how much anger caused her eyes to spark with such raw energy. "The banana plantation is more than a financially secure plan, Jenny," he explained.

There was a tight, constricting pain in his chest as the words slipped out. "It's an opportunity to prove myself."

"To who? You or Samantha?"

He ignored her question. "It's going to be a success."

The discomfort growing inside him would go away if he let her up. Take her back to the hotel and call Samantha. Part of his brain argued that was the most sensible plan. As much as he'd love to deny it, Ric knew why the tightness grew inside him.

The pain in his heart matched the glow in Jenny's eyes. For whatever reason, he suddenly saw deeper into her soul. She was angry. The strong emotions churning over inside her were suddenly in his face, impossible to ignore. Jenny cared. About him. Maybe more than she, or he, wanted her to. And because she cared, she also feared he was using her, seducing her so she would fight his battle.

He wouldn't ask her to do that.

"Go to your meeting, darling. Give your speech. Don't worry about Samantha or which bed-and-breakfast will serve the island a year from now."

"You don't want me to ask her to loan you the money to pay for all the restoration and renovations needed to launch your new business?"

He shook his head slightly and ached to kiss her. Jenny tried freeing her hands. Ric tightened his grip and brought her hands over her head.

Jenny didn't struggle. "Do you think this will change my disappointment in you?" she asked, raising one perfectly shaped eyebrow.

"It's not easy asking for a loan, from a stranger or from someone you know. No, I don't want you asking Samantha. That's my job—I'll do it."

He loved how the color of her eyes changed according to her mood. When she was pissed, they turned almost violet. Yet now, with her hands pinned above her head and her nipples hardened points pressing against her cotton dress, her breath coming faster, her bright eyes were like sapphires, radiant and captivating.

"You are not having sex with me in the back of this truck."

He moved his hand, stretching his fingers over her abdomen. "Have you ever had sex in the back of a pickup?"

"Let me up!" she hissed, and rolled her hips underneath

him. She struggled with a bit more intensity this time. "I'm not fucking you. You're using me!"

He'd begun moving his hand lower, keeping it pressed against her body, but froze at her last words. "Using you?"

"Let me up, Ric."

"Wait a minute. Do you really think I'm using you?"

"You lured me into that house feigning interest in me, hoping I would be so entranced with the place my description of it would make Samantha instantly love it, too."

He remembered telling her stories as he led her from room to room, saving the better stories for last and knowing if he played his cards right, she would convince Samantha to support him without even asking.

"I didn't feign interest in you."

"So you admit to using me?"

"I'm not using you. I want you."

Jenny shoved hard, pushing him onto his back, then jumped up. She leaped to the ground, falling to her hands and knees. Immediately pushing herself to her feet, she swatted at her knees before marching away from him.

Ric was on his feet in a minute, racing off the truck and landing on his feet as Jenny neared the road ahead. She turned, pointing a finger at him. Even at that distance, her blue eyes pierced like daggers deep into his soul. A wall tightened around his heart, damn near cutting off all air to his lungs. The pain was unbearable.

"You just said you can talk to Samantha. There's no reason for us to be together anymore. Leave me alone, Ric."

He stopped, almost stumbling. It wasn't the first time he'd heard those words or the first time a lady had looked at him with pain and anger in her eyes. But it was definitely the first time his insides had recoiled at the words, tightening and adding to the pain already weighing down in his chest.

"And don't follow me," she added, then turned fast enough her hair flew over her shoulders as she marched away from him, heading for the highway and a rather long walk back to her hotel.

A large drop of rain splattered onto Jenny's cheek. She ignored it, letting it slide to her jaw, then her neck. She was sick of breathing in the smell of the ocean, her feet hurt like hell, and her dress was itchy. There was a long curve of the highway ahead, and she knew the hotel was a couple miles past that.

*It's not that bad of a walk,* she thought, reminding herself the island had only forty-seven miles of coastline. Once she was around the curve, the beaches would be more populated. It was barely seventy degrees outside, but die-hard beach junkies, traveling to the island for the sole purpose of lying out on the white sands without being surrounded by hundreds of other beach junkies, would have descended on the beaches as soon as the sun was up.

She squinted at the clouds overhead. All she had to do was pull out her cell phone and call Sean. He would be right there. She wouldn't have to take another step. But if she called Sean, no matter what the explanation she offered, he and Marc, and Samantha, would hate Ric.

God! Her feet were killing her.

Jenny glanced over her shoulder. There wasn't a car in sight. She'd told him not to follow her.

She thought of the look on his face, outrage, awareness—betrayal. Had she seen betrayal? And if so, did that mean her accusations were wrong?

"I wasn't wrong." She bent down to pull a small pebble out of her shoe and rubbed the bottom of her foot through her sandal.

It was starting to rain again. At this rate, in her cotton dress, she'd look like a drowned rat by the time she returned to the hotel. Jenny pulled out her cell phone. Her anger had ebbed enough to allow her to think straight. She glanced off the road at the rows of pineapple bushes with their speared leaves. They weren't a very attractive plant. She imagined the generations of Karakas who had worked this land, raised their kids, and been happy. Who wouldn't fight to be part of that legacy?

Jenny looked ahead of her. Ric's pickup was parked on the side of the road, the front of it facing the highway. Ric leaned against it, watching her with his arms crossed over that broad, muscular chest. He was waiting for her.

Her heart flip-flopped as her tummy twisted with a mixture of nervous anticipation. He cared, a little voice in her head pointed out. He could have said the hell with her and moved on to the next woman. Jenny focused on the gorgeous and complicated man waiting for her to approach.

Damn it. She couldn't fall in love with him. But how could she stop it from happening?

The rain was steady now and drops of water clung to her eyelashes as she studied Ric. A quick look indicated the dirt road he was on disappeared back across his property.

Jenny blinked raindrops from her eyes, then wiped her face, knowing if there was any makeup left, she was smearing it all over the place. There wasn't any way she could pull out a compact and inspect her appearance before reaching Ric. He would figure out she cared how she looked to him, which would give him an edge when they continued their argument. And there wasn't any doubt they weren't done with this conversation. She'd accused him of using her, which was a severe stab to the fragile male ego.

The look on his face as she neared him told her it had been a direct hit.

She glanced up at Ric, who still leaned against his truck, those well-formed muscles stretching in his forearms as he watched her with an unreadable expression on his face. His eyes, however, told a completely different story. They were dark pools of scrutinizing determination.

His black hair was damp and straight and looked shiny, even under the cloudy sky. It reached the collar of his shirt. And the way his shirt clung to that muscular torso . . . Jenny fought the urge to walk a bit slower and brush her legs together just so she could offset the pressure growing and starting to pulse. If only she'd worn shorts instead of a dress. At least that way she could get the seam to press against her clit.

She blinked, once again fighting raindrops, and almost stumbled just imagining that kind of friction against her pussy. In spite of the rain slowly soaking her, a whole different type of moisture welled inside her underwear.

God, he was making her nuts. Jenny was mad at him and turned on by him at the same time.

Suddenly she was a lot closer to Ric than she realized, her thoughts having distracted her to the point where she hadn't paid attention to nearing him. At the same time, she became aware of the twitch in his jaw, the way his lips were pressed into a thin line, how his shoulders seemed a bit broader than usual, and, with the rain having flattened the hair on his arms, the way his muscles were acutely outlined under his dark skin.

Ric was pissed as hell.

Jenny cleared the last twenty feet, raising her attention to his face and holding it there. Why was he so mad?

Obviously he didn't like her suggesting he was using her. Maybe he didn't see it as using her, but how could he not?

Yet here she was, ten feet away and still walking. He sure didn't appear ready to apologize. If driving from somewhere on his land to this side road, which she now saw led to the highway, in order to be there when she'd walked this far was his way of apologizing, she would hear what he had to say.

Jenny slowed, came to a stop, and held his gaze. Her anger was gone. That didn't mean she had nothing to say. He'd hurt her. She had herself to blame for that. In just a few days, he'd managed to damn near claim her heart, and she'd allowed that to happen. She didn't hold that against him. The pain he'd caused occurred when he admitted how he would have handled his initial meeting with Samantha. Since she hadn't been here, Jenny had become his tool of necessity to see his venture with the banana plantation take place.

Ric finally moved, reaching for the passenger door and opening it for her. He didn't look at her as he held it open. She could either stand there and allow her dress to become a second skin or get into the cab of his truck.

Colby's tail thudded against the bench seat when Jenny stepped toward the truck. Ric grabbed her arm as she passed him to climb inside.

"What?" she asked.

His grip wasn't so tight it cut off circulation, His touch was hot, sizzling against her soaked skin. It wasn't as hot as his mouth was when he dragged her to him, slid his other hand into her soaked hair, and captured her mouth with a kiss so demanding and passionate it robbed her of all rational thought.

Was this an apology? Or was this simply Ric's reaction to her storming off on him?

He crushed her body against his, bending her over backward and feasting as if he hadn't been able to live without her since they'd parted, which had been all of ten minutes ago. Her brain was a foggy, oversensitized mess.

She needed time to analyze her thoughts. But analyzing things indicated she wanted a relationship. Her fingers were curled into his soaked, thick hair. God, she couldn't think. She opened for him. Her tongue darted into his mouth, greeting him as greedily as he had her. When a deep, commanding growl escaped him, vibrating its way up his torso and electrifying every nerve ending in her body, she moaned in response.

What the hell was she doing?

She might as well be telling him that she didn't care if he used her or not.

But damn! This sure beat the hell out of trying to figure out what to say when she climbed into his truck. Was she that bad at navigating her way through the stages of a relationship? Although, if she forced herself to remain focused on the simple fact he'd been using her, there probably wouldn't be a relationship at all. Was she then capable of becoming the kind of woman who could throw all care to the wind and submit simply because her body craved it?

Because that was basically what they had here. Two souls brought together by circumstance. The physical attraction was off the charts. Maybe Ric was trying to show her what happened when she let her feelings get wrapped up in a hot, sordid affair. And now she got to experience what it felt like pushing those emotions to the side and letting her physical needs rule the moment.

Her fingers were wrapped around thick strands of wet hair. She grasped his head, pressed her body against his, and ravished in the heat and sizzling desire consuming her. Every inch of his body pulsed with raw, carnal need.

His cock, hard and solid, pressed against her soft tummy. Her breasts were swollen and heavy. Her nipples ached for attention. Jenny swore every raindrop that hit them evaporated immediately and rose as steam, adding to the fog of lust enveloping her.

Ric's hands moved through her hair, the pinch against her scalp creating rushes of desire so intoxicating she was barely able to stand. She thought the kiss was over when he nipped at her lower lip, but then his hands moved down her back and cupped her ass. He lifted her, pressing her against his raging hard-on, and once again ravaged her mouth.

All she could do was hold on. She should end the kiss, make a few demands, and learn if this was physical or something more. They couldn't have more. Her brain got that, but her body refused to listen.

"Don't stop me," he whispered into her mouth, his scratchy baritone a rush of powerful energy when his lips moved over hers. "Berate and yell, chastise me all you want after, but, sweetheart, don't break this off now."

Jenny didn't understand what he meant at first. His fingers were under her dress and lifting it. When he did end the kiss, his lips seared her tormented flesh as he worked his way down her neck.

"We both want this, and it won't be a distraction after," he added.

He was turning her while scraping his teeth along her collarbone.

Jenny blinked when her back was to him, and she stared at Colby, who was stretched out on the bench seat. Comprehension sank into her frazzled brain as she watched the bloodhound lift her head and look at her curiously.

"Colby. Floor." Ric's command wasn't fierce. He spoke quietly to his dog, who cooperated immediately.

At the same time, Ric found her underwear and eased it down past her hips. "Bend over, sweetheart."

"Someone will see us." It was the first thought that came to mind as she turned her head, still dazed, and stared at the rain-smeared windshield.

"They won't see you. And they won't think a thing about my truck being parked here. The open door blocks the view." One hand slid up her back, pressing gently and easing her down against the seat.

She wasn't even considering telling him no. Worse yet, her next thought was to order him to hurry. Jenny went up on tiptoe and rested her elbows on the seat. Ric had pulled her dress up to her waist, and the rain splattering on her bare ass heightened her senses. It was cool, contrasting with his warm fingers.

When she heard him tear open the condom wrapper and sheath his dick, she wondered if he made a habit of keeping condoms in his jeans pocket. She would worry later how easy this made her look. Ric placed his hands on her rear end and stretched her open. She'd never felt more exposed, or more alive. Jenny was acutely aware of every raindrop, of the breeze as it moved past her pussy and her ass. Every tiny hair on her body stood at eager attention. Every nerve ending sizzled with energy.

In spite of how wrong this was, she'd never felt more alive. Her feet didn't hurt anymore. She focused on how swollen and heavy her breasts felt, and her nipples rubbed against her strapless bra. Her thigh muscles were taut, her legs straight as she stretched her body and arched her back.

She felt so . . . sexy. It was amazing how exhilarating it was breaking rules, consenting to have sex when they could get caught.

Ric's fingers moved closer to her entrance, moving over her flesh as if she were some cherished object. His breath was ragged, but he didn't say anything else. Jenny tried guessing his thoughts. Brushing her hair out of the way, she looked over her shoulder at him, trying to see his face.

Black hair bordered his dark expression. Shadows made it hard to learn his thoughts, and the way his soaked hair clung to the sides of his head gave him an even more rugged look. Ric was focused, staring at her pussy. He slid his fingers inside her. She hissed. His gaze shot to hers.

"Damn, darling." His voice was rough, raw with need.

"Now." It was the only word she could get out.

He stared at her a moment longer. Jenny was going to drown in the sensations rippling through her. She dropped her gaze, unable to keep her head twisted far enough to see his eyes. The moment she did, Ric entered her.

"You're soaked," he growled. He brought his head down so it was right behind hers. "Maybe I should piss you off more often," he whispered.

She gritted her teeth, refusing to let him chastise her while fucking her.

"Faster," she ordered. "And shut up."

Ric's chuckle was contagious. But he obliged. He built the momentum, creating a rhythm that forced her forward on the seat, again and again. If anyone was close enough to see Ric's truck, they would see it rocking sideways. Yet more proof she was nuts; she smiled at the thought.

Rain continued dribbling down her ass. Her legs were wet, but not as soaked as her pussy. A fire ignited between them, raging hot and spreading until it consumed her. Jenny closed her eyes, fisting her hands against the seat, and rode out her first orgasm. The moment she came down from it, another one was in its wake.

Ric took her places she didn't know existed. He made love to her, hitting incredibly sensitive spots deep in her womb and creating sensations almost too intense to handle. She'd lost count as to how many times he made her come. But each time was at least as incredible as the last, if not better.

When she was sure she would pass out in a blissful state of sexual ecstasy, Ric slowed his movements.

"You were right," he whispered into her ear, leaning over her and pulling her hair away from the side of her face. "I thought if I sold you on the banana plantation, you'd convince Samantha how wonderful a place it was and do my work for me."

Jenny opened her eyes, staring straight ahead but not seeing anything. Ric just admitted he had used her. And he was fucking her. She'd wanted him to fuck her.

"Once we spent time together, made love for the first

time . . . ," he continued, moving slowly inside her, pulling out with painful consistency, then easing back into her heat, filling her completely.

The steady, deliberate way he fucked her would either bring her to the biggest orgasm of her life, or make her insane, or both.

"Talk about it later," she muttered, squeezing her eyes closed and not wanting to dwell on what didn't exist between them.

"No. Now," he insisted, and pressed his lips against the side of her neck, just below her ear. "Something has started between us. You aren't going to run away from that."

Jenny blinked again, taking a minute to register what he'd just said. Her mouth was too dry to respond. Her brain wouldn't put together words anyway. Not that Ric gave her a chance. The moment he finished speaking, he picked up speed, once again taking her hard and fast, reigniting the fire between them and taking them both over the edge together.

As she was floating in that special place she didn't ever want to leave, Jenny swore she heard Ric say, "I'm sorry, sweetheart. I won't ever hurt you again."

# 10

---

Jenny gave herself a final once-over in the full-length mirror in her hotel suite. She'd pulled it off. Unbelievably so, but her reflection was proof. Her hair was pulled back in matching barrettes. Soft auburn curls flowed over her shoulders. The sleeveless blouse she'd chosen looked crisp after she'd ironed it. And her khaki capris showed off her slender figure. She chose low-heeled, closed-toe shoes, which gave her a professional, conservative look. Jenny didn't want to stand out during the luncheon.

She glanced at the digital clock next to her bed. Fifteen minutes left.

"Damn," she breathed.

It had been a whirlwind morning. Ric had driven her back to the hotel and walked through the lobby with her, encouraging her to laugh along with him so anyone watching would think they had enjoyed a walk in the rain. Both of them were soaked. He'd pointed out in the elevator that no one paid any attention to them.

At her hotel door, he'd planted a promising kiss on her lips; then he was gone. That had been almost two hours ago.

For whatever reason, Marc hadn't come to see her yet. That was a blessing in itself. If he had seen her soaked and laughing earlier that morning, Jenny was sure it would have ruined her day. As it was, she headed down to the meeting room in the hotel where the ladies' luncheon would be gathering about now, without anyone calling out for her or hurrying after her to remind her of her duties and obligations.

In spite of the relief she felt, Jenny paused outside Marc's room, then glanced at Sean's hotel room door across the hall. She almost knocked on Marc's door. Maybe turning the tables and demanding where he'd been all morning would help keep her spirits high. As it was, she knew she was floating in a surreal state after coming so many times, making love outside in the rain, an adventure she never would have asked for but was thrilled she'd experienced.

Since arriving at her hotel room, she'd tried not to dwell on her feelings, or her reaction to the events of the morning. There would be time soon enough after the luncheon to analyze everything said, every scene, every emotion, and every facial expression. Jenny had no doubt she would do just that. Even as she hurried past Marc's and Sean's rooms to the elevators, Ric was on her mind.

After they'd made love, he'd helped clean her, put her underwear back on, and straighten her dress. Ric had lifted her into his truck, as if he were as in tune with her body as she was and knew her legs were weak and wobbly. Then he'd shut her door and hurried around the front of his truck. The wind had picked up the moment he was in front of her. She imagined it wanted to flow through those thick, inky black strands as much as she did. His hair was smooth, silky, and strong, just like the rest of him.

He'd stared ahead of him, not ducking from the rain or appearing concerned about the increasing wind. His long strides brought him around to the driver's side in seconds, but the image of him in front of her, walking to the other side, seemed branded in her mind.

He was physically perfect. Every inch of him. Now that they'd made love twice with him behind her, she ached to be on top, have control and the ability to explore every inch of his body. He had a tattoo on his right arm. It was a band that went all the way around his arm. She hadn't noticed any other tattoos. He probably knew her body better than she knew his. Soon she would change that. That thought had brought her pause.

The elevator doors opened. Jenny hadn't remembered getting into the elevator. She blew out a breath, trying to put Ric out of her head. As much as she knew where she and Ric were headed, thinking about that would bring her pain. She'd intentionally headed to the meeting room early with hopes of learning what her speech was supposed to be about. Apparently taking the easy road wasn't an option for her in any aspect of her life. It would have been a lot easier to have called Samantha back and asked her what she was supposed to talk about or find out from Marc, who was sure to know. Just as it would have been easier to have confronted Ric when she'd been in the back of his truck, instead of storming off and getting soaked. And it would have made life easier in the long run if she'd broken it off with him instead of their making love again.

Maybe she wasn't as easy as she thought she was.

Jenny moaned over her warped humor and started across the lobby toward the meeting rooms. A black limousine was parked outside, and she slowed when she saw Marc. He stood next to the sleek black car as an old lady climbed into the backseat. Jenny froze. The old woman looked just like Samantha.

Marc closed the door once the old woman was inside, then opened the front passenger door and let himself in, closing it behind him. The car pulled away from the entrance and disappeared from her sight.

What the hell?

Her stomach did a few flip-flops as she hurried to the other side of the lobby and down the wide hallway with meeting rooms on either side. The ladies' league meeting was in the first room. Jenny's mind went blank, and she faltered at the entrance. How in the world was she going to pull off a speech in front of all these women when she hadn't prepared for it at all?

What had she been thinking?

"May I help you?" A heavy-set woman with a pleasant smile and beautiful caramel-colored skin stood next to a table filled with name tags and leis. Her bright, flowery dress flowed around her when she moved.

"I'm Jenny Rogers," she began.

"Oh, my dear! Aloha," she exclaimed, opening her arms and pulling Jenny in for a warm hug. "We're so excited to have you join us today. Here is your name tag, and these flowers are perfect with your outfit."

Jenny was immediately surrounded by a handful of women, all of whom were talking at the same time and finishing each others' sentences and laughing loudly as they bombarded Jenny with questions she wasn't able to answer before another one of them answered it for her.

"Samantha Winston has been a member of our ladies' league since my mother used to come to our meetings," a tall, thin lady named Pearl Lea told Jenny as she wrapped her arm around Jenny and escorted her out of the group of ladies. Together, they started across the large room, which was filled with round tables occupied by ladies of all ages, chatting contentedly. "When she informed us you would be talking today, sharing your impressions of our beautiful island, I promise you, the excitement among all of us skyrocketed."

Pearl Lea was either a very nice woman or one hell of a good marketer. Jenny looked in the direction they headed—toward the podium. It mocked her and filled her with apprehension and fear of embarrassment. She would be standing next to it, possibly leaning against it, stammering and faltering her way through her speech. While she made an ass out of herself, that podium would remain standing tall and proud.

She really had no one to blame but herself. Jenny glared at the podium, managing to listen as Pearl rambled on about events that had happened at previous meetings. There was only one thing to do. In the amount of time it took them to eat their lunch, Jenny would have to create one kick-ass speech in her head and present it without notes.

Giving a speech on her impressions of Lanai wouldn't be that hard. It wasn't as if there were right or wrong answers. They'd paused to join another group of ladies, and Jenny snapped to attention when she overheard one of them speaking.

"By keynote speaker, you mean me?" Jenny asked, smiling at the woman who looked at her, startled.

"Brenda Hopper, may I present Jenny Rogers," Pearl said formally as she gestured between the two women.

"Good grief, Pearl. Why didn't you tell me?" Brenda was all grins. The woman, who appeared to be in her midthirties, held out her tanned hand in greeting. Her wedding ring had the largest diamond Jenny had ever seen. "Don't let that get to you," Brenda added, gripping Jenny's hand and holding her smile when she caught Jenny staring at the ring.

"It's really beautiful." She was sure she was blushing all shades of red.

"It snags on everything," Brenda said, leaning forward and lowering her voice to whisper the confession.

Jenny smiled, deciding she liked Brenda. Her ring was another story. It was hideous as hell, and apparently Jenny was a better liar than she thought. Brenda took the praise of her wedding ring to heart.

"It is beautiful, though, isn't it?" she continued, holding her hand out for both of them to admire the gigantic rock on a gold setting. "That's my Clifford. When he goes after something, he goes for the best."

"Which is why you are his charming bride," Pearl announced, taking Brenda by the shoulder and turning her away from Jenny. When Brenda began commenting on something another lady said, Pearl gave Jenny a knowing look and ran her finger across her throat.

Enough said. Jenny hadn't wanted to base an entire conversation around the wedding ring anyway. When Pearl gestured again, Jenny moved closer and found herself being introduced to about five other ladies. By the time they reached the opposite side of the room where the podium was, Jenny was positive she would never remember the names of everyone she'd just been introduced to. She accepted her seat at a round table nearest the podium and fidgeted with her name plate, which had been set across her dinner plate. Slowly, all the other women began finding their seats.

Coffee, iced tea, and salads were brought out as Pearl Lea, who'd sat next to Jenny, went to the podium and gave a greeting speech. It was actually pretty interesting learning about the league and how they helped with Lanai affairs and also their involvement with state affairs. Pearl spoke of how so many of their mothers and grandmothers volunteered their time helping wherever help was needed, getting their hands dirty and not worrying about what others might think of them. Jenny became aware of the strong sense of pride around the room. Pearl named names, calling out someone's grandmother, who had since passed, and reminding everyone how that woman had carried out some courageous event. Each woman mentioned sat a bit straighter as her smile grew serious. Without being boastful, the speech reminded everyone in the room how simple charitable acts accomplished so much more than some of the largest checks ever written.

It was a beautiful speech, powerful and moving. Jenny had no idea how she could top that and was grateful when Pearl finally announced to the room that they were to enjoy their meal now, and the guest speaker would be presented after dessert. Which gave Jenny less than an hour to think of the perfect presentation to move the room just as Pearl had.

Every time she looked across the room, someone met her gaze and smiled with pride. Pride over family. Jenny had that. She had always been very proud of her grandparents, and grateful for them. They'd taken on being parents a second time around and raised their granddaughter. If they hadn't, she would have become a ward of the state.

Which was what had happened to Ric. If Samantha had known he existed, would she have taken him in? And if she had, how much different would he be today? Would he seem so haunted by a past she knew so little about? Jenny wasn't sure about the answers to her questions. Samantha had known Ric wanted to meet with her; in fact, he'd shown up at the hotel the first morning she'd been there.

Jenny remembered his reaction when he'd learned Samantha wasn't on the island. She understood now what she'd seen that day. Ric's expression had been a mixture of pain, confusion, and betrayal. He'd found his grandmother and she'd declined to come to the island and meet him. She stared down at her lap when she pictured his face from that morning, with his hair wet and his eyes ablaze with fury. Jenny didn't understand how anyone could turn down meeting their own flesh and blood.

Someone made a comment and the room broke out in laughter. Jenny looked up, needing to keep Ric out of her thoughts. It was the only way she'd be able to save face and keep Samantha from looking like a fool for suggesting Jenny take her place.

*Focus on your speech.*

Marc appeared at one of the entrances. Jenny was positive he stared only at her when he looked in her direction. He rocked back on his heels, an action Jenny had learned meant he was very satisfied with something he had done.

Jenny looked down when her cell phone vibrated. Slipping it out of her handbag, she touched the screen to read the text message.

*When you begin your speech, announce that you'll have a guest speaker joining you. This is Ric.*

She stared at her screen, reading the message several times as she tried making sense out of it. What guest speaker?

Jenny glanced around the room, then at the door leading into the large meeting room. Marc still stood at the doors where she'd entered, but he wasn't looking in her direction any longer. Instead, he was scowling at something, or someone, down the hallway. There were two other entrances to the large room, but those doors were closed.

Waiters began serving the main entrée, a delicious-smelling fish lunch.

"I don't know which looks better, the mahimahi or the waiter," an older woman sitting opposite Jenny announced.

The waiter set her plate in front of the woman, then winked at her, and everyone at the table burst into laughter. Jenny jumped. Her nerves were too frazzled.

Did Samantha somehow find out that Jenny had never given a speech before? But how would she find out, unless she called and asked Nana? Samantha wouldn't do that, would she?

Her cell phone vibrated again, and her heart did a triple beat in her chest. She stared at the meal placed before her, positive she wouldn't be able to take a bite, and tried to make herself appreciate the tantalizing aroma of the thick sauce draped over the fish.

No one seemed to notice when she glanced at her phone again and read the next message.

*Begin your speech by saying you've been on the island a few days and have fallen in love with its beauty. Then say you'd like to bring someone to the podium who has been here over a year so he can give his impressions.*

Jenny tapped in her response: *Who is this guest speaker?* She sent the message, then placed her phone on her lap and sipped her iced tea. It was sweetened and cold and wonderfully wet against her dry throat.

"This is to die for," Pearl said, sitting next to her. She gestured at the food with her fork. "Give it a try. You'll be surprised how delicious it is."

Pearl thought Jenny wasn't eating because she didn't like fish. She imagined many tourists turned their noses up at much of the local cuisine. Jenny thought about running with the idea and whispering something to Pearl about not being able to stand fish, but the truth was, so far everything she'd sampled since being here was absolutely delicious.

"I admit I'm a bit nervous about my speech," Jenny admitted.

Pearl patted Jenny's hand with hers. "Understandable," she said, then scooped more food into her mouth.

Jenny stared at her a moment, thinking she would say more. When Pearl continued eating, Jenny focused on her own food. She would at least make a show of eating and broke flakes of the fish apart with her fork, then took a bite. The array of flavors exploded in her mouth. It was delicious.

"It's good," she said to Pearl, and at the same time her cell phone vibrated in her lap.

"I told you. Be sure you include how much you enjoy the food on the island. That will go a long way with the ladies."

Jenny nodded, her tummy once again twisting into hard knots. She brought another bite to her mouth before checking her phone. It was rude to sit and text someone while eating. None of the other ladies had their phones at the table.

Jenny tried thinking of an acceptable excuse why she kept using her phone as she once again glanced at it on her lap.

*I'm going to give your speech.* Ric ended the sentence with a smiley face.

*Why would you do that?*

*I overheard a little rat gloating about how he would watch you fall on your face while giving a speech you obviously didn't have time to prepare. I'm not going to give him the satisfaction.*

Jenny was both pissed and embarrassed. She wanted to know who Marc was speaking to when he said that, if it was in fact Marc whom Ric had overheard.

*Was it Marc?* She had to know.

*Yes. I have half a mind to permanently remove that smug look off his face.*

Jenny hid a smile. Ric would be the kind of man who would fight for the honor of his lady. He possessed so many good traits. He was a proud man, confident and capable of providing for himself and determined enough to make his dreams happen. Jenny had no doubt, with or without Samantha's help, he'd find a way to make the banana plantation into whatever he wanted it to be.

Ric hadn't hesitated in using her to reach his goals. Then, when necessary, he admitted what he'd done and told Jenny he wasn't using her now. She believed he meant what he'd said. He wasn't a liar. But his truth was how he saw it, how he interpreted the world around him. Only time would show if he was using her. Unfortunately, she wouldn't be on the island long enough to see it played out.

She ate more of her fish, finding that it went down easy. She ate the asparagus and cashews that were the side dish and even enjoyed the hot roll, complete with whipped honey butter. More than once, she shot a furtive look toward the open doors where Marc continued standing. He was waiting to gloat at her expense and would probably immediately report to Samantha.

Jenny sat back and fingered her phone, staring at Ric's last message. Her thoughts shifted to Samantha and seeing her before coming to the luncheon. She'd only seen her from behind, but Jenny would swear it had been Samantha. What was she doing on the island? Did she think Jenny was somehow failing her? If so, she should have let Jenny know what it was she wasn't doing to Samantha's satisfaction and not flown to the island without telling her.

Samantha had offered Jenny the deal of a lifetime. Jenny knew it and Samantha knew it as well. Jenny understood the conditions. But there were things that Samantha could have been clearer about. It might have been being a woman in a man's business world, or maybe it was living with so much money—whatever the reason, Samantha cared a lot less about people's feelings than Jenny originally thought.

Samantha was using Jenny for her own gain. By Jenny giving her first impressions of the people she met with, people Samantha would do business with, it gave Samantha the upper hand. Jenny had to admit it was a clever idea. She'd probably do a whole lot better in life if someone else gave her insight on the nature of a person before she interacted with them.

As soon as that thought landed in her mind, another immediately pranced on top of it, bringing her pause. Would she listen to someone if they told her Ric was a user and a manipulator? If she'd been told Samantha would take advantage of her and place her in awkward, uncomfortable situations, would she have turned down the trip?

It was very likely she would have ignored the sound advice

anyone might have presented to her prior to coming to the island. Jenny would want to draw conclusions for herself.

At least she hoped she would have ignored someone else's impressions. Ric wasn't perfect. He had issues. But then so did she. If she were ever introduced to a perfect man, she'd probably hate him. A bit rough around the edges was a turn-on. Ric had lured her into his home and given her the grand tour of the banana plantation. She remembered how he shared stories as they entered each room, turning the old place into something alive and passionate. Ric had a good sales pitch. If he gave the same spiel to someone else, quite possibly he'd get his backing for his bed-and-breakfast.

When she turned her head, Marc met her gaze from across the room and grinned broadly. If he'd predicted Jenny would make a fool out of herself during her speech, had Samantha suggested he watch and report back to her? It would be Samantha's style, someone else's impressions and all. If Samantha was on the island, she would know exactly what Marc was doing and where he was. Jenny returned the smile.

Then, glancing down at her phone, which was resting on her leg, she tapped the screen and sent Ric a message.

*Thanks for the offer but I'm good. Wish me luck!*

Jenny stuffed her phone in her handbag before she could see how Ric might answer. It was a done deal.

The next few minutes seemed to drag on forever. Suddenly Jenny couldn't wait to get to the podium. Pearl gave her a reassuring smile and patted her leg when she scooted her chair back.

"Ready?" she whispered.

Apparently it was a rhetorical question, since she stood and started for the podium. Another lady joined Pearl and messed with the microphone, sending a few shrill squeals across the room. Jenny snapped and unsnapped her handbag, fidgeting as her mind raced. She never quit watching Pearl as she began mapping out one event after another, laying out her first impressions of the island. They wanted her to speak of Hawaii, of this small, somewhat reclusive island of Lanai. Her thoughts spilled over each other.

"That was a great meal, wasn't it?" Pearl asked, leaning into the microphone, her voice booming across the room.

Jenny snapped out of her thoughts, out of her fears of the unknown, and watched Pearl as she straightened and adjusted the microphone. Pearl lowered it an inch or two before speaking again.

Jenny had never taken a crash course in anything. She'd researched, taken notes, memorized, practiced and recited. It was her preferred method of studying during high school and had allowed her to make almost all As. But she'd never taken a speech class.

Pearl continued talking about the food, then shifted the topic to the waiters, which ended in an energetic round of applause in appreciation for the great service. Jenny peeled her attention from Pearl and scanned the room, watching the many smiling faces, who likewise watched Pearl attentively.

"We're thrilled today to have a very special guest with us," Pearl announced.

Jenny had just shifted her attention to Marc, who was leaning against the open door, focusing on his fingernails and looking almost bored. The moment Pearl started announcing Jenny, his bored look disappeared and he straightened. Jenny watched him pull something from the inside pocket of his suit jacket. It looked like a small handheld tape recorder.

"Please, ladies, give a warm island welcome to Jenny Rogers, a dear friend and protégée to Samantha Winston, and a beautiful young lady." Pearl held her hand out to Jenny as the room began a heartfelt round of applause.

Jenny stood, dropped her handbag on her chair, and moved to the podium. Her palms were sweaty. Her knees wobbled and her stomach was twisted in so many knots there wasn't room enough for the food she'd just enjoyed. It began churning, causing her throat to burn.

"Thank you." Jenny shook Pearl's hand, then gave her a hug, her body going through the motions while her brain continued whirling as an outline began taking shape in her mind.

Then she stood there, alone at the podium, the moment of truth facing her. Expectant faces, friendly, content, stared at her. There wasn't an empty seat in the large meeting room. Countless numbers of round tables were arranged in several rows shaped in half circles, allowing each person to see Jenny without having to crane her neck or twist too much in her chair.

The room grew quiet. A sudden rush of panic flooded her system as somewhat organized speech seemed to evaporate from her mind. Marc stood at the open doors, holding the small device out in front him. He was recording her speech, or rather, her lack of a speech.

Jenny shifted her gaze to the microphone, staring at it as she struggled with the mounting panic. This was it, the climax of her trip to Hawaii and her unexpected vacation to the island of Lanai. She'd lived through experiences she never dreamed she would have, and it all came down to this, giving a speech she didn't want to give. Of all the adventures she'd had while here, this was her final event, and she was about to blow it all to hell.

She cleared her throat. The sound erupted throughout the microphone, sounding incredibly unladylike. A few women close to the front glanced at each other. Jenny swore she felt their discomfort, the way a person felt when they were witnessing someone endure an embarrassing, humiliating moment. She wondered if racing out of the room—in complete and utter disgrace—would be the final scene of her trip to Hawaii. Jenny saw Nana in her mind, watching attentively as Jenny shared with her all the details about her trip. Nana would look just like the ladies sitting in front of her. Uncomfortable, awkward, unsure of what to say or how to comfort Jenny.

She shoved the unpleasant thought out of her head. Nana wouldn't endure that level of torture. Jenny wouldn't allow it.

"I've never given a speech before," she confessed.

Immediately the tension that was closing in around her dissipated. The women at the table in front of her exhaled, relaxed, and smiled, nodding at her.

"I wasn't sure what to expect once I was standing up here."

More women relaxed, grinning at her, leaning back with their full tummies and watching Jenny. She'd broken the ice—now to make her way through what she would say.

The mental outline she'd lost in her head reappeared, and Jenny began speaking. Her body was wound tight, her knees locked, which was the only reason she didn't stagger or take flight and run out of the room for the safe, secure haven of her private suite.

"My name is Jenny Rogers, and I live in Parkville, Minnesota. I was born there, and after my parents' death when I was an infant, I was raised by my grandparents. I've been to Minneapolis a few times, and the last time I was there, I was on the game show *Last Chance for Happiness.*" Jenny sucked in her lower lip, feeling her insides relax and the knots in her tummy untwisting when the ladies staring at her smiled, nodded, and began to whisper among themselves. "The game show host, Joe Jobana, is definitely better-looking on TV than in person."

The room filled with laughter. Jenny grinned. She was going to pull this off. Turning her attention to Marc, she grinned broadly but then looked away quickly before he could remind her with a look that she hadn't gotten to the point of her speech yet.

Before the room was quiet again, Jenny started explaining what happened at the airport while waiting for her flight.

Everyone watched her. They really seemed interested in her story. She continued with meeting Samantha and her first impression.

"And that is what she asked of me," Jenny added, after explaining how Samantha had insisted Jenny ride on her private jet. "She has put me in her shoes, which has been quite a learning experience."

Everyone was waiting to hear what she'd learned, what experiences she'd gone through. It was the moment of truth. Jenny plowed forward, everything she had to say coming out easily.

"It amazes me that I hadn't realized what I'd learned, and truly seen and experienced, until sitting here this afternoon and deciding what to say." She leaned against the podium, recalling each event since she'd arrived and how looking back on them now brought everything into perspective. "First of all, I have to say this island is just about the most beautiful place I've ever been to in my life. And maybe being in paradise made me feel everything I was doing and experiencing wasn't quite as real. After all, soon I'll be home and back to my life with Nana, and all of this will just be a memory." That thought brought her pause. She opened her mouth to continue and almost choked on her next words.

Pearl mistook her faltering and grabbed a glass of ice water.

Jenny mumbled her thanks and sipped. It did feel good going down but didn't get rid of the empty feeling suddenly filling her gut. A void spread through her at the realization she would never see Ric again, and at the same time, she wanted to kick herself for reacting to the obvious truth as if it were something she hadn't known, and been repeating to herself, all along.

"I'm going to take home some incredible memories, though," Jenny continued, determined to finish her speech and say what she'd wanted to say. "And although I come from a world that doesn't compare to yours in beauty, I won't regret leaving here." She sipped the water again, aware of the many faces staring at her. "Your island is so close to paradise I can only imagine how hard it is for many of you to keep others from exploiting it. In the last few days, I've been bombarded, as the representative of Samantha Winston, a very wealthy patronage, by those who would take this island and turn it into a financial gold mine intended to line their own pockets. Very little would go back into the island."

The women's smiles faded, and Jenny knew she was being heard. She continued, letting the words fall out, knowing she could only speak her mind and pray it would do some good.

"I can honestly say, with the short time I've been here, I could easily have made the decisions necessary in the appointments I've attended on behalf of Samantha Winston."

A few women at different tables leaned forward, their smiles fading and their expressions growing concerned. Jenny's tummy twisted a bit but no longer from fear of speaking.

"I see why Samantha visits the island as often as she does. Everyone who lives here is so friendly. I feel as if I've come home." She fought to keep her voice from cracking and took a breath to keep her voice calm. "Samantha must feel the same way. That's why I know what her answers would have been during these business meetings."

She paused, sipped her water, then fingered the edge of the podium as she continued. "There are a lot of very powerful people out there who want Lanai to be an island for the extremely wealthy, no one else. And they might very well pull it off. If they do, I hope they don't ruin the heritage that runs so deep here on the island. Everyone living here is so friendly. I think they are strong enough, also, to keep outsiders who don't care about the heritage from taking over."

"So if this were my home, I would want to make sure that any business on this island, any venture undertaken, was done to keep Lanai for Lanai. Where I come from, if outsiders try to set up shop, and take the profits out of our community, we fight them, and we don't stop fighting them until we win. My advice to you—a large group with some say-so—is to do the same. Look around you. Maybe you take all this beauty for granted; maybe you've grown immune to it. I don't know. What I do know is your heritage here is as incredible as the flowers blooming outside. I hope I can return here someday and see that all this beauty has remained."

Jenny walked away from the podium, aware of all the whispering around her. They wanted to know what she meant. They speculated, began arguing, and no one applauded or moved from their spot. She took advantage, grabbed her purse, and kept walking, heading straight for a door leading out of there. It went into the kitchen but she didn't care. All she knew was she had to leave before she started crying.

She would never return to this island, wouldn't know who won or lost. But she'd done her part. Nana would be proud. The first teardrop fell when she reached the elevator.

# 11

Ric wanted to leap into the air. He wanted to yell and hear his voice bellow off the ceiling. He wanted to grab the nearest person and pull them into a bear hug, swing them around in a circle, and laugh out loud. No one had ever gone to bat for him before, and the experience was beyond exhilarating. He wanted to race into that large meeting room full of every wealthy woman from the island and grab Jenny, kiss her senseless in front of everyone.

Maybe she hadn't mentioned the banana plantation, but he couldn't have given her speech any better than she had. Jenny planted the seed. She created curiosity, and in a room full of those ladies, it would spread like the plague. Ric would give them five minutes tops before that entire room began demanding to know what Jenny was talking about. He wanted to barge in there and announce loudly that his banana plantation would make the perfect bed-and-breakfast and keep Lanai heritage good and strong.

Instead, he remained standing where he'd been throughout Jenny's speech and waited. When after a moment the room remained silent, Ric couldn't stand it any longer. He stepped over to the doors that were almost closed. He'd propped one of them open with a doorstop just enough so he could hear Jenny. Now he stepped inside, positive Marc would still be down the hall at the other doorway, standing there stupefied. What he wouldn't give to get a look at that prick's face after Jenny's glorious speech.

He stepped into the large hall and began clapping. It didn't take a second for the room to join in, which was all he wanted. Then stepping out, he planned on leaving the room when he noticed no one stood at the podium. A lady began moving toward the center of the room, glancing over her shoulder and looking rather stunned.

"Apparently our Miss Jenny Rogers doesn't like to hear the praise of her moving speech," she said when she reached the microphone. "But we must give her another round of applause. She's given all of us something to think about."

Ric frowned, scanning the room. He then searched more closely, scrutinizing every lady at every table, searching for Jenny. He didn't see her. The applause grew annoying when the lady began speaking again. Ric wanted to hear her. She had to be saying something about Jenny. She kept glancing to the side of the large room, toward the waiters who kept entering and exiting through a swinging door that probably led to the kitchen.

An older woman dressed in a business suit entered the room from the kitchen door and hurried over to the lady at the podium. Finally the room had quieted down enough to hear what was said.

"It appears Jenny was a bit overwhelmed by her first speech," the woman explained apologetically. "She's retired to her room."

"Do you know what she was talking about?" A woman stood at one of the tables in the middle of the room and called out. The other women looked at her, then at the woman at the podium expectantly. "Jenny made it sound as if she knew about a business trying to move onto our island, and it was clear she didn't approve."

Ric wanted to applaud the woman. He wanted to bound into the room and make it crystal clear exactly what Jenny had been talking about.

"I know Samantha Winston," the woman continued, straightening now that she had everyone's undivided attention. She was the kind of lady who wouldn't give Ric a second glance. She seemed full of self-importance and probably judged the world on a sliding scale based on their annual income and who they knew. She was also the kind of woman Ric wouldn't normally give a second glance. Right now, though, he'd attack anyone who tried interrupting her.

"She's a shrewd businesswoman whose taken a family fortune and turned it into one of the most successful businesses on the planet. She's endured generations of prejudice against her being a woman and being a major stockholder and a corporate giant. She lives in man's world and has done so successfully for many years."

She paused only long enough to look around the room, her gaze never settling on Ric in spite of her turning in his direction.

"What Samantha has done—bringing a young woman out of her sheltered life and planting her in a world she knows nothing about—is nothing less than genius. Jenny Rogers went to meetings in Samantha's stead. She attended luncheons, such as this one, and walked in the shoes of a very wealthy woman, who is adored because she is wealthy. A young lady, who is accustomed to being judged, liked and disliked, based on her personality, was flooded with attention and adored because of a status she didn't ask for or earn." The woman's voice grew louder as she drove her point home. "Jenny Rogers has been approached by someone, or a group of people, who want to use Samantha Winston's money to start a business on the island. And Jenny Rogers doesn't approve. I want to know, and I want to know now, what business this is. If Jenny, who has an innocent, fresh, untainted view on life, has a problem with it, we should all pay heed and listen."

Once again the room exploded with applause, and many of the women standing also demanded the same. Ric was ecstatic, overwhelmed with happiness. At the same time, he watched the woman at the podium hurry to the side of the room. She started talking excitedly to one of the waiters, who continually shrugged helplessly. Could they not find Jenny?

Ric had heard enough. He'd witnessed the seed Jenny had planted take root and grow. Now he needed to find her. He left the meeting room and started down the hallway. A group of employees stood huddled in the middle of the lobby, and Ric went around them. They dispersed when Ric neared the elevators. As the doors slid open, the group hurried past him and filled the elevator, pushing the button and closing the doors on him before he could push his way inside.

"Hell," he grumbled, turning toward the stairs.

As Ric came out of the stairwell on the second floor and stepped into the hallway, the elevator doors opened. The group he'd seen in the lobby downstairs were coming toward him, pushing carts filled with luggage and once again filling the elevators. The doors closed and he glanced up, watching the buttons light up above the elevators and descend to the lobby. Ric glanced down the hallway in time to see the door at the opposite end of the hall close.

"Jenny," he yelled, then bounded toward the door to Jenny's suite. "Jenny," he repeated, knocking firmly on the door. "Sweetheart, you were amazing."

He stopped his fist in mid-knock when the suite door opened and he stared at a middle-aged woman, who tilted her

head and looked at him with a mixture of amusement and ag-
gravation. She wrinkled her brow and pressed her lips into a
thin line.

"Yes?" she demanded, her voice sharp, that no-nonsense
tone teachers used when he was in grade school. "What did you
want?"

He didn't know Jenny had any of Samantha's staff working
with her, although they'd never discussed what she did in her
hotel room when she wasn't with him.

"Jenny Rogers," he said, reaching over her to push the door
open and starting past her.

The woman was stronger than she appeared. "Young man,"
she snapped. "I have not given you permission to enter."

Ric froze in his steps and looked down at her. He took a step
back, slowly removed his hand from the door, and stared at the
rigid-looking lady. Her hair was streaked with gray and pulled
back tightly into a perfectly round bun. The straight-cut dress
she wore, along with her stockings and flat shoes, were all the
same color. She was the spitting image of every caseworker,
every school teacher, every social worker who ever invaded his
life and possessed too much power to yank him out of it and
toss him into another life he'd be forced to get accustomed to
and toughen up against.

He gave himself a firm mental shake. The system had permanently severed him from their cruel grip twelve years ago.
He'd never looked back and he wasn't about to now. Ric held
the reins to his life now. No one controlled him. That didn't
mean he was incapable of interacting with people. Ric had manners. "Forgive me," he said with a nod, and because no one
could shatter his good mood right now, he smiled. "Please tell
Jenny that Ric Karaka is here." He stared into the woman's ice-
cold eyes.

She didn't appear a happy woman. That wasn't his problem.
If he'd learned anything growing up, it was happiness wasn't

handed to anyone. If a person wanted to be happy, they had to take the path leading in that direction. There were people out there incapable of seeing that, for whatever reason. Some people didn't have the right signals in their brain and would be condemned to a life of depression and bitterness. Others intentionally chose to be bitter, finding reason to blame anyone and anything for their miserable lives. Ric wasn't sure which type of person this lady was. She stared back to him with cold, pale blue eyes that looked empty. Nor did he care. All she was to him was an obstacle between him and Jenny.

"Let her know I'm here," he added, facing her and hoping his stance showed her he wouldn't allow her to close the door on him. He might have let her prevent him from initially entering, but that didn't mean he couldn't force his way in if he decided to do so, and without hurting anything other than the pride the woman used to keep her back as straight as a board.

"Jenny isn't here," she snapped.

When the lady took a step backward, and it was clear Ric was being dismissed, Ric made his move. Once again the woman surprised him, this time with her speed. She leaped into his path, letting go of the door and putting her hands on her hips and turning her icy blue orbs on him.

"Young man, Miss Rogers doesn't entertain scoundrels. Now, you turn around and go back where you came from. She wouldn't see you if she were here."

He hadn't been called a scoundrel since the eighth grade, when he'd graduated to the title of delinquent. Once again he shoved his past back where it belonged. Today he was a good man, honest, hardworking, and very undeserving of the treatment this hired help was giving him.

"I'm not a scoundrel. Jenny does entertain me." He leaned forward, bending slightly so he was almost eye to eye with the prude. "And if I weren't a gentleman, I promise you'd lose at the game of insult slinging."

"Well," she huffed, stepping back and looking at him as if he were a leper or something.

"If she isn't here, where is she?" He'd guessed she'd run from the meeting room downstairs to the safety of her suite, but if Jenny knew this hired help would be waiting for her, it wouldn't surprise him if she found solace somewhere else. Did she take off looking for him? "Do you even know where she is?"

"Jenny has left the hotel." She narrowed her icy blues on him. "Young man, I'm being generous with my information. Now turn around and leave. This is no longer her room."

Ric straightened, looking past the lady and into the room. He saw the plush carpet that spread across the spacious hotel suite, but could see little beyond that. When he returned his attention to the woman, she'd apparently decided her words might have distracted him enough that she could escape back into the room and finally have her moment of satisfaction by slamming the door in his face. Her words hit him with strong clarity.

"Why isn't this her room anymore?" he demanded, the menacing chill he felt rising inside him coming out in his tone. If that little weasel of a bastard Marc shared Jenny's speech with Samantha and his grandmother didn't appreciate her words, they might as well not be related. Ric would hunt Samantha Winston down and have his say if the old woman kicked Jenny out of her room. "And where did she go?" he asked, raising his voice and not giving a damn who heard him.

"Let him in, Ethel."

Ric wasn't quite sure he heard the soft-spoken instructions until Ethel, the blue-eyed, cold, calculating woman, who continued assessing Ric and apparently finding him lacking, moved.

"Let me in, Ethel," he whispered, once again reaching for the door over Ethel's head and this time pushing it open. He was pretty sure who he'd meet once he entered Jenny's suite.

The excitement he'd known a week ago over meeting his maternal grandmother had faded. The anticipation of knowing his life was finally coming together and he was reuniting with family had disappeared when he'd learned Samantha had chosen to not come to the island. Since meeting Jenny, and feeling a connection building between them, he wasn't as concerned about his grandmother as he was learning where Jenny was and why she'd been kicked out of the room.

He moved around Ethel, ignoring her when she leaped out of his way as if he might crush her in passing. Ric completely intended to give the old lady a piece of his mind. However, when he stepped into the room, he came to a halt as he stared at the petite, elegant old lady who slowly came to her feet.

"Ricardo," she said, speaking in a soft, rather husky tone. Samantha pushed on the armrests of the chair where she'd been sitting, and another woman, this one with red hair that was cropped short around her face, hurried to assist her. "Margo, I'm fine." Samantha waved the woman off. "Prepare coffee for me and my grandson." She looked up at Ric. "Or would you prefer something else? You young people have given up the coffee addiction for other vices these days. Would you prefer tea or a Coke?" She looked at Margo. "We have Coke, don't we?"

"Yes, ma'am," Margo confirmed, then left Samantha and headed to the other side of the suite where the kitchenette was.

"Let her know what you want." Samantha waved in Margo's direction but then beckoned Ric toward her. "I'm an old woman, Ricardo. Don't make me come to you for a hug."

Samantha's watery gray eyes beamed with happiness, and she smiled at him and held out her arms. She truly seemed happy to see him. He approached, somewhat warily, then bent over to give the old woman a hug. She smelled of roses and something minty. Her body was brittle and her hands cold when she patted his back before releasing him and gesturing to the matching chair facing her. Ric sat, staring at her. This was what he'd expected a week ago, had been certain he'd receive. Samantha's warm welcome and the happy, content glow in her eyes were everything he'd imagined over the months of writing to her. And although he'd been certain just seconds ago any type of welcome from her would be too little too late, his heart swelled in his chest and rose to his throat, making it hard to say anything.

"I know you're brimming with questions," Samantha said, patting the hand he'd placed on the round table between them.

Ric stared down at the blue veins traveling under her skin and the age spots darkening the back of her hand. He imagined this petite woman once had been someone to reckon with, and probably still was in spite of her frail state. In fact, at this moment it appeared she had decided that now was the moment to begin their reunion and to make it a happy, tear-shedding event. He couldn't give her that power.

"Where were you a week ago?" he asked, his voice a bit deeper than usual—not that Samantha would know that.

When he looked into her eyes, she stared back at him, moistening the pink lipstick that had dried on her lips. She took her time, letting silence build between them, and Ric had no intention of breaking it. Let her find the answer to appease her grandson, her blood relative who'd sought her out and waited anxiously for this meeting.

He sat there, watching her watch him, and was aware of Margo approaching, hesitating, and waiting. Even the hired help saw that Samantha needed to rectify herself before a man who would never be in her class and had no regrets about that fact.

"You look just like her," she whispered.

Ric blinked. "Who?"

"Your mother. It's uncanny. Has anyone ever told you that?"

"Nope." No one in his world had ever met his mother. Up

until a year ago, when the Karakas had shown him the few pictures they had of her with their son, his father, he hadn't known what she'd looked like.

"I brought pictures. Lots of them. I thought you would want to see your parents. I have their wedding album with me. It's yours now, of course."

He wondered if she'd made that decision before seeing him, or now, after staring at him for a minute, ignoring his question, and deciding he was in fact a blood relative.

"Thank you." He glanced at Margo, who took that as a signal to bring forward a large tray she placed on the table. "But I've already seen pictures my grandparents have shown me." They weren't wedding pictures but casual shots taken or sent to his grandmother when his father sent a letter.

"I guess you never told Margo what you preferred to drink." Samantha easily changed the subject and maintained her friendly smile as she looked up fondly at her servant. "Which do you prefer, Ricardo?"

"Call me Ric," he said, then glanced at the tray. There was a carafe that probably held some expensive coffee by the smell of it. Margo had also prepared a pitcher of soft drink, which he guessed was Coke. "And, honestly, I'm not very thirsty." He knew he was being difficult, but his grandmother didn't seem to care that she'd shown up a week later, and on the brink of Jenny's sudden disappearance, although he wasn't sure yet that she hadn't gone to his house.

"Leave the coffee, dear." Samantha waved at the contents on the tray as if she could magically see to the order herself with a gentle movement of her hand. "You two go in the other room."

Ric waited until Margo and Ethel obediently disappeared into the bedroom, and the sound of a TV began as the door closed behind them. Then, unable to stand the formalities his grandmother insisted upon, he practically leaped out of his chair and began pacing as he studied Samantha.

"Where is Jenny?" he demanded, stalking to the open glass doors and barely noticing the view outside before turning and pacing back to the table. "What have you done with her?"

"Done with her?" Samantha shook her head, her soft smile becoming an annoyance. "I believe I helped her out."

The look on his face must have shown enough anger for his grandmother to quit playing her control games. She sighed, reached for her coffee, and poured a cup.

"A moment ago you wanted to know why I waited a week to come see you," she said stoically as she poured. "That is rather interesting and something I didn't anticipate. Maybe I should have shown up sooner." She glanced at Ric, this time impervious to his seething look. "Or maybe not."

"Where is Jenny?" he asked again, barely moving his mouth and feeling his teeth aching to clench. He was beyond irritated with how Samantha was treating him. Her initial greeting threw him off guard, but she was trying to manipulate him now, and it pissed him off when he couldn't guess her motives.

Samantha placed the carafe on the tray and picked up her cup, sipped, then placed it in front of her, a lipstick stain now planted on its side.

"Jenny's grandmother had a heart attack late last night. I had been in touch with her since she's very close to her granddaughter and the two haven't been separated much during Jenny's life." Samantha took another drink. "I found out early this morning and flew out here, knowing Jenny would want to leave and be with her grandmother right away." She nodded past Ric to the door of the suite. "You started demanding to come in right after her luggage was carried out. Jenny didn't wait for it, though. We hustled her out the door right after her speech."

"Crap," Ric hissed, once again pacing as he pulled out his cell phone.

"She won't be able to receive your call." Samantha glanced

at the elegant watch on her thin wrist. "She'll be boarding now. They're rushing to get her home."

Ric found the love seat along the wall and collapsed on to it, suddenly feeling deflated. Jenny was gone. He looked at his grandmother, the woman he'd been so anxious to meet and knew he should start talking about something, anything, other than Jenny. Although all he wanted to know was if she was coming back. But he knew the answer. Jenny coming to the island was a one-time deal. Now it was over.

"Why did you change your plans and not come out when you said you would?" he asked, changing to the only other subject he could think of. He was numb inside, though, and honestly didn't care what her answer was. It would be several hours before he could talk to Jenny.

"If I had, you wouldn't be so worried about Jenny right now."

"You didn't send her in your place just so she could meet me."

"True." Samantha leaned her frail body back in the chair and relaxed her arms on the armrests. "She's changed all our lives."

"All of our lives?" Ric wished the numbness would go away. He was sitting and facing Samantha Winston, the woman who could make or break his future. And although the numbness continued to consume him, it dawned on him that that wasn't true; Samantha couldn't make or break his future. A week ago, maybe, but Jenny had set him straight. His insides constricted. Would he be able to tell her that?

"She's changed yours and mine," Samantha said softly.

"I was nervous to meet you." She studied him with heavy mascara lining her eyelashes, making her eyes stand out.

"I'm sure," he said dryly, and realized he was looking for a family resemblance. It didn't bother him when he didn't see one.

When Samantha laughed, the wrinkles in her cheeks and her

crow's feet became a lot more apparent. It gave the impression she laughed a lot, which was a good character trait. Ric didn't want to like her. Not yet. He wanted her to make amends before he sat and chatted like family over coffee.

"I know what you're thinking and you're right." She waved a hand at him, her delicate fingers as laced with blue veins as the backs of her hands were. "And you're right. But there was history . . . ," she said, and her words trailed off for a moment.

*What history?* He almost asked, but couldn't motivate himself into conversation.

Ric waited it out, watching her, willing to hear anything she had to say.

"Maria was perfect, the daughter most mothers only dream of having. She adored me and I adored her right back." Something changed in her tone, her voice turning gravelly. She quit looking at him and lowered her gaze, staring across the room as she continued. "Maria had the perfect grades, was valedictorian, and had scholarships waiting for her at several of the best Ivy League schools in the nation. She had the opportunity to study abroad, and although I gave my blessing, my Maria decided against it because she didn't want to be that far away from me. Most daughters can't wait to part ways with their mothers, and vice versa. She decided on Harvard and used the family jet to fly home for weekends. Over spring break her freshman year, instead of partying on the beaches with the other kids, she chose to come to Hawaii with me."

"Which is where she met my father." He hadn't meant to get so wrapped up in Samantha's story, and the words slipped out. "And she chose him over you," he added, since he'd already slipped into the memory with her.

Samantha nodded and sucked in her lower lip. When she blinked, a lone tear slid down her cheek. Ric held his ground. But the picture was becoming clear to him.

"Julio was good-looking, just like you." She raised her watery gaze to his. "You're better-looking, actually. You've got your father's size and stance but your mother's perfect bone structure. He swept my daughter off her feet, and he had nothing, not a dime. Not even a dress jacket to wear when she brought him to meet me."

"And you were sure he was taking your daughter from you and was after all her millions."

"I saw to it that that wasn't the case. After learning she didn't even finish out her freshman year at Harvard but dropped out a week after spring break to return here to be with him, I fired my entire staff for helping her make the move and not telling me." Her voice grew bitter, and she gripped the arms of her chair until her knuckles turned white and her blue veins bulged in her hands and wrist. "My precious Maria deceived me. I would have rather her been a rebellious teenager and broken my heart again and again than to have her pretend to be perfect only to stab me in the back. I've never had a business deal go sour. Not once have I miscalculated when it came to the market, or buying, or consolidating any transaction. But my daughter threw me the biggest curve ball of all when she ran off with an island bum. I froze all of her accounts, cut her out of my will, and refused to send her a dime. She wasn't going to give that gigolo a chance to take her for her money."

"You're talking about my father," he reminded her.

"He killed my baby!" she cried out, her voice shrill.

The bedroom door opened, and Margo stepped into the room, Ethel right behind her, with her piercing glare pinned on Ric. He kept his attention on Samantha, seeing no reason why they shouldn't have this all out right now.

"The way I was told, I killed your daughter," he said morosely.

Samantha leaned forward, her expression having transformed into what he imagined was a look that made many successful businessmen cringe and cower. It was a damn good thing he wasn't a successful businessman.

Samantha wasn't the only one who had suffered over the past thirty years. He hadn't curled up in a ball and wallowed in a state of misery when he'd been told the truth about his day of birth, but it had struck deep nonetheless. Today he could live with the knowledge that it had nothing to do with him. His mother had made choices that killed her, plain and simple. Once he'd accepted that, he'd lived with years of hating her for not going to a hospital when she'd gone into labor. They wouldn't have turned her away even if she was penniless. How different his life would have been if his mother had lived. That wasn't how it happened, though. Ric had taken the hand he'd been dealt, and he had made it work. Samantha wouldn't berate him, place blame on him, or make him stand here why she sobbed over her terrible loss.

"Forgive me if I don't feel your pain," he added.

"You resent Maria for dying," she accused.

Ric shook his head, aware of the two servant ladies edging closer. He wasn't worried about them. If they thought he would hurt Samantha in any way, they were poor judges of character. He cut Samantha a bit of slack for her false accusation because she didn't know him. But he wasn't feeling too sympathetic.

"My *mother*," he began, stressing her role in his life when Samantha referred to her as if she were someone connected to her but not to him, "died giving birth to me in a shabby motel room because she believed she had nowhere to turn. I'm the only one not to blame, and all I can do is believe she didn't have any options."

"Of course she had options," Samantha wailed, the bite in her tone gone.

"You just admitted cutting her off. Did you later make

amends with her? Did you go to her wedding? Were you there with her to celebrate when you found out she and her husband were going to start a family?"

"You have no idea what you're talking about," she whispered.

Ric stared at her. When there was a pause in the accusations, Margo and Ethel went to their employer's side and Margo bent over, whispering something in a concerned, hushed tone. Samantha nodded and reached for her coffee. Ric exhaled, feeling the two of them had said enough for a first meeting.

"It was nice meeting you, Grandmother," he said, keeping his tone flat.

Samantha looked up at him, her eyes still watery. He didn't doubt she felt a lot of pain over losing her daughter, and Ric probably caused those wounds to open again. There wasn't much he could do about that.

"I'm sure you know where the banana plantation is. So you know where to find me." He wasn't sure why he extended an open invitation for her to seek him out again. Something told him she wouldn't. However, despite how aggravated the old lady made him, she was family. After thirty years of having none, Ric wasn't ready to sever connections with any relative, regardless of what they thought of him.

Samantha didn't say anything but didn't look away. Ric gave it just a couple seconds, then turned and walked out of the hotel suite.

It was later that evening when Ric relaxed on his couch with his cell in his hand. He'd jumped into work after leaving the hotel. Jenny was gone. He'd met his grandmother. There wasn't a chance in hell she would finance his bed-and-breakfast. Therefore, Ric needed to work. He needed to hustle up more jobs, keep the mortgage paid on the banana plantation, and come up with a new game plan and time frame for turning his home into a bed-and-breakfast. Jenny's speech had stirred up some talk in town. It would take time to learn if it had done any good. He had no choice other than to sit and wait. Ric doubted any damage control Pritchard might implement would do any good. But again, time would tell.

He stretched his legs across the coffee table and remembered fucking Jenny in this exact spot. She'd been so incredibly hot. Ric had a thing about taking ladies doggy style. It did keep the sex less personal, although he wasn't in the mood to analyze why he'd always preferred that type of sex over more intimate positions in the past. When Jenny had requested fucking that way, it had made him even harder.

And it wasn't just the fact that taking a woman from behind was considered more casual on the fucking scale. Ric loved how it felt sliding in from that angle. He could go deeper, feel her constrict around him as she sucked him into her heat. He was able to watch her long hair drift down her back. God! He loved Jenny's long, curly hair.

If he wanted, he could make the position more intimate, pull her back against him, turn her head slightly and devour her mouth while easing his way deep inside her. It wasn't as if he had intimacy issues. He hadn't ever wanted a serious relationship, but that didn't mean he had problems with them.

Leaning back against the couch, Ric lifted his phone and stared at it. He needed to call Jenny and at the same time get her out of his head so he could focus on a new plan for the banana plantation. Even as he held his phone before his face and scrolled down to Jenny's number, he lifted his gaze to appraise his living room. This place would be a bed-and-breakfast. If he had to replace each piece of rotted wood himself, landscape the yard outside with his own bare hands, and take on each room in the house until he had the place ready to open, he would do it. Hell, he might need that much time doing it by himself if he had to finance each project on his own. He wouldn't be able to hire anyone to help him. The sooner he began prioritizing his projects, the better off he'd be.

"Crap," he groaned, heaving out a sigh and closing his eyes.

Jenny was immediately there in his mind, consuming all his thoughts, smiling at him. They'd barely had time to get to know each other, and she was gone. He needed to accept that she wasn't coming back.

"Damn, call her already." Part of him wondered what the point was. But his heart was still swollen against his chest, throbbing painfully, and he knew there wouldn't be any getting past this until he spoke to her, even if it was to put closure on their way-too-brief love affair.

Love?

Ric cringed, refusing to dwell on the slip of his thoughts, and pushed the button to call her. It rang once, twice—

"Samantha's Winston's phone. May I help you?" a scratchy older woman's voice said into the phone.

"What the—"

"Excuse me, young man. If you're trying to reach Miss Jenny Rogers, I'm afraid you've dialed the wrong number."

"I didn't dial the wrong number. What the hell is going on here?" he bellowed.

"Sir, if you're going to use profanity, I will hang up," the woman said tersely.

Ric couldn't tell which of Samantha's hired ladies he was speaking with, but he didn't care. He leaned forward, letting his feet fall off the coffee table and hit the hardwood floor, causing loud thuds that echoed through his almost empty living room.

"Then why are you answering Jenny's phone?" A glimpse of hope rose inside him.

Was Jenny still on the island? He wanted to believe that so bad he didn't take time to rationalize his thoughts. Ric jumped up and hurried to his front window, staring at his dark front yard and willing Jenny to appear. Maybe Samantha had arranged some ploy to keep the two of them apart. He'd much rather believe that than accept the fact that Jenny was thousands of miles away and never returning.

"This isn't her phone. She was allowed to use this cell phone, which is the property of Samantha Winston, while she was here on the island."

Ric was a good judge of character. He always had been. Samantha, his grandmother, wasn't a bad person. He muffled the stream of obscenities that he wanted to scream at the top of his lungs. Jenny wasn't here. His grandmother hadn't deceived him. If anything, she quite possibly had been more honest, and open, with him in admitting fear in meeting him. It had opened old wounds for her, and the pain from losing her only daughter.

Ric pinched the bridge of his nose and squeezed his eyes shut. "Would you please give me Jenny's phone number?" he asked, and sounded calm.

"I'm afraid I don't have it."

His swollen heart couldn't get any bigger. Already it pressed against his ribs so painfully he could hardly catch his breath. He was pretty sure he mumbled something akin to good-bye before hanging up. Ric headed into the kitchen to his laptop. One of the things on his list was securing DSL for the banana plantation. For now, all he could do was pray this was one of those times he'd be able to get online with dial-up. Ric had to find Jenny's number.

Colby had wisely given Ric space, having determined his mood wasn't to her liking and finding a comfortable spot somewhere in the house. When she came bounding down the stairs and into the living room to the front door, Ric stopped what he was doing and leaned back in the chair.

"What is it, girl?" he asked.

Colby answered with a deep bark, the bark she used only when someone she didn't know was on her property. Ric got to his feet, moving stealthily into the living room and peered out

222 / Lorie O'Clare
222 / Lorie O'Clare

the front window. He stared at the black limousine parked in the curve of his driveway and watched Sean move around it to the rear passenger door.

For a moment his heart leaped to his throat as he swung open the front door. He was down the steps before reality kicked in and he realized it wasn't Jenny returning home. Damn. This wasn't her home.

Samantha stepped out of the car but then watched warily when Colby came bounding down the porch steps toward her.

"Colby, no," Ric ordered.

Colby stopped, sat, and stared at Samantha, who remained guarded by Sean, who looked at the dog, then at him. Ric mentally agreed with the driver. Even if Colby offered greetings with the best of intentions, his large bloodhound was way too much for the fragile old woman.

"Inside, Colby, now."

She obeyed but gave him a rather scathing look as she walked past him and into the house.

"Your dog is very well trained," Samantha said in form of greeting as she accepted Sean's hand and headed to Ric's porch steps.

"What are you doing here?" Ric asked. He knew his mood was foul, but he'd had about as much as he could take from the world for one day. If he couldn't get online, he was ready to head into town and find Jenny's number.

"I brought you the pictures I told you were yours," Samantha began, pausing on her trek and raising her head so she could look him in the eye. "And I know your plan was for me to see your banana plantation, so here I am. Will you give me the tour?"

Ric opened his mouth, ready to tell her to turn around and go back to her hotel. From inside, he heard his cell phone ringing and turned to stare at his screen door. It rang a second and third time, but he wasn't in the mood to talk to anyone, let alone give a tour.

"This isn't really a good time," he began, trying not to sound as pissed as he felt.

"I do apologize for not announcing myself. Sean was taking me on a ride, and when he pointed out your land, I grew curious." She looked across the span of his front porch, squinting at the darkness. "I hear you want to turn this into a bed-and-breakfast. It would certainly offer a taste of local culture once it was fixed up."

Samantha smiled. She grinned up at him, and the twinkle in her eyes showed no hidden agenda, only sincerity. He was grumpy and wanted to stay that way, but Samantha was here, offering the two of them a second chance. Not to mention, she was right. He hated thinking it and would be damned if he'd admit it out loud, but here was his chance to sell her on the place and gain his financing.

His cell phone started ringing again.

"Don't mind me," she said, waving her hand at him. "Someone obviously needs a minute of your time. Sean, be a dear and help me up these stairs. I think a moment on that porch swing staring at this incredible scenery will do me just fine. Go answer your phone," she told Ric, dismissing him as if she owned the place and not him.

Ric needed a minute to get his thoughts in order, whether he answered the phone or not. Turning, he stalked into his house, at the last minute grabbing his screen door with his hand so it wouldn't slam behind him, and ignored Colby's anxious stares as he moved around her to his phone.

It had quit ringing when he retrieved it off his kitchen table. As he held it in his hand, staring at the number and area code he didn't recognize, it began ringing a third time. It was the same number. Ric didn't dare allow his heart to trip him up yet again that day. He'd had enough of this damn emotional roller-coaster ride. It was time to buckle down and get his thoughts in order so he could function around others, especially in front of his grandmother, who'd just shocked the shit out of him by showing up unannounced and requesting a tour. Something told him she enjoyed the upper hand and surprising him with her visit.

He pushed the button to answer the phone before it went to voice mail yet again. "Hello," he snapped.

"Ric," Jenny said into his ear, her voice breathless and sounding incredibly far away.

He damn near tumbled into the kitchen chair at his table. "Jenny," he said, his own voice reminding him of an excited schoolboy when the most popular girl in school just called.

"Ric," she repeated. "My grandmother just died."

# 12

———————

Jenny pulled into the driveway and parked. She was getting used to every movement feeling as if she were dragging a very heavy ball and chain along with her. Getting out of the car almost seemed to be too much work. And she honestly didn't care if she walked up to the house or remained sitting in her car.

One of her friends at work told her it was depression and would pass. Jenny didn't care if it passed or not. Everything that was dear to her no longer existed. Nana had been gone for three months, two weeks, and four days now, and the only man she'd ever wanted to spend more time with was halfway around the world. Heaving a sigh, she pushed her door open and stepped out into the crisp evening air. It was probably sunny and warm in Lanai.

A cold wind whipped around the house. She hadn't showered that morning, and her hair was limp, heavier than usual. At least the wind didn't blow her hair in her face as she trudged from the driveway to the path that led to the side door of the house. Jenny held out her key to unlock the door, then noticed it was ajar. She stared at it, tilting her head and seeing inside to the mudroom through the partially open door.

Had she forgotten to lock it and the wind blew it open?

Jenny pushed the door open and stepped inside, closing it behind her, before it crossed her mind she might have been robbed. She cringed at the thought that if she had, at least Nana hadn't been here. Glancing around her, she grabbed the broom leaning against the wall by the door, the only thing she could find that resembled a weapon. Then, with her purse sliding off her shoulder to her arm, she gripped the broom sideways with both her hands and walked silently from the mudroom into the kitchen.

Everything appeared okay.

Her laptop was on the kitchen table where she'd left it.

She stepped gingerly into the dining room. Nana's silver spoon collection still hung on the wall. The TV was in the living room. Maybe she hadn't been robbed.

Jenny continued from room to room. When she stood in Nana's bedroom, turning slowly to make sure all was in place, it dawned on her this was the first time she'd been in her grandmother's room since she'd died.

"I miss you so much, Nana," she whispered, and prayed the room would answer her.

She smelled Nana everywhere. Moving to the bed, Jenny traced the lace border to the throw pillow neatly placed over another pillow. Tears welled in her eyes.

"Why did I let you talk me into going to Hawaii?" she demanded, staring at the white lace as it blurred from her tears. "If I'd stayed here, I would have had another week with you."

And she never would have met Ric.

And she wouldn't be mourning two losses right now.

Jenny stomped out of the room but closed the door carefully. Nana hated doors slamming. They shook the pictures on the walls. Except there weren't any pictures on the walls. Heading down the flight of stairs to the first floor, she stared at the many rectangle shapes on the wall. Two weeks ago she'd taken all the pictures off the wall since almost all of them were pictures of her grinning from ear to ear, and she couldn't bare seeing herself so happy. Or they were pictures of Nana, which tore at her heart just as bad.

She'd done the same thing in the living room. Every wall hanging had a history to it, which Jenny didn't want to be reminded of. She'd packed up all of Nana's handmade doilies and had taken Nana's rocking chair and packed it in the back room along with a lot of the other furniture in the house. Jenny stared at the living room. It was almost empty. She returned the broom to where it always leaned against the wall, just inside the door, then dropped her phone and purse on the kitchen table. Jenny had been walking around in a stupor for months. Heading for the dining room, she began taking down the silver spoons. They might as well go in with everything else. If she'd become so forgetful that she wasn't closing or locking the door to Nana's house, she might as well pack up the valuables so they wouldn't be stolen.

She'd done away with most of the dishes in the kitchen, their flowery pattern having been one of Nana's favorites. By the time she made it back into the kitchen, she'd taken two more boxes of Nana's things into the small back room that had always been used for storage. Jenny slid into one of the two kitchen chairs and immediately wanted to put the remaining chair in the back room. With the back of it facing her over the edge of the table, it made her feel someone else should be sitting at the table with her.

And there was no one else.

Her purse was on the table and her cell next to it. For a moment she thought about calling Ric. They'd spoken daily for the first few days she'd been home, so he knew her home phone number. But with the funeral plans, and with Ric having to lead his own life, more days had slipped by without them talking. She hadn't spoken to him in eleven weeks and three days. Not that it mattered how much time passed.

What was the point?

Every time she talked to him, it opened up the wounds in her heart all over again. Which wasn't fair. There had been men in Parkville she'd dated for longer than a week. Each time the relationship ended, there was a day or two of pain. But it faded and she got on with her life. Jenny scowled, trying to remember the breakup of her last relationship before meeting Ric. She drew a blank.

But that was good, right? It meant this pain would end, too, and eventually she'd never remember experiencing it.

"You'll forget all about this three and a half months of pain," she said to herself, and knew immediately that it wasn't the truth, no matter how much she argued with herself that it was. She tried another theory on for size. "The only reason you miss Ric so much is because Nana is gone." It was another lie.

Jenny stared at the newspaper, laid out flat in front of the empty chair across from her. She'd never understood how deeply Nana had missed Papa until now. The newspaper was her grandfather's. Once, as a child, Jenny had made the mistake of opening it and clipping out pictures for a class assignment before her grandfather had a chance to read it. She'd had to walk three blocks to the grocery store, the store where she'd now worked since high school, to buy another paper, and that was before she'd been allowed to sit at the table and eat her dinner. Nana had fussed around her for a good hour after she'd returned home. But Papa had been stern, making it clear sending her to buy another one was the best way for Jenny to remember never to touch his paper.

Jenny's grandfather had been dead five years, yet Nana had religiously placed his paper at his chair at the table every morning. It always remained there until the next morning when she'd throw it away and replace it with that day's paper.

"You two are together now," she murmured, leaving the paper where it was. It was from three months ago. Jenny had stopped the subscription along with Nana's subscriptions to *Good Housekeeping* and *Reader's Digest.* "I'm going to have to throw you away soon, you know?" she said to the newspaper.

She reached for her laptop and booted it up. Her stomach growled and she ignored it, knowing there was no way she could eat. Not to mention there wasn't any food in the house. Which was pretty bad considering she worked at a grocery store.

As she did every time she was on the Internet, she went to the home page for Lanai, then clicked on the link for their local online newspaper. Soon she would quit torturing herself. Soon she could pack everything about Ric into a back room in her brain, just as she was doing with Nana's things.

Until that point, she would scour every line of the online newspaper searching for anything that might have to do with him. She didn't need to be a psychologist or have fancy degrees to know the stages of grief and healing. But this was working for her—sort of.

Jenny didn't realize she'd clicked on the classifieds section until she caught herself scanning jobs on the island. An entry caught her eye, and she read it a second time, then straightened, staring at the small font and few lines.

> Full-time manager needed for soon-to-open
> local bed-and-breakfast. Responsibilities in-
> clude but are not limited to booking rooms,
> supervising the menu, and housekeeping.
> Pay based on experience.

Jenny read the phone number, then continued looking at it until her vision blurred. Not that she needed to see it. She'd memorized that number three and a half months ago.

"He's opening his bed-and-breakfast," she said, feeling a rush of emotions tumble through her insides. At the same time, her tummy fluttered with excitement. "I could do that job."

But how could she get there? She had this house, her job at the grocery store. It might suck right now, but she had a life here. She couldn't just walk away from it.

"You've already started packing."

Jenny wasn't sure what made her come to that obvious realization and then voice the truth out loud. It was the truth, though. For the past couple months she'd been packing up everything in the house without acknowledging that was what she was doing. Maybe if she sold the house, it would give her the money to move.

She started to open a new browser window so she could search for a Realtor but then realized she couldn't put it on the market until she knew she had the job.

The classifieds section had a place where she could fill out a generic job application, which she began doing. Her heart was racing. She felt more alive than she had since she'd returned home. Without Nana, this wasn't a home but a capsule of memories she couldn't bear to live with. She finished the application and submitted it. Now all Ric had to do was hire her. Somehow, the rest would fall into place.

By the end of the next day she couldn't stand the wait any longer and contacted a Realtor. She'd reached for her phone to call Ric so many times she'd lost count. Each time she stubbornly put her phone back down. She would have to face the fact that he might not want her to work for him. Jenny prayed it wasn't the case, but it was possible he'd moved on. If so, she would, too. But not here, not in this big old rambling house clogged with too many memories. One way or another she would start a new life. Her current life wasn't working out so well for her.

Friday morning, she paced the living room waiting for the Realtor to show up. Her boss had reluctantly agreed to her coming into work late. It didn't bother her the way it had since the day she'd started working at the grocery store, when her manager looked incredibly put out at having to run the store without Jenny there to do everything. Jenny had a nine a.m. appointment so the Realtor lady could do a walk-through and start the process of putting the house on the market. The only way to meet with the Realtor was to miss time at work. The only way to sell the house was to meet with the Realtor.

"You can do this," she told herself firmly.

Sitting at her kitchen table for the tenth time, she cleared her screen and stared at her in-box. There was a new message. At first it didn't make sense to her, but she clicked to open it.

That's when she realized it was a response to her application. It was sent via the Web site on which she'd applied to the classified ad. The e-mail didn't make sense. It appeared to be automatically generated with Xs marked next to certain comments. Jenny tried making sense out of it until she spotted a link toward the bottom.

*Employer comments to applicant.*

Jenny clicked on it and stared at the new box that popped up in front of her e-mail. At the same time, there was a firm knock on her front door. She couldn't move. Her heart had stopped beating and was now swelling in her chest, robbing her of breath and creating a pressure she had no way of stopping.

All it said in the box was, *"How soon can you be here?"*

Unlike the last time Jenny flew to Hawaii, this time she didn't wait hours for a plane destined to never leave the ground. Arriving three hours before her scheduled flight, she spotted an earlier flight leaving in forty-five minutes and almost ran to that end of the airport to catch it. She had hauled quite a bit of luggage and by the time her flight landed on Lanai many hours later, the energy she'd had earlier that morning had dissipated and she was now groggy and in desperate need of a shower.

Since she'd come in on an earlier flight, Ric wasn't here to meet her. When she'd first reveled in her luck at securing the earlier flight, the thought of surprising Ric by showing up sooner than planned sounded great. Now, as she gathered her luggage off the conveyer belt and started dragging it through the airport, she wished he were here.

Over the past few days, talking to him on the phone after reading the message he'd sent, new life had ignited inside her. She still missed Nana terribly, but today the pain was bearable. Only because it was countered with joy and excitement over seeing Ric again.

She made it outside the airport and waved down a taxi driver. The house back in Parkville was on the market, but until it sold, she was on a very tight budget. This time when her stomach growled, she wanted to eat. Airport food was ridiculously expensive, though, and not an option on her budget. The taxi ride, however, was a necessary evil. Lanai might not be a huge island, but it was way too big to haul three well-stuffed suitcases on foot.

"Take me to the banana plantation, please."

She grinned when the driver nodded, secured her luggage in the trunk, then held her door as she slid into the backseat. Everyone on the island knew about the banana plantation. Ric's bed-and-breakfast would be an incredible success. Jenny wondered if Mr. Pritchard and Mr. Sagawa's idea for the resort that would honor Samantha Winston had been shot down. She stared out the window when they reached the highway. Everything looked the same. She would have loved to have been part of that conversation when the two crooked businessmen were told to take their idea and shove it. At least she hoped that was how the conversation went.

When the cab reached the end of Ric's long driveway, Jenny leaned forward, her jaw dropping. Near the highway was a wooden sign with letters burned deep into it. BANANA PLANTATION, BED-AND-BREAKFAST. She only focused on it a second, though, as the cabbie turned into the drive and slowed.

She barely recognized the place. A crew of at least ten workers were all over the house, roofing, painting, landscaping. Jenny wondered when Ric started the project, because at the rate they were working, they would likely be done soon.

"Here you go, ma'am. Are you new hired help?"

Jenny snapped her mouth shut when she realized she'd been gawking out the window. "I sure hope so." She grinned, then opened her door and got out.

She paid the cabbie, then stood, staring at the transformation of the beautiful old house as he pulled around and headed back to the highway. Several men on ladders, bare-chested and wearing jeans, were painting the wood a beautiful, dark shade of rustic red. With the sun high in the sky, the fresh paint radiated and almost appeared to glow. Already the place had been covered with a primer or something, because instead of old wood showing, underneath was a rich gray. All the windows were new and gave the house a more alive look. But what impressed her the most was the incredible flower garden that had recently been planted around the house.

The sidewalk from the drive to the front porch was new, and Jenny rounded up all of her luggage and worked her way toward the front porch as she continued taking in her surroundings. If she hadn't seen the old house before they'd started, she never would have believed how much it had been transformed.

"Let me help you with those." A short, stocky man hurried down the porch steps, which were also brand-new, and reached for her luggage. "If you're looking for a room, I don't think we're open for business yet." He had a cheerful smile and a twinkle in his eyes when he grinned at her.

"Looks like you'll be open soon," she replied, unsure how to introduce herself. Ric hadn't officially hired her, just demanded she return as soon as possible.

"I'm Joe Seal," he offered, herding her luggage away from her, then lifting them easily as he made his way back up to the porch. "Are you a new employee?"

"I'm Jenny," she said, distracted by how clean and fresh the porch looked with its floor painted and white wicker chairs lined up against the house. "I can't believe how wonderful everything looks." She stared longingly at the porch swing at the far end of the porch. Another one hung at the other end. If this place brought in decent business, she doubted there would be many nights when she'd be able to relax, cuddled next to Ric and breathing in the sweet aroma of the flowers. The thought caused a quickening deep inside her gut and she sighed.

"Jenny?" Joe pulled her out of her daydream when he stopped, looked at her, then gave her an appraising once-over. "So you're the one . . ."

"Huh?" she asked, but then couldn't stop from blushing when he gave her a meaningful look. God, she hoped she was the one. She felt as if she were coming home.

"I've known Ric as long as he's lived here. No one's ever affected him like you have, little lady." He was frowning at her but then grinned, showing off white teeth. "So aloha, my dear. We're glad you're here so he'll quit brooding and feeling sorry for himself."

# 13

_____

Joe had no idea how incredibly good his words made her feel. She almost danced through the screen door, which no longer slammed loudly when she let it close of its own accord behind her. She'd lost Nana and had spent over three months of her life doing a fair share of her own moping, but she would get through her mourning. Everyone always said with the end of a life starts a new one.

"Oh, wow." She took a moment, turning slowly and taking in the incredibly large living room. "I don't believe this is the same room. It can't be," she said in disbelief.

"Thank you," Joe shot over his shoulder. There was a crashing sound out back, and he cursed under his breath, then deposited her luggage in the corner of the living room. "You're on your own figuring out your sleeping arrangement." He winked at her. "That is out of my pay grade," he teased, but then thumbed in the direction where the crashing sound came from as he backed away from her. "Sorry to leave you on your own. Ric is here somewhere. Obviously I can't leave my crew alone for five minutes before they try tearing the place apart." With that, he stalked out of the living room, fisting his hands at his side.

Jenny followed slowly, still distracted by the dark varnish that glowed over the hardwood floors and the crisp, pale, burned-orange paint that was the absolute perfect color for the walls. When she reached the kitchen, she stopped short. Two men were hanging cabinets, banging hammers against nails in an off-rhythm beat. One of them looked at her, and for a moment she thought he was Ric.

He was as tall and as well built with dark skin and thick black hair. His jawline was different, though, and although he looked young, there were barely noticeable crow's feet on either side of his eyes and a haggard look on his face Ric didn't have, as if he'd seen some bad things in his time.

Someone started yelling outside, obviously pissed about something. She edged her way around drop cloths spread over a table and across the floor. The kitchen wasn't as far along as everything else she'd seen so far.

"Is there something I can do for you, Miss?" the man asked, lowering his hammer and looking at her curiously. When he gave her a crooked grin, she was sure more than one lady had swooned over that look. "I wouldn't go out there if I were you. My nephew is on the rampage."

"He's being a dick," the other man, who hadn't looked at Jenny yet, muttered. "He keeps this up and I'm out of here."

"No, you're not," the good-looking one said.

"Who are you?" A third man she hadn't noticed faced her now.

He didn't look as much like Ric as he did the man who was standing next to him. There was a family resemblance, though. Whereas the older man looked a lot like Ric, the younger one with the attitude looked a lot like the man standing next to him.

"My name is Jenny Rogers," she began.

"You're Jenny?" the better-looking guy of the lot asked, his crooked grin broadening when he started toward her, then clicked his tongue when he walked around her, making a show of visibly giving her a thorough once-over one side and then the next. "Might have to cut our prick some slack," he said to the other man, who stood, arms crossed, scowling at the good-looking one. "She is hot."

The older of the two men, possibly old enough to be the father, rolled his eyes and shook his head. Jenny noticed streaks of gray lining his black hair when he faced her.

"He has no manners," he offered in place of an apology.

"I was complimenting her," the good-looking one complained.

"I'm Jose Karaka, Ric's uncle." Jose, the older one, wiped his hand on his jeans, then extended it to her. "Aloha, Jenny. Ric is outside. Just follow the yelling. This is my brother, Jacob."

"Aloha," Jacob said, straightening and brushing sawdust off his clothes, as if suddenly intent on proving he did have manners.

Jenny nodded, shook hands, and started to retreat. "Aloha," she remembered to say as she headed to the back door. It was getting a bit overwhelming how everyone seemed to know who she was.

There was continual yelling outside, and Jenny turned to the back door. She had her hand on the door handle and was opening it when the two men behind her started swearing under their breath.

"Fool is going to blow a gasket," Jose muttered, following her out back.

She noticed a paved road leading around to the back of the house and a parking lot that hadn't been there three months ago. Next to it a structure was going up, almost appearing to be a second house. Jenny walked across the yard, perplexed, but forgot her curiosity when she saw Ric.

He stood with his back to her, shirtless like the rest of the men working around him. As she watched, he nearly attacked a ladder as he lunged at it, then climbed it with a grace that belied his size. Jenny tilted her head and fought not to drool when he reached the roof of the structure and began lecturing about nails versus screws being used in the skeleton structure of a house.

She barely heard a word as he yelled. His dark body glowed against the sun. Lean muscle stretched across his back, and she swore his arms were more muscular than they'd been last time she saw him. His faded jeans hugged his legs, hinting at the taut, perfectly shaped man-muscle underneath. She stared at him, almost feeling a need to pinch herself. Even his thick black hair lay perfectly around his head.

Every inch of her body responded to the glorious view on display before her. Her womb quickened with anticipation, and her mouth went dry. She tried swallowing, and instantly her mouth was too wet, as if she would start drooling if she didn't lick her lips and prevent it. That wasn't the only part of her that was soaked. A pool of moisture spread between her legs, soaking her pussy. Shifting her weight didn't help matters either. The pleated shorts she'd worn during her flight rubbed against her suddenly very tender and sensitive shaved flesh.

"I swear I'll yank this all apart if it isn't done right," Ric was bellowing. He hit his fist against a wooden plank that was part of the skeleton of the structure.

Three men on the roof along with him all appeared appropriately chastised. Jenny wasn't sure what it was they were doing wrong, other than it had something to do with nails. She wanted to run up to Ric, get his attention, and make him climb down the ladder. But at the same time, she worried that her arriving earlier than expected might put him in an even fouler mood. Conflicted, and throbbing with a ravenous desire she hadn't felt in over three months, Jenny stood there, watching.

One of the men on the roof noticed her, and his sober expression brightened. He winked at her and gave her an impish grin. The man continued watching her, ignoring Ric as he began explaining the correct way to do the job. If he was family, too, there wasn't any resemblance.

"Jimmy, are you listening to me?" Ric roared. "Your entire section is fucking crooked. If this is how you work, so that you're guaranteed jobs down the road when the roof starts leaking, I'm sure as hell not interested."

The man flirting with Jenny with his eyes shot his attention to Ric, busted and not pleased. "I'll do it over," he said. "And I was just smiling at the pretty lady."

His comment caused the other men on the roof to immediately turn their focus on her. Ric turned, looked at her, and his jaw dropped.

"Jenny," he gasped, sincerely surprised.

"Hi," she said, wishing his workers would quit leering at her.

Ric turned farther and his ladder pulled away from the roof.

"Crap!" he hissed.

"Ric!" she howled.

Jacob and Jose rushed past her as Jenny froze, her hands flying to her mouth as she tried to hold in a scream when she was sure she would witness Ric falling off the ladder and breaking his back.

His uncles grabbed the ladder, and everyone began yelling at once. Jacob and Jose were shouting at Ric, telling him what to do. Jenny didn't hear a word of it. She witnessed the scene in slow motion as the ladder came farther away from the roof of the structure. The men on the roof scampered across to help.

"Oh my God! Ric! No!" She couldn't hold back her screams.

Joe Seal, the first man she'd met on the front porch, moved incredibly fast for a short, stocky guy. Out of nowhere, he was at the bottom of the ladder, helping to brace it.

It appeared the three men were trying to lean it back against the structure. Ric didn't wait for them to complete their task. He leaped from the ladder and was airborne. Jenny watched, horrified, as her legs went weak underneath her.

As instantly as everything around her played out in slow motion, it just as quickly returned to regular speed and time. Ric fell to the ground, landing on two feet but going down so his hands hit the ground as well.

"Oh my God! Are you hurt?" Jenny found strength in her legs and rushed to Ric.

Before she reached him, Ric pushed himself to his feet and met her halfway, grabbing her and lifting her off the ground.

"Jenny!" he gasped, winded as he wrapped strong arms around her and held her against his chest.

She didn't know whether to laugh or cry. "You're hurt," she insisted, trying to touch him everywhere at once and focus on his face at the same time. All while hanging suspended, pressed against his incredibly virile body. Both of his hands cupped her ass, stretching her, opening her, and causing the throbbing to shift to a swollen desire that stole her ability to think.

"I'm not hurt." His voice was raspy, and his dark, forest-green eyes began to glow as emotions soared to life inside him. A small, crooked grin appeared on his unshaven face. "But you're early."

"Yeah," she whispered, unable to form any other coherent words.

Ric apparently was cool with minimal conversation at the moment. When she thought his eyes would darken from green to black, they blurred before her as he lowered his head and captured her mouth.

His kiss was hot, enticing, and made her want to curl up against him and feast to her heart's content. Ric's tongue probed between her lips, soft at first, but the kiss grew demanding, needy, filled with promises to satisfy. And she wanted that promise fulfilled soon.

It took her a minute to realize the men around them were whooping and hollering, cheering the two of them on. When Ric broke off the kiss, he adjusted her in his arms so she was cradled against his chest.

"Get back to work," he yelled over his shoulder, and made it to the back door in several long strides.

"Ric," she cried out, laughing, when he pulled the screen open with one hand, entered the house, but didn't let her down. "I can walk."

"I remember," he grunted, hitting the stairs and making it to the second floor in record time. He didn't let her down until they were in his bedroom, and he'd kicked the door closed with his foot. "Why are you early?"

"I found an earlier flight when I got to the airport." She stood next to his bed and watched as he sat next to her and began pulling off his work boots. When he stood and unfastened the top button of his jeans, all she could do was stare. "I didn't want a recurrence of the last time I flew out here and had to wait so long for my flight."

"Good thinking. I doubt there would be a rich, willing old lady ready to give up her seat for you twice," he said, catching her watching him and grinning. "I was going to shower and come get you," he added, pausing before he pushed his jeans down his hips and reached for her.

"I took a cab." She shrugged, knowing she'd wanted to surprise him and since she had, not feeling a need to admit it.

He reached for her, took her shirt at the waist, and pulled it over her head. Jenny raised her arms, allowing him to undress her while her pussy began throbbing with eager anticipation. There were no more words as he finished the job, tossing all of her clothes on the floor in a pile with his.

When she stood naked before him, once again drooling over how magnificent every inch of his perfect body was, including his hard, swollen cock that stretched toward her eagerly, Ric gripped her arms and guided her backward, until she lay on the bed with him on top of her.

His dick immediately found its place between her legs, its swollen tip pressing against her entrance. Jenny hissed in a breath, doing her best to spread her legs underneath Ric to allow him entrance. She was noticeably disappointed when he adjusted himself and moved his dick away from her pussy. He rolled to his side, exposing her and touching her nipple when both of them hardened into hypersensitive peaks.

"You don't realize how much you need someone until they're gone," he murmured, staring down at her body with a hooded gaze as he ran his finger lazily over her body. Then as if realizing what he'd said, his eyes shot to hers. "I'm sorry about your grandmother."

"Me too." She didn't want to think about what caused her pain. Not right now. Jenny rolled to her side so she faced Ric and began her own exploring. She lifted her finger to his jawbone and ran it along his unshaven face.

"I was going to shave before I left for the airport," he grunted, defending his rugged look.

"I like it." She grinned into his brooding expression. There wasn't anything about him she didn't like.

"Just like?" he asked, raising his focus from her breasts to her face, taking his time, until he stared at her with dark, intense orbs.

Jenny swallowed, understanding his question, at least she thought she did. "I'm not sure yet," she admitted, whispering, although she was pretty sure she was. "Possibly more."

He was on her then, and just as he'd done outside, he captured her mouth without warning. This time, though, his hunger was obvious, demanding, and when she almost fell to her back, his arm went swiftly around her and pressed her against his hot, muscular body.

"Definitely more," he growled into her mouth. Then his hand was tangled in her hair, and his other hand found her breast. He was tugging, pinching her nipple, torturing and offering pleasure at the same time.

"God," she cried out as her head fell back, the kiss ending but his pursuit of her body just beginning.

His lips were hot upon her neck. He pressed his hand into the center of her back, encouraging her to arch into him as he continued feasting on her, moving lower until he captured a nipple between his teeth.

Jenny's world crashed around her. All the pain from losing her grandmother, the dual suffering she'd endured after coming home and being alone and so far away from Ric dissipated. The house she'd grown up in now empty and no longer feeling like a home suddenly didn't bother her. Just as it had become a shell she needed to shed, so did all the pain she'd endured over the past few months. It washed out of her, leaving her feeling giddy, light enough to float, and grounded only by Ric.

She had power, though, too. When she brushed her fingernails over his flesh, Ric shivered, and his breath was quick and hot on her nipple. In spite of shivering along with him, which apparently gave him immense pleasure because he groaned, she held on to her power. Running her fingers over his body, she began exploring, learning where he was more sensitive, where she could touch him and make his body tighten with need or cause muscles to constrict under her touch.

Jenny also learned what parts of him she loved most, although every inch of him was damn near perfect. Other than the rough stubble on his chin, which was now doing wicked things to her breasts, the tight, black curls spanning his well-sculpted chest brushed over her body when he moved, heightening her senses even more. His legs were long, roped tendons as hard as steel when he moved one between her legs and forced her to open for him.

But it was his hands and his mouth that were partners in crime as they explored and drew out the passion in her she'd tried so hard to extinguish after leaving the island. Ric now brought the fire simmering inside her to full flame, making each flame dance, stretch to be taller than the one next to it, until every inch of her was on fire, burning from the inside out.

Ric cupped both her breasts in his hands, brushing her damp nipples with his thumbs as he lifted his head and stared down at her.

"You're incredibly beautiful," he said, his voice rough and raspy. "Too beautiful, actually."

"Too beautiful?" she countered, making a face at him to keep herself from floating with his flattery. "That sounds like a bad thing."

"It is," he told her seriously.

She would drown in those incredibly intense dark green eyes, bordered by thick black lashes. But she also saw his dominance, the power gleaming just behind his black pupils. Ric was a man who took what he wanted and made it his own. This banana plantation was proof of that. He hadn't said but Jenny guessed he'd persuaded Samantha that backing his bed-and-breakfast was a financially sound move. And it was. She wouldn't argue that fact, and although she didn't yet know the details, she bet he'd pay Samantha back before whatever terms they'd negotiated came due.

Jenny also saw that he was a perfectionist, and for some odd reason, she met that criteria in his eyes. If she wasn't careful, he'd possess and control her. And she knew instinctively that they wouldn't make it if she allowed that. They would have to be equals, which meant she had her work cut out for her.

"So therefore I'm a bad thing?" She saw the glow in his eyes and couldn't help grinning as she continued watching him.

"Very," he grumbled, then dragged his chin down her body as he continued kissing and torturing her flesh.

Jenny drew in a sharp breath. Her vision blurred and she wasn't able to hold his gaze, in spite her efforts to try.

"If I'm bad, then you're wicked," she managed to utter before his mouth clamped down on the most sensitive bit of flesh on her body. "Oh!" she wailed, bucking against him.

Ric was ready for her reaction. He was a step ahead of her, giving him the edge and the lead. She told herself this wasn't a game. Not when it came to her heart. He would lead, and she would let him. But there would be other times when he would follow her lead. Which was just how it should be.

Ric performed magic with his tongue as he dragged it over her entrance, then dipped inside her and began making love to her with his mouth. It dawned on her that this was the first time they'd made love facing each other. She remembered wanting this moment so she could see his face, stare into his eyes as she came and watch him when he did the same. Before, she'd wanted sex with him to remain casual so she wouldn't lose her heart to a man who lived so far away. Obviously it didn't work.

Jenny blinked, raised her head, and focused on Ric. His hands were still on her breasts and his dark skin contrasting with her pale flesh looked incredibly hot. Visuals did a lot for her, and watching him crouch between her spread legs, his black hair bordering his face as his long lashes draped over his eyes, made her want him even more.

Ric dipped his tongue inside her one more time, then returned his attention to her clit. He sucked her swollen flesh into his mouth, and again she bucked against him.

"Let go, Jenny," he instructed, his gravelly whisper as hot as the view she offered. "Come for me."

"I'm not holding back," she told him.

"Yes, you are. Relax and allow the pressure to consume you."

There was no way he understood her body better than she did. "It happens when it happens," she said, her teeth clenched tight. She finally let her head fall back, the sensations ripping through her growing too strong for her to keep her head up and manage the growing tidal wave ready to spill over inside her. "Just keep doing what you're doing."

Ric chuckled and lashed at her clit with his tongue. This new affliction hurled her to a place too intense to handle for very long. She willed her body to relax, but the attention he was giving her clit was too much. Jenny barely managed to raise her head, once again trying to watch him, and locked gazes with his when he stared up at her.

His eyes were dark and glowed with powerful passion that stole her breath. He was taking her over the edge, and it was getting him off as much as her. She wished she could see how hard his dick was at the moment, but there was no way. And she couldn't reach it either.

Before she was able to contemplate switching positions so she could give him the same pleasure he was giving her, that tidal wave inside her reached the dangerous level.

"Ric," she gasped, and watched his eyes widen as a small grin played at his lips.

"That's it, sweetheart," he whispered against her soaked flesh. "Just like that."

As if she could do it any other way. Wave after wave of heated bliss swept over her, each one stronger and larger than the one before. Dark colors brushed the world around her, giving her tunnel vision. Her world became just the two of them. His eyes locked on hers. Hers on his. And when the tidal wave finally broke loose, racing through her and bursting in a climactic explosion of incredible satisfaction unlike anything else she'd ever known before, Jenny wasn't sure she'd recover from it.

As it waned and her body went limp, she was powerless when Ric crawled over her, bringing her legs up with him until she was almost folded in half and his throbbing, harder-than-steel, swollen dick was pressing against her. He was definitely affected by what he'd just done to her. As he glided inside her, he locked gazes with her, then immediately took her to the explosive edge once again.

Before when they'd had sex, it had been physical, carnal, lustful, and raw. This time was all those things and so much more. Jenny wasn't sure she'd ever admit to anyone that love for another person could so fully consume her that quickly. But there wasn't any denying the obvious. The way he looked at her. The way she knew she was looking at him. If this wasn't love, she wasn't sure what was.

Losing Nana had torn her world apart. But going months without Ric had destroyed her inside. They'd spent a week together, and during that time she'd known she needed so much more. Like the rest of their lives. He was everything she'd imagined a man should be. Strong, determined, motivated and driven, beyond sexy, and in love with her.

Hadn't he said he wanted more when she'd told him she liked this? And everyone had known who she was when she arrived today. His uncle mentioned he'd be less grouchy with her here. Those had to be signs of him missing her as desperately as she had him. And when she'd applied for the job at the bed-and-breakfast, he'd demanded to know how soon she could return.

Jenny stared into his eyes, drowned in the adoration she saw there as he began making love to her. She spread her legs, willing him deeper, wanting nothing more than to feel him come inside her. Using a condom had denied her of that sensation. It was a minor part of showing love for each other, but she didn't want anything between them ever again.

"Say it, Jenny."

She blinked, wondering if she'd voiced out loud her thoughts but knowing she hadn't. Ric gave her a slow, crooked grin. As he lowered his head to hers, his black hair shrouded them in a world big enough only for the two of them.

"Say what you're thinking."

"How do you know?" She couldn't elaborate further on her question when he impaled her, grunting as he did.

She loved the sounds he made. Loved the way he looked when he made love to her. Loved everything about him.

"Say what *you're* thinking," she managed when he began pulling out of her.

"We'll say it together."

She kept her eyes on his, pretty sure she knew his thoughts but knowing how embarrassing it would be if she was wrong.

"Say it, darling."

"Together."

He nodded, filled her again, closed his eyes briefly as if the pleasure was too much for him. When he opened them, Jenny was sure she saw the love in him that she felt inside her.

Jenny opened her mouth. "I love you," she whispered.

"I love you, darling," he said at the same time.

It was enough to trigger the tidal wave in her once again. Her pussy tightened around him, and his eyes widened. Jenny felt a rush of control even as she came. Ric exploded right along with her, consummating a love Jenny knew would be strong enough to last forever.

Keep reading for a
sneak peek at Lorie O'Clare's
enticing new erotic romance,
ISLAND OF DESIRE

Available February 2012!

# 1

---

"The Mr. Desire Pageant is the fastest growing in the history of pageants." Windsor Montgomery spoke as if he were solely responsible for its success.

Andrea stared at her red, closed-toe heels that matched her Betsey Johnson dress, a bright red thing that was off-the-shoulders sharp. She crossed her legs, then pressed her hands on her dress, pushing the cool material down an inch, almost to her knees. "I'm impressed," she offered, knowing Windy, as he liked to be called, was waiting for her praise.

"In its six years, it's grown in popularity so that today each of the fifty contestants is loaded with sponsors." Windy paused, looking at his file.

Andrea had already looked over the figures, or she wouldn't be here. She also wouldn't be here if it wasn't for her success working with the Miss Florida Beauty Pageant for the past six years, as many years as the Mr. Desire pageant had been in existence.

"Miss Denton knows the facts about the Mr. Desire Pageant." Julie Ward, Andrea's accountant and the closest person Andrea had to a friend, leaned forward in her high-backed chair and slid the contract she'd prepared across the oblong table.

Her target was Mark Tripp, Jr., but Frank Benison, his lawyer, snatched the stapled papers with his thick hand. Windy watched the contract slide from one end of the smooth, highly glossed table to the other. He shifted in his seat, looking rather proud of himself, as if his speech about the Mr. Desire Pageant had secured this contract. Although straight, Windy presented himself to the world as if he were gay, then acted baffled when more men came on to him than women. Andrea caught herself before she started fidgeting and remained perfectly still. Body language could be so misleading. It was one of many lessons this line of work had taught her. She didn't have a problem with Windy but wished he would quit being a hypocrite. More people would like him.

"I believe we made it clear Miss Denton's salary was non-negotiable." Frank Benison spoke with what almost sounded like a fake British accent. His white, starched, button-down collar was cutting into his neck, and his skin was too red.

Andrea imagined it was due to high blood pressure. Mr. Benison had no idea how many lawyers tried intimidating her on a daily basis. All part of the job. She ignored his pointed glare and instead focused on Mark Tripp. She'd learned about Junior only after arriving at this meeting at the Tripp Mansion. In spite of her impeccable track record of always showing up for a meeting prepared and knowing what she would gain from her time, Andrea was surprised to meet Mark Tripp, who was somewhere around thirty. Apparently, although Mark Tripp, Sr. had a passion for pageants and was using his butt loads of money to ensure the pageant was on his private island, he didn't have a passion for boring meetings.

Junior didn't appear to be any more impressed. He stared out the windows that lined the west wall and offered a view of well-manicured gardens. Andrea studied his profile. He was distractingly good-looking but seemed rather distanced from the meeting. Maybe it was his father's money, and not his, that would be backing the event, and his family's privately owned island where the pageant would take place. Regardless, Mark didn't appear to be paying attention to anything being said. He hadn't spoken a word since their meeting began.

Which made him a mystery. And a damn sexy one at that.

Julie and Mr. Benison began haggling over the details of Andrea's contract. Andrea knew every word of the agreement and knew Julie wouldn't allow one word to be changed, unless it was for more money. Andrea knew everything about the Mr. Desire Pageant. Six years ago, the Mercury Energy Drink company took the most eligible bachelor contest, as often reported in magazines, a step further, encouraging cities to hold their own pageants. No longer was the most eligible bachelor strictly a movie star or a celebrity. Now the guy in the next cubicle, or who taught kids in school, or who possibly delivered mail, might be the most eligible bachelor. With enough propaganda and the proper promoting—Andrea remembered the commercials being top-of-the-line—the Most Eligible Bachelor pageants sparked to life all over the country. Within the year almost every state was holding the pageants with as much reverence as that for their state pageants that sent one of their young ladies to Miss America.

Mercury had one hell of a marketing team, although she wasn't sure sales spiked all that much with their energy drink. What did spike was the need to take these pageants to the final level. The Mr. Desire Pageant was created, not by Mercury but by an independent team, which Andrea soon learned was backed by the Tripp Foundation. Each state presented their Most Eligible Bachelor to compete in the nationwide Mr. Desire Pageant. Now, in their sixth year, they had passed Miss

America's television ratings two years running. Andrea had no problem joining the winning team, especially when they had sought her out.

And she'd also done her homework on the Tripp family, although she was now kicking herself for not researching Junior.

They were old money, reclusive, and owned half of Florida, as well as a few islands off the coast. Mark Tripp, Sr., had been in the public eye with some venture or another most of Andrea's life, although he seldom made public appearances. There were never pictures of him in the newspaper or magazines, and nothing online. Nor were there family shots. Andrea had surfed the Web prior to this meeting for any and all available information and had gone over information she already knew about the family, which was basically all business related. There were no articles about the Tripp family, Mark Sr., his children, or his wife. She wondered if Junior would be involved with the pageant. What a bonus that would be!

"I'll sign the contract." Mark looked away from the window, proving he'd been paying more attention to the meeting than Andrea had guessed. He looked directly at her, showing off green eyes brimming with power.

Andrea had done what she'd swore she would never do—judge someone on their appearance. Granted, how a person dressed, what labels they leaned toward, spoke volumes in this business, but she had no proof Mark was in the pageant business. As far as she knew, he wasn't. His casual attire—jeans, a button-down shirt with no tie or jacket, and loafers with no socks—made him look anything but a businessman.

"Excellent," Windy breathed, clapping his hands together and grinning a toothy grin as he looked to her and nodded.

"Mark," his lawyer, Mr. Benison, said under his breath, barely moving his lips as he turned to his client. "I'm not through."

"I am. Miss Denton is the only person we're willing to consider to run this pageant. Her terms are fine." He didn't look away from Andrea when he pulled the contract out of Mr. Benison's hands, lifted a pen from the table, and poised it over the contract. "You'll agree to give notice to your current employer and work exclusively for us within thirty days."

He didn't make it a question. Andrea wasn't sure he knew she'd been studying him, but she made a show of taking him in now. Mark's soft brown hair was long enough to wave around his strong facial features. He was tan, and not from tanning booths. He looked like the kind of man who was outside a lot more than he was in an office, if he ever was in an office. In addition, the top button of his shirt was undone, revealing a glimpse of enticing chest hair.

"You'll spend all of your time on the island," Mark continued, his voice crisp with authority. In the blink of an eye he'd taken over the meeting as if he ran the show on a daily basis. "Of course, you'll be provided with living quarters I think you'll find suitable." He finally looked away from her, focusing on the contract and pressing the pen to the paper. "Contact my secretary to schedule a move-in date."

Mark signed the contract and a strand of hair fell over his forehead. He had a long, narrow, straight nose and just a bit of shadow lining his strong jaw. When he pursed his lips, his expression grew more serious. She now saw indication of a man capable of running the family ventures the Tripps were known for. His lawyer huffed, puffed out his chest, and grew even redder as he watched Mark sign the contract. Mr. Benison didn't challenge Mark, which showed he knew Mark was a man who could not be pushed.

"Andrea," Julie whispered, leaning closer.

Andrea blinked and quit looking at Mark. Julie's natural golden light brown hair, a color to die for, reflected the sunlight streaming in from the windows. She had pretty blue eyes but downplayed them with the brown eye shadow she always wore. Andrea ached to do Julie's makeup but didn't want to offend her by suggesting she could do Julie's face better.

"What do you think about living on the island?" she whispered. "There's nothing in the contract about living arrangements. You don't have to if you don't want."

Andrea liked the loft she rented, which was only a few miles from her office. Although she would be giving notice as director of Florida Pageants, Inc., where she'd worked since moving to Key West from Miami, she hadn't considered moving out of her home.

"Your job requirements will require you be on the island full-time," Mr. Benison interjected, watching her and Julie pointedly. "We'll type up an amendment, if necessary."

Mark was watching her, his eyes not moving from hers. Not once did she catch him checking her out. He was all business, something Andrea knew how to be as well. She worked in an industry that focused on beauty and sex appeal and that was filled with manipulation, deception and greed. She could always spot a player, a two-faced bitch, and a bad deal. Andrea knew how to think on her feet and go with the flow when plans changed.

"That's fine," she decided, and forced herself to relax. "Everything should be in writing."

The moment Mark finished signing the contract that sealed Andrea's future, a woman in her fifties wearing a straight-cut gray wool dress that oddly enough looked good on her too-thin body, entered the conference room from one of the closed wooden doors behind Mark and Mr. Benison. The woman moved silently, pausing when Mark slid the contract across the table to Andrea.

"Would you like a tour of the island?" he asked when Andrea accepted the pen Julie offered her.

"That would be a good idea." She realized it was the first

time the two of them had spoken to each other directly and found herself being pulled into those commanding eyes of his.

"We can head out now. Your pageant headquarters need to get used to functioning without you," he added. "Give copies to Ms. Ward and Mr. Benison," he instructed the woman standing next to him, and pushed his chair back. "Shall we?"

Andrea glanced at Julie when she pushed her chair back as well. "Thank you," she said quietly.

"Give me a call." Julie gave Mark an appraising once-over when he appeared behind Andrea. "We'll get together this evening so I can go over your letter of resignation. You need to get that turned in before the press gets wind of this meeting."

Julie was right. Timing was everything, even when it came to resigning from a position. Julie would also interrogate her about Andrea's time with Mark Tripp. Julie worked at least as hard as Andrea did, usually putting in twelve-to-sixteen-hour days. Very few people had a clue how much work went into a pageant. Unlike Andrea, though, Julie maintained a healthy social life, always having dates and often boyfriends who hung around for months on end. Andrea was good at her job, damned good. She started working within minutes of getting out of bed and finished shortly before putting her head on the pillow at night. There wasn't time for dating. She wasn't sure how Julie pulled it off. Andrea saw the glint in Julie's eyes and knew she would hound her about spending the afternoon with such a good-looking and wealthy man.

Mark's loafers didn't make a sound when he walked ahead of her out of the conference room and through his family's mansion to the front door. When they'd arrived, she'd been taken in by the beautiful rooms they'd passed through to reach the conference area. Now Andrea stared at Mark's backside, his broad muscular shoulders that tapered down to a trim waistline, and his blue jeans that hugged his hard-looking ass.

"In spite of the popular opinion that all beautiful men are gay, it isn't true."

"What?" She stopped as they reached the front door and stared at him.

Mark's expression was neutral, his eyes pinning her gaze so she couldn't look away. He was definitely a man used to controlling his surroundings. She was forced to tilt her head back in order to maintain eye contact.

"What's that supposed to mean?" Andrea saw no reason not to hide her confusion. His statement came out of nowhere and made no sense. If he was making a comment about Windy, he was being too forward.

Mark opened the front door. The butler who had been so attentive when she and Julie had arrived was now nowhere in sight. She stepped out into the early spring sunshine, welcoming the warmth of the day. Mark moved ahead of her but faced her when a driver moved around a sleek black limo and opened the back door for them. Did every servant in this household so successfully predict their employer's actions?

"You're an incredibly beautiful woman," he explained, lowering his voice, since the driver was still easily within earshot. "Your mother was Miss Florida and your sister was a runner-up. You won three pageants by the time you were twelve. I look forward to hearing why you're a director of pageants, yet chose not to continue participating in them."

Mark ignored the driver and gestured for her to enter the car. He looked away before she could catch his expression after informing her how much he'd researched on her. It crossed her mind to tell him she would follow in a different car, then grab Julie, who had driven them out to the Tripp Mansion. Julie was incredibly perceptive, and her uncanny ability to read people was extremely useful. But Andrea didn't want to be drilled as to why she was suddenly shaky and dry-mouthed. It would be better to sit in the limo with a stranger.

Andrea gave silent thanks that the only person who knew her dreadful secret was as mortified and as equally disgraced as she was. Today there wasn't quite as much pain. She worked too hard to dwell on her past. Someone as sexy as Mark might think he could trip her into spilling information that wasn't public record, but he wouldn't succeed. He already knew enough about her past.

She slid into the car, the smooth cool leather stroking the underside of her legs as she adjusted her red dress, taking a moment to regain her composure as she watched Mark grab the seat facing her.

"I love what I do," she said, keeping her voice soft and offering an easy smile as she crossed her legs and watched his gaze lower. "But, Mr. Tripp, it's rather late for an interview, don't you think?"

Mark had a smile that could make her melt inside. She fought the urge to clench her legs together when his bedroom eyes rested on her face, studying her.

"This is your business, not mine, but I intend to learn everything about running a pageant before the contestants arrive on the island." There was a shift in his expression, the commanding, rather dominating glint returning. It made his green eyes appear to glow. "I hope you're a good teacher."

Mark's cell, which he'd been holding in his hand, rang. "Excuse me," he muttered, then flipped it open and stared at the number on the screen. It was too hard to tell if he was angered by whoever called or because they interrupted them.

Andrea pulled out her iPad, giving him as much privacy as possible in the confines of a limo, and checked her messages. Julie had already sent her an e-mail. Andrea kept her phone on silent, which is where she'd had it during the meeting, deciding they would never get their tour of the island over with both their phones ringing every few minutes.

She glanced at Julie's short and to-the-point e-mail. *I've at-*

*tached a file of information on Mark Tripp, Jr. Check out the articles when you get a chance. There is some interesting stuff on Mr. Stud Muffin.*

Andrea fought a grin over Julie's nickname for Mark. She also wanted to know what Julie viewed as interesting.

"We'll discuss that later, Dad." Mark's tone was so firm Andrea wouldn't have guessed he spoke to his father if she hadn't just been pulled out of checking her messages by Mark calling him *Dad*. "Yes, we're heading to the island now. And don't do that. I'll meet with you later and fill you in." Mark hung up without saying good-bye.

The island was as breathtakingly beautiful as Andrea had imagined. She wasn't prepared for long walks in her heels and was about to tell Mark as much when they stood at the dock. She followed him to a new Excursion, and Mark pulled keys from his pocket and pushed the button on his key chain to unlock the doors.

"I'm really curious to know," he began after opening her door, then coming around to the other side and sliding into the driver's seat. "The increase in income you requested in your contract isn't enough to make it worth your while if we choose not to renew it after this pageant is over. I need to know you aren't tired of being surrounded by sexy ladies and have decided an island of sexy men might be more appealing."

Andrea looked at him. Mark started the SUV and put it into gear. He focused straight ahead, not glancing her way even as she stared at him.

She took a deep breath. It just figured Mark would be an asshole. There was no such thing as a perfect man. Mark turned them around, then headed down a straight, paved, one-lane road lined with tall palm trees on either side. He continued looking straight ahead.

"Did I offend you?" he asked when a moment of silence passed. He still didn't look at her.

"Did you mean to offend me?" There were bushes growing along the bases of the palm trees with large, bright pink flowers on them, already in bloom. She turned and gazed out her window to get a better view of the flowering bushes. When she faced forward again, she caught Mark looking at her.

"No."

Andrea captured his gaze before he could look away. He quickly did, and continued driving along the narrow road, which appeared to go on forever.

"No," she said, repeating him.

He didn't say anything.

"To answer your question." She glanced down at her dress. "I took this position because it was a smart career move."

Mark didn't say anything. His straight jawline and nose, along with his high cheekbones and that hint of a five o'clock shadow, created the perfect mixture to make him easily the sexiest man she'd ever laid eyes on. And regardless of his accusation, Andrea had directed pageants for men in the past. None of the contestants held a flame to this man sitting next to her.

But his personality was complex—possibly too complex. She hadn't ruled out the possibility of him being a pure asshole. Once she could look over the file Julie had sent her, she might have a better clue.

"What's your role in this pageant?" she asked, deciding if she knew how closely involved with him she would be while on the island, she could determine how much time to dedicate to figuring out his personality.

"Role in this pageant?" He cocked an eyebrow and shot her a quick glance. "I have no role in this pageant."

Andrea wondered at the sudden pang of disappointment that clutched in her gut. Mark Tripp would distract her, and taking on a new pageant would require 100 percent of her attention. She didn't need some gorgeous guy coming around and distracting her.

The road ended at a parking lot alongside a very large home, equally as magnificent as the mansion where they'd just had their meeting. The house had a burnt-orange terra-cotta roof and was apparently three stories, judging by the windows. Instead of facing the parking lot, the home faced the ocean. A rock garden stretched out past the terraces to the beach.

Mark pulled into a carport alongside the middle of the mansion. The house was huge, Andrea realized when she climbed out of the Excursion as Mark came around the front.

"This place is amazing." Andrea couldn't imagine living in a house this big, let alone owning two homes this size.

Mark tilted his head, looking at the home as if it were the first time he'd ever seen it and was trying to decide if he agreed. "Thank you," he murmured, sounding serious. Once again the predator was apparent when he bore into her with his intense green eyes. "Let's show you your new home."